I0652845

MADE IN THE IMAGE

Mickie Turk

HOUSE OF MYTH BOOKS

Cover Design by Benjamin Hovorka

DEDICATION

To my writer's group:
Caroline Ore, Susan Hastings,
Kristi Belcamino, Laurie Walker,
and Alex Kent.

Your stories gladdened my heart and filled my imagination. Every two weeks for a whole year, you witnessed my attempts and stumbles and triumphs. Your honest critiques and unwavering support made the process of completing this book immensely satisfying. I'm sending you warm embraces and lasting friendship. And something else— a thousand wishes for a lifetime of joy in the writer's life.

PROLOGUE

Andy O'Keefe knew he was being watched, but not by the blue-grey uniforms assigned to the lines.

He had felt Sasha's limpid stare tracking him since early morning. It started when he finished retrieving data from a frozen hard drive. While putting his tools away, Andy dropped a screwdriver behind him. When he turned around, the gangling Russian slave was holding it in his hands standing like a bird of prey, blinking hard. Andy had felt naked, like bait. During lunch, Sasha watched him eat his whole sandwich before going outside to smoke. Was he on to him? Was this really how it would all end? After six months of dogged surveillance, wiretaps, and countless man-hours and resources poured into undercover police work, to be outmaneuvered and trounced by a twelve-year-old? Or was the boy just curious about the outsider. A non-Russian, looking anything like but what you might expect in a techie. Andy refused to wear a uniform, just stuck to jeans and a tee.

His hair was always in his eyes, too long, and subject to cowlicks. A real live American.

Maybe the kid was lonely and wanted a friend. But he didn't speak English. And they both knew that the illegal factory made for a lousy neighborhood meet-and-greet. A cavernous space laid out in twelve rows, eight boys to each. Serious looking goons walking back and forth making sure no one dropped a stitch. A place where young supple hands and small dexterous fingers—ideal tools for quick and efficient assembly—attached small parts to circuit boards. The new startup company, *MotionAmerica*, specialized in motors and drives used in semiconductor technology. Andy had it on authority that ever since sales had started to soar, more and more of the company's profits had to be laundered. Not much of a surprise when the biggest overhead, salaries and benefits, had been eliminated. When you only employed itinerant workers and human slaves, anything was possible. Hear! Hear! America was about to become great again.

No, Andy didn't think it was safe to chummy up with one of the kids, not yet. Not with so much at stake. But at the end of the day that is exactly what the undercover cop would do.

Andy closed the cover on the main server. The motherboard inside the installation computer was as good as new. He looked at his watch. Just enough time to check in with the captain and make it to the World Series game. Not just any World Series, but the first of the season played at Marlin Park, where, if there were any justice in the world, the Marlins would soon be thrashing the Minnesota Twins. But just then, flailing hands and pointing fingers beckoned him to the back of the room. Now he would be late. Shit, those tickets cost $250.00 each.

He walked over to the Sasha's computer expecting the worst. The page was open to Google Translate. Andy glanced at the computer screen, back at Sasha who for once was not looking at him, then back at the screen. With a simple keystroke Russian morphed into English and, for the first time, Andy felt the crust of everyday routine lift. The air crackled with promise.

I KNOW THINGS. I CAN HELP.

It was time to call in their secret weapon.

Lydia.

ONE

Ten months later

Special Agent Lydia Angelova wished she could take off her jacket. The air conditioning in the truck was no match for Miami summer heat and humidity. But that would give her away. She looked in the rear view mirror and liked what she saw. A ball cap pulled down low over her forehead and oversized sunglasses camouflaged her delicate feminine features. She looked just like another UPS driver. She looked like a guy. Satisfied, she pulled high-powered binoculars to her head and scanned the horseshoe-shaped warehouse across the interstate. Two-story square buildings attached by a series of steel garage doors, lined up like concrete cutouts. A half-dozen unwashed white vans lounged at a deserted loading dock. The small parking lot was full but quiet. On the western side, men and boys stood around eating sandwiches. When they finished, they smoked. As soon as two boys came out of a door at the opposite end and sat down on the stoop to eat their lunch, Lydia slid into drive.

She parked at an angle, positioning the UPS truck to keep her and the informant concealed from the rest of the warehouse and most of the parking lot. She studied the two boys. Where Sasha was tall and fair, golden-eyed like a cat, Tadzio was dark haired, short and stocky, with round mournful brown eyes. While he ate his sandwich, the younger boy kept his eyes on the ground, trained on a sketchpad and broken pencil. When Lydia stepped out of the truck, Sasha smiled at his friend and then gently elbowed him in the ribs. Without a word, the younger boy swallowed the rest of his sandwich, gathered up his drawing materials, and clambered up the stairs.

Only then did Lydia speak. She loved the guttural resonance of Russian but had few opportunities to use it.

"Где же вы были? Я ехал сюда пять раз в две недели фиктивные поставки. Я не смел спросить о вас. Даже не—"

"Where on earth have you been? I drove here five times in two weeks on bogus deliveries. I didn't dare ask about you. Not even—"

They watched the departing Tadzio shut the door behind him.

"I imagined the worst. You had me so scared," she said.

"They sent me to another facility to learn a new computer program. Right now I'm their star pupil. That's good, don't you think? I can be more help to you."

Lydia didn't want more help from Sasha. She wanted it to be over. To be able to break the case and free all the boys. The case to break all cases. If everything went right, this bust would lay the foundation for identifying future crimes before they even happened. Not only would mid-and high-level Russian traffickers go to prison, their slaves would be freed and given a new chance at life. And best of all, everyone would find out about it. Word would leap across continents that the Russian crime syndicate was invadable. When news broke out that mere children fought back and snitched on their captors, world traffickers would lose credibility. In the future, it wouldn't be so easy to rely on complete submission from their victims. Lest one betray them, like Sasha had.

Sasha wrinkled his brow when he saw Lydia's eyes dart back and forth. He knew that's what she did when she was deep in thought, but he never liked it. It took her away from him. Then he saw her reach inside her pocket and he beamed.

"New iPod. For me? What do I tell the others?"

"Tell them I'm a perv trying to get next to you."

Sasha laughed. "Good plan. Thanks, everyone will be jealous."

Lydia said, "Anything new I should know about?"

"No, the delivery is still going down like I said before. Same place, same time. In a week. It's big, the biggest, I think."

Sasha tore his gaze away from his present to scrutinize Lydia. He raised a slender finger.

Before she could stop him, her ball cap slid off. As it did, long dark chestnut tresses fell past her shoulders. She took off her sunglasses and smiled.

"You remind me of my mother. But not so tired. What's going to happen to me? I can't go back. There's nothing there for me anymore," the boy said.

Lydia knew Sasha was right. He had no one. And now he was working as a slave for the same people that had annihilated his family only two years earlier. Back in Russia, his father had been murdered for turning state's evidence against the mob. At first his mother tried to keep it together, but they soon ran out of money, then food, and finally she had to sell their apartment to settle debts. Out on the streets, Sasha's mother gave up and began disassociating from reality. Right before pneumonia killed her, she had stopped talking to her son, because she no longer recognized him.

Lydia quickly wrapped up her hair, popped the ball cap back on, and adjusted her sunglasses.

"Don't worry. I gave you my word. I will find you a good home. I promise, you're going to love it."

"But I want to live with you, Lydia."

Sasha's gaze strayed upward. Lydia followed it and detected a slight movement in a small round window on the second story stairwell. The noonday sun appeared to melt the glass, but they could still make out the chubby round cheeks mashed against windowpane. As quickly, they slid their eyes past the truck when they heard footsteps on the tarmac. Lydia grabbed a package from the passenger side and mumbled, "I better get going."

Sasha got up to follow when a strong hand gripped his neck.

The man was a human block and he matched the building. Grey, nondescript, and square. The block snatched Sasha's iPod and scowled.

"Из драйвера ИБП. Я думаю, что он любит меня."

"Where did you get this?"

"From the UPS driver. I think he likes me."

"Don't you know anything about pedophiles? First they give you gifts, and then they want blowjobs. Maybe you want that too?"

Sasha said, "You're sick. Give it back. He tugged at the electronic device. The block spat at the ground. A sickly yellow mass pooled next to Sasha's foot. He let go of the player but not before jabbing the boy in the back. "Just be sure you're not, or Markiza will feed you to the wolves."

Tadzio couldn't wait any longer for Sasha in the stairwell. The bell rang for the second time and he had to go back to work. They would be expecting him to restart the all-day task of shredding paper. The boy trod up the last set of stairs and was almost through the doorway when someone blocked his way. He had to point his chin way up to the ceiling to see the top of the man's head and then froze. Markiza. He wasn't scowling for once; instead he smiled before bending down to pat his head. When he saw the behemoth reach for his sketchpad, Tadzio quickly drew his hand back. The boy slid between the man's legs and was almost free when another man sandwiched him. He looked back to see Markiza waggle his fingers.

"Дай мне это мальчик."

"Give it to me boy."

This time, while the back of his throat began to close and small tears formed in the corners of his eyes, Tadzio let go and as he did, something smooth and cool pressed against his palm. A clear plastic bag with an unmarked drawing pad and a box of brand new colored pencils. Tadzio immediately forgot about his sketchbook.

Markiza carried Tadzio's sketchbook to his office, sat down, and began flipping through the drawings. The first pages detailed the factory space—young boys at work, their handlers standing over them. On a separate sheet, the same room, same perspective, but Markiza was in it this time and shown shouting at a subordinate. He was the biggest thing in the room. Markiza liked that. The boy had talent. His friend Sasha dominated many of the next pages—standing, sitting, or working at a computer. All normal observations until he got to the drawings of the UPS truck. There were dozens of renderings detailing a variety of angles and perspectives of the vehicle. Much like what a photographer might do if he were obsessed with a delivery truck. In the last sketches, Tadzio inserted a driver. In one, the UPS driver had just stepped out of the vehicle carrying a small package under his arm. He wore a ball cap and sunglasses. It could have been a mock-up for the company's ad campaign. In another, the driver had climbed back into the truck with Sasha waving behind him. The next one showed the same driver leaning against the truck grinning, smoking. Sasha stood next to him, also smoking. In the last one, the driver's half-closed eyelids exposed long curled eyelashes like a doll's. Here, Tadzio's cartoon-like motion of Sasha flipping back the ball cap, revealed a shock of thick luxuriant hair flowing past the narrow shoulders of a female.

TWO

Darryl King sank his body deeper into the earth and was barely conscious of Andy next to him until the other man chirped.

"Darryl, sting and stakeout are two different animals. A sting is art. You create diversions, misdirections, traps; then you storm the citadel like a Roman. That's art. But stakeout is only a distant relative of surveillance; it comes from the practice of surveyors, who mainly measure stuff before a project commences. This here, what we're doing, is a stakeout. But this here, should be a sting."

"Don't let Lydia hear you say that," Darryl said.

"I'm just saying, if it's coming, it better come soon. Besides, she doesn't scare me," Andy said.

"Really? Because she does most people." Darryl said.

They continued to lay at the top of an earthen berm above the interstate in companionable silence. Thanks to a night sky that was both moonless and cloudless, neither man could see the other's expression nor read his thoughts for once. But they were thinking the same thing. The Russians weren't coming.

They had been watching the frontage road that led into the industrial park for almost three hours. At the bottom of the steep embankment, Lydia and Captain Carlos Sans sat cramped together inside a mobile unit monitoring video images of the deserted loading dock. Further back in an empty field, a convoy of squad cars and armored trucks filled with police in riot gear, sat at the ready. When Sans gave them the order, they would drive their vehicles over the berm and across the freeway to do their own version of rushing the fortress.

Lydia called on the radiophone, "Darryl, what's Andy doing?"

"Same thing he was when you asked two minutes ago. Looking through night vision goggles at concrete and seeing nothing. Right Andy? He says, right."

"Fuck you two reptiles. You're missing something."

Darryl said, "You can't fool me. I know you love us."

Sans took the radiophone away from Lydia. "Just let us know when you do see something."

For the third time, Darryl wondered how much longer Sans was going to let this charade go on. His gut told him nothing was going to happen tonight, and it must be obvious to everyone else that something had spooked the Russians. Otherwise they'd be here already. He knew how disappointed Lydia would be.

Sans trusted Lydia like she trusted Sasha. She had promised to deliver Markiza, arguably the world's biggest and shrewdest trafficker, so Sans threw unprecedented dollars into the investigation. On top of everything else, he had called in his last markers to get a judge to run a wire on the warehouse. They had taps on the factory, the enjoining dormitory, and two of Markiza's lieutenants' cell phones.

Lydia was known among police investigators as the Miami architect of confidence games. If she had enough manpower and dollars to work with, no criminal was safe from her. Responsible for everything from design to delivery, she had exposed government fraud, brought down a major international banking system, put away a psychopathic killer, and got a high-level drug lord to rat on another. But that was before she got emotionally involved with an informant.

Darryl mused that at one time he been the recipient of that much care and love. Once, months after they had broken up, Lydia had asked him what had been the happiest time of his life. He answered truthfully. The six months they spent together. Without saying another word she patted his forearm with forgiving strokes and then kissed him on the cheek. She knew what it had cost him to tell her that. She wasn't greedy or vindictive; it was just that occasionally she needed to know that her own love hadn't happened in a vacuum.

Not in all the years he'd been married to Karen had he been that happy, or felt that comfortable around another human being. So it was with something like amazement that he'd discovered himself determined to quit the relationship. He always knew the pervasive reason for his decision, but on occasion, such as now, he questioned why his heart had allowed his brain to surrender so easily. When it knew the brain was telling brazen lies.

That morning seemed like yesterday. His hands had been full of Lydia—her luscious taught body, that riot of unruly first-thing-in-the-morning thick hair—as she dragged him into the brightly lit bathroom to show him their reflection. From the side, they looked like a single braided human in two color strands. She leaned into him lolling her head across his broad chest; one of her legs was pulled up seductively balancing the heel and ball of her foot against his calf. While she encircled his neck with arms pulled back and stretched like a gymnast's, he had his hands wrapped around her waist, his chin dipped into her shoulder. Their chiaroscuro portrayal glistened from the night's lovemaking, and Lydia said she recognized a magazine cover when she saw one. The last thing Darryl expected was for that same likeness inside the looking glass to jump out and mock him.

Flesh of my flesh, bone of my bones. Not on your life, baby. Where the hell had that come from?

His face was all dark angles across features that since childhood family and friends had told him were striking, and so far his forty-year-old body had not betrayed him. It was still lean and muscular like a long-distance runner's. He eased out of the embrace and saw Lydia as if for the first time. Yet he knew it was a trick, and that some part of him was deliberately sabotaging the best thing that had happened to him. And he allowed it.

Shape and proportion gave way to color. Or the lack of color. Before this he had thought of her as olive-skinned with plenty of pigment because after all, Lydia had been the only progeny of a Mexican artist and a Bulgarian banker. But here standing next to him, her skin resembled fine alabaster. He was too shocked to feel any shame for what he was thinking about.

How could he move past the color contrast between them when he finally glimpsed what others must have always seen? His mother and sister—the looks, the hushed tones whenever he first brought Lydia around. He remembered how he tried to ignore their occasional white-people jokes, their not-so-subtle suggestions to sign up with a black dating service. And then his mind traced dinners at fashionable restaurants that he and Lydia shared, the walks on the boardwalk afterwards, and so many Sunday afternoons on the beach. People always stared at them and he thought it was because they were so damned good looking together. Could he have been that naïve? Even at that juncture, he could have easily shut off the thoughts that lead to hell. Later . . . it really would be too late.

He could see now that wasn't what mattered. Truth, it didn't bother him what others thought. And his own family couldn't help themselves; they fell in love with Lydia about the same time he did. His sister said later that she had been expecting wedding bells to chime.

The elephant in the bathroom had never been about their color differences—even though he did think about that sometimes. It was a self-created obstacle. It was his fear of failing again and becoming like his father. If fear were energy, the anxiety and dread that coursed through him when he stared at the reflection of their intertwined bodies, could have fueled a small planet. To get away from the fire that was about to consume him, he excused himself from love by drawing a bogus race card and then for good measure, told himself that he could never fully trust Lydia.

When Darryl stepped back from the mirror, peeling apart their photo op, Lydia knew what he was thinking and had screamed a defiant No. He'd left that morning without an explanation but sent her a letter a few days later. She answered it with two sentences.

I think I'm going to die. Nothing has ever hurt this much.

Darryl was pulled back from the past when his partner poked him in the shoulder. Andy held a finger to his tightly closed lips and pointed with another to his headset. He pulled off one ear bud and handed it to Darryl. Together they listened to an argument that should have remained private. It seemed either Sans or Lydia forgot to shut off their transmitter.

"Look Lydia, we can stay a little longer, but these riot squads guys, they're getting paid in gold bullion. I can't justify much more overtime for them."

Lydia's voice began calmly enough, "Something's holding them up. You know for a fact that Sasha has never been wrong before. Thanks to him we've identified mob lieutenants, Miami business partners, banks, holding companies—all linked to Markiza. He's got this too. We have to be patient."

Sans said, "I think he was right."

With a start, Darryl pictured Lydia's stomach clenching.

"You think they're onto him? But how? He's discreet. Never talks or sees anyone. No computer searches could lead back to him. He's too good."

Sans said, "They might have spotted something between you two. Held the shipment back to see what would happen."

"But Andy . . . he would have known before anyone. God, Captain. Schedules change. Besides, we know that the boys are in the country. And they're coming here."

Sans shrugged. "Maybe, maybe not. Distribution might have been relocated. If that happened, we're back to square one."

"No. They'll be here."

"Lydia, it's not your fault. I'm not holding you responsible. Listen, if—"

Andy pulled up his binoculars and adjusted his microphone, "Captain, Lydia, two vans rounding the corner. Watch where they go."

After a beat, Lydia said, "I see movement, I told you." It sounded like she smacked something hard because the ear buds popped like firecrackers in their ears.

Darryl and Andy continued watching as two ordinary looking, white-paneled vans drove slowly into the parking lot. They parked side by side. A man got out of each van and shook hands with the other. They pulled out cigarettes and lit up. The detectives watched in disbelief as one of them found a flask, took a swallow, and handed it off to the other man. Ten minutes went by. The men talked, smoked, and laughed.

"'Captain, what are they saying?" Andy asked

"Lydia says they're swapping gardening tips."

This time Darryl and Andy looked at each other and clearly saw what the other was thinking. Darryl grabbed the mic. "Shit. They're throwing it in our face. Giving us the finger. And you know what's next, don't you?"

They all knew. A stink bomb. They heard Lydia shout, "So what! We have them."

Darryl's voice snapped over the radio. "What the hell's going on?"

Sans said, "You two can belly on down now. We're leaving."

Lydia said, "NO!! You can't. I'm primary on this. I say when. Besides, two minutes ago I had more time. Now just because the thugs are taking a cigarette break, you call it quits?"

"You might be primary but I'm your superior officer. So pull yourself together. You know what happens next. It won't be worth it."

Lydia cried, "Look!!"

The men flicked their cigarette butts into the air and strode to the back of the vans. Out of each vehicle they pulled out six sleepy boys and lined them up in a row. Next they marched them across the parking lot to the eastern end where they shoved them through the delivery door Sasha always used whenever he met Lydia.

Sans spat. "I knew it. See, that's the stink bomb. They throw a few kids in our face, but they know we know it's not enough."

Lydia said, "Are you insane? They're little boys about to be sold into slavery. We have a legal and moral obligation to help them. I gave Sasha my word."

"Since when do you report to a child? You report to me and your obligation is to follow orders." Scraping and shuffling noises made it sound like Sans was on the move or wanted to be. "Your source promised me two-hundred boys. You know we can't make our case with just a few. We'll never get Markiza this way."

"Plus the seventy kids inside," Lydia said.

"You're forgetting something. If we move now, we'll never find the others. Ever. So we have to wait."

"For what? For more innocent children to get abused? To die? You bastard."

"Lydia—"

"If they're onto Sasha, they'll kill him. It'll be on you."

"No, special detective, it's on you. You've completely lost your objectivity. Your emotional hang-up with this Russian boy has overshadowed good police instincts. What the fuck happened to you, Lydia? How did you lose the ground beneath you?"

"I walked up on a bigger stage."

Sans sounded bewildered. "You were trained to withstand the effects of emotional involvement. You're better than this."

"You can't know what's really inside until something like this case opens you up."

Forgetting that they were still eavesdropping Andy cut in. "Lydia, it'll be okay. Captain's got a point. We have to find all of the kids. And Markiza."

"Fuck you."

Darryl said, "Lyd. I hate this just as much as you. But you know it's not over. We're going to get them, right? Just not tonight."

Lydia said, "It never occurred to me that you two would sandbag me. How stupid was I?"

THREE

When Lydia walked down Biscayne Boulevard people gave her wide berth. Not because they were afraid of her—although some might be—but mainly to get a better, longer look before she turned into an afterimage and then disappeared altogether.

The Special Intelligence detective was tall and leggy with a slim athletic build; today she wore her hair gathered into a thick ropy braid that switched like a nervous pony's. She wore a faded jean jacket with a white tank underneath, fitted chinos that molded to buttocks like they had been ironed onto her body, and rugged black lace-up boots. Green-tinted, mirrored shades accentuated a mixture of delicate and sharp features. She had skin that was tawny and as soft as a chamois cloth, and full pink lips that glinted in the sun. People always looked. But the manner in which she got scoped depended on who was doing the scoping.

Lydia knew she invited attention. She didn't really mind because she likened her fast walking, strong body to a traveling mirror that could secretly record the city's social yearnings. Along the roadway while men and women examined and passed judgment on her, often heaping on flirtatious leers; others showing disapproval or even jealousy, Lydia sensed escaping memories, secret dreams and desires, unspoken sadness and loneliness, and the unwinding emotional toll of being alive.

The old Cuban men always took the full snapshot and almost immediately withdrew their ogling eyes when Lydia returned their stare, but not before something shifted behind clouded gazes. Behind the ruins of their old selves lay hidden memories of strolling down Havana's romantic seafront promenade with a girl who might have looked a lot like Lydia. During a time when war and embargo had not collided with their youth, managing to lock out childhood dreams forever.

The younger Cuban males, who never had to witness bloodied history right outside of their front doors, assessed Lydia with everything from overbearing gaping to whispered catcalls. She thought their actions were typical of the unemployed youth; they belied a bored, unfulfilled existence that no amount of swagger or machismo could mask.

Cuban women with small children often smiled up at her shyly, as if hoping that a drop of her essence might imbue their progeny with the same kind of confidence and success she seemed to possess. Sometimes Lydia looked back to see the women still watching her. They could never dream that even though she had the right kind of exterior packaging, inside and on most days, she felt as helpless as any one of them.

Black and dark Latino men watched her obliquely but took the most time. They hardly ever smiled but something in their gait slowed and altered, as if their thoughts were being invaded; for a split second they thought they might know her. Might stop and talk to her. But they never did. Because even though more than thirty years had passed since the savage beating and death of Arthur McDuffie by white Miami police officers, the hurt was still too deep, the cultural divide still too wide. Lydia was more white than Latino and, if they looked closer, they would know that the bulge under her jacket could only be a gun belonging to a cop.

Black and dark Latino women appeared to ignore her but managed to slide their eyes sideways for the quickest release of the shutter. It was enough. She was an attractive giant who posed no threat to them.

It took Lydia thirty minutes to walk from her apartment in the run-down neighborhood of Park West, to the downtown Miami police station. She needed the brisk workout to tease out the memory of the nightmare. Something that was happening now every day since she left Sasha locked up at the factory a week ago. She dreamed of children climbing aboard a carousal in an amusement park. As the platform turned in a circle and painted wooden horses bobbed up and down, the children laughed and pretended to gallop. But when the calliope music started and the horses turned into white vans, the children began to scream. The vans sped off quickly towards a high cliff above the ocean. She had waited at the precipice holding out her hand to open the doors for the children to escape, but they had locked themselves in. She could only watch helplessly as each van toppled over the promontory onto the deep abyss below. Afterwards when Lydia awoke, the images remained.

Only the early morning August heat could melt away much of the terror and panic she felt. While she strode down the boardwalk of one of America's most traveled highways, ancient royal palms lined up like sentries to guard towering hotels, million dollar condominiums, international banks, and bustling office plazas. She discovered she could ignore block after block of despicable displays of ostentation by simply gazing at the ocean. Today Lydia noticed the rising sun had stippled the water with a silvery coat that glittered like a million teardrops. Miami's unapologetic commercialism bracketed by breathtaking vistas. It was this city's paradox that managed to retain Lydia as a resident for most of her thirty-four years. All except the one year that she spent in Minnesota.

As she headed west on Coral Way, she encountered the usual long line of people waiting to get into the Museum of Contemporary Art. The familiar Dominican man covered by a yellow and red umbrella, was pushing his stainless steel cart and doing a brisk business. He trundled hot cups of coffee and homemade sweet rolls to sleepy waiting tourists. When he saw Lydia he waved and poured her a large espresso. As she paid him she noticed two women in line, both with fiery red hair, talking excitedly. It was time, she thought, to come up with a new disguise so she could see Sasha again.

As she got closer, Lydia frowned at the three-story police headquarters, arguably the ugliest edifice in downtown. The first two stories, which were made of brick and glass, were only boring. But some misguided architect decided to add a white ridge of crenellated, jutting offices at the top. From a distance, it looked like the building was wearing a chef's hat. Lydia pushed through the revolving doors and walked into Miami's epicenter of police activity. Besides offices for administration, field operations, information technology and internal affairs, the mayor's department also let out a few rooms in the chef's hat for Sans' special task force. Woven with staff from Special Victims Bureau and The

Violence Crime Inspector's office, the four detectives and their captain were affectionately referred to as MAGS, short for *Markiza's Ass Goes South*.

Inside the lobby Lydia got icy reception. And not just from the over-amped air conditioning system. The regular cops didn't understand her and didn't like her, so they ignored her. That suited Lydia just fine. She rode the elevator to the third floor and waited for the doors to open to the MAGS atrium.

Lydia punched in her code and a tall glass door slid open. MAGS looked like a banking center. A semi-circle of wood and glass partitions complete with computers and phones banks served as working stations for the detectives and Marla. Dwarf palm trees had been brought in to fill up some of the wasted space in the atrium between the cubicles and the office. Sans' office was a notch between two points of the chef's hat. It looked out over downtown and had an actual door.

Noticing that Darryl wasn't at his desk, Lydia walked over and searched its contents until she found what she was looking for. Before she could sit down though, the detective snatched the copy of *Essence* magazine out of her hands.

"Hey, that's my fashion magazine," Darryl said.

Lydia let out an exasperated sigh. "Why can't you buy porn like normal men?"

Darryl shrugged, "I like these women better. Besides, if I did, there would be nothing for you to steal."

"That's just stupid."

That brought a laughing spasm from Marla Stanfield. A short round African American woman pushing forty, with a cherubic face which at times like this, could pass for seventeen, was Lydia's favorite person in the world. Lydia wished everyone could be as smart, decisive and fair, and funny, as the communications manager on their team.

"What's up, Marla?"

"You just kill me girl. Don't you know by now that ever since you broke his sorry heart, our man about-town here—Darryl, only dates between the pages of magazines?"

"Now Marla, that would be hilarious if only one word of it were true. Everyone knows damn well," Lydia pointed fingers at Marla, Darryl, Andy, who just walked in, and the captain behind his closed door, "that it wasn't me who did the leaving."

Darryl cleared his throat and smiled good-naturedly. "Stop picking on us, Marla. That was a long time ago. Young puppy love. Back when we were both in Major Crimes, working up the homeless serial killer case. Remember Lyd, when you cut your hair and wore street rags for three months? I'd sneak into your crib in tent city and cozy up, even though one of us hadn't bathed in weeks. But we cracked the case. Remember?"

Lydia's took off her sunglasses letting her melt-in-your-mouth chocolate brown eyes harden into marbles. Puppy love indeed! She remembered that they had been hopelessly smitten with each other, believing that their love and idealism could conquer the woes of all of humankind. *Darryl and Lydia against the world.* Then one day he woke up to discover she was white. Some excuse. He broke it off and never looked back. The clueless man at one time had been the great love of her life. Lydia shut off the memory and turned her attention to the closed door.

"What's going on in there," Lydia said. Their supervisor had a literal open door policy. It was always open whether he was alone, on the phone, handing out assignments, or even reprimanding a detective—everyone was privy to that conversation. But not today.

Marla crossed her arms and shook her head. "I don't like it at all. Naaah. They've been in there since I got here, and that was almost two hours ago. Ever since he got chair of the Justice Committee, Senator Lex Kastle wants more and more updates, and how he likes to put it, 'to be part of the process'. He's a meddler if you ask me, and the captain puts up with it."

"Maybe he's got good reason since it was the senator's recommendation that got us open-ended funding for the task force," Darryl said.

"Personally, I think he's compensating." Marla said.

The three detectives waited patiently for her to go on.

"That senator in there used to be a big thing in this town. Movie star looks, football hero, beloved high school teacher, freshman senator, all that and he ends up a cripple. A cripple in a wheel chair."

Lydia burst out laughing from embarrassment. "Marla, no one says cripple anymore. It's handicapped or disabled. You know better."

"Would calling Kastle disabled make him less of a cripple?" Marla asked. Lydia punched her lightly in the arm.

Andy said, "I remember the case. Unsolved hit-and-run eight years ago. Kastle's first year in office and he was just leaving the state capitol on the way to the courthouse. He started crossing the intersection when a speeding van mowed him down and kept on going. It was lunchtime with lots of people around; still few saw what actually happened. In a written testimony, one bystander swore that the truck was turning the corner at a normal speed, but when the driver saw Kastle, the driver accelerated and hit him on purpose.

Darryl said, "Didn't another eye witness say that after hitting Kastle, the driver backed up and ran over his legs? But the coroner stated his injuries were not consistent with that kind of collision."

"In any case, Kastle's spine was crushed, but he made it. Took a whole year in rehab. Next term, he won by a landslide."

"Wicked. Sounds like he had a target on his back. Did anyone ever connect him to organized crime?" Lydia asked.

"Nah, he's a choir boy." Marla said.

"Maybe a disgruntled voter," Darryl offered.

"Or a warning." Lydia said.

Before anyone could add two more cents, the captain's door swung open followed by a soft beeping of an electric wheelchair working itself out of the narrow passageway. Sans walked close behind.

The handsome senator nodded at the detectives and Marla but kept his gaze on Lydia when he spoke.

"I'd like to say how sorry I am that you did not find all the boys at the warehouse. I can't imagine how hard it was to leave the rest of them behind like that, but you all did the right thing. Remember Markiza is the prize, and when you get him you'll have everything else.

"And don't worry, you will always have my full support, and I'll make sure you get everything you need to keep this operation going. I wish I could stay longer, but I have to get back to Tallahassee for a subcommittee meeting later this afternoon." Kastle waved his hand behind him as he rolled out to the corridor where an aide and an opened elevator door waited for him.

When the elevator door closed, Sans asked everyone to come into to his office.

They all sat down and Sans said, "Our intelligence was too good. First, Andy working inside. And then Sasha. We know the boy always had good intel. I'm telling you now what I told the senator. Inside this operation lies a mole and a huge goddamned leak. We'll have to start completely over. New surveillance, new wire taps, the whole nine yards.

"But first we have to hunt down the mole and eliminate it."

"Any suspects?" Darryl asked.

"Not yet. I want us to concentrate on citizen informers and technology. Andy and Marla, you two are in charge of proofing our communications. Darryl, check out the CIs, anyone at all connected to this case. Lydia, talk to Sasha again. And stay uninvolved. Do you think you can do that?"

Lydia cut her eyes icily to Sans. "Does the senator suspect any of us?"

"No, of course not." Sans turned to go. "Reports on my desk by the end of the week. Let's move on this."

Andy, Darryl, and Marla groaned as they got up and went to their respective desks. Lydia followed Sans into his office.

"What am I supposed to tell Sasha?"

"Tell him the truth, that we were sabotaged."

"I owe him. We all do." Lydia said.

"Just do your job."

"He's a human being who feels things. Do you even remember what that's like?" Lydia didn't wait for a response but strode out of the room grabbing her jacket on the way to the elevator. She stopped when she saw Andy. He got up from his desk and headed for the water cooler.

"Hey, why do you walk away every time we're alone together in a room?" Lydia said.

"I don't." Andy said.

"You've been a jerk to me ever since—"

"You walked out on me."

"Don't give me that. I don't want to date you. You don't want to date me. But we used to be friends. It's something else. Tell me what it is."

Andy picked up a file, sat back down at his desk, and fired up his computer. "Some other time, Lydia. You heard the captain. I gotta get busy on these."

Darryl held the phone to his ear and took a swig from his coffee mug. He couldn't hear what the two detectives were saying but watching them through the break room window, it was easy to imagine. Lydia was painting the air with lots of expressive gestures that seemed to articulate her unhappiness over something Andy did or didn't do. Andy's response was to turn into a turtle and hide his head. Seeing anything bad happen to Lydia always tugged at Darryl's conscience.

He said into his cell, "Yeah, mom. Sorry about that. I'm listening. There's a lot going on around here today. I'll be there. Because when you describe them, I can smell all those delicious sauces right through the phone. Makes me hungry just thinking about it."

It wasn't going well out there. Now Lydia was tugging on Andy's shirtsleeve, but he shrugged her away. When Lydia finally walked over to the elevators, her head was down and she was pulling on her sunglasses.

"Mom, that sounds great. I've got to get back to work. See you Friday then. I love you. Bye."

Darryl clicked off the cell and noticed a missed message from Karen. Oh no, not today. Not any day, he thought. He erased the message without listening to it.

FOUR

Lydia timed it so she could arrive at the warehouse just as Sasha was coming out to smoke his final cigarette of the day.

Today, she pulled up from the opposite direction in a blue Ford Focus with large magnetic signs plastered across the doors that read, *Crocodile Couriers*. Andy had ordered a transfer cable for his computer, insisting he had to have it by the end of the day.

When she was parallel to the stoop, Lydia rolled down her window and was so close to the boy she could almost touch him.

He wouldn't look at her.

Sasha said, "I stayed up all night waiting for you. What happened, why didn't you get me out? You promised."

"Oh god, Sasha. You have to know how much I wanted to. They wouldn't let me because only a handful of kids showed up. We were expecting two-hundred."

"That's what I heard."

"Sasha no one blames you. Please try to forgive me; my hands were tied. What do you suppose happened to the other boys?"

Sasha shrugged. "I wish I knew. Do you have a Camel?" Lydia handed him a cigarette and took one for herself. After they lit up, Sasha still wouldn't meet her eyes. It wasn't like him not to remark on her new disguise. Today she had on a bright red wig that tapered into an A-line bob, tortoise-shelled eyeglasses, and her midriff was wrapped with cotton batting making her appear pregnant. He should have been acting like a smart- ass by now, piling on jokes and laughing.

"We have to quit these, you know," Lydia said.

Slowly Sasha looked back at his old friend and lifted a brow. "Why?"

"Because my building is going smoke-free the first of the month. We won't be able to smoke inside the apartment, not even on the grounds."

Sasha tried to smile, but it didn't make it to his eyes.

"Something strange is going on around here. They've taken half the workers to other plants. Only three guards left and Markiza never comes around anymore."

She could tell something was off too. "Where's Tadzio?"

"I don't know, he doesn't hang on me like he used to."

"Did he finally make new friends?"

"No, most of the other boys still think he's a twerp. Tadzio just draws all the time now with those new colored pencils."

The hair on her neck and hands stood up. "Colored pencils? When did he get them?" Lydia asked.

"I think the last time you were here."

Lydia leaned her head out the window and looked around. She saw the bullet before she heard it. Her eyes followed the *frisson* of movement until it reached the stoop.

Sasha sank into the concrete, his cigarette still clutched between his fingers.

One hand on her automatic, Lydia tore open the door and catapulted out of the car on her stomach pulling Sasha off the stoop. She rolled on her back covering the body as she fired two rounds into the staircase window above. The sniper moved out of the way, but she could hear shouting. Any minute they would come down the stairs and kill her too.

Sasha had died instantly. The first two bullets exploded his head, the next three tattooed his chest. She picked Sasha up by the shoulders and cradled his body for the first time in her life, even as his own life was exiting the human world. It was dangerous to linger, but Lydia thought if there were such a thing as a soul, she would stay long enough to let him know that at the end, he was not alone.

Reinforcements did not come down the stairs. Instead, two vans started up from the far end of the parking lot and were accelerating for the stoop. She scrambled into the car and gave the round window one last look. Small splayed fingers clenched and unclenched, sending a cascade of broken colored pencils raining on her windshield and hood. The car went screaming down the tarmac, the tires pulverizing the splintered wooden pieces.

One idea guided Lydia. She needed to get to the frontage road before the Russians did.

A volley of artillery fire ricocheted off of both rear quarter panels. The rear window shattered spraying glass over the back of her wig. She was so close. She swept her eyes over her inflated stomach and legs and then caught her reflection in the mirror. Face and neck were coated with drying blood. Sasha's blood.

She was there. The frontage road was segmented by a series of hairpin S-curves and Lydia blasted through them. It was only when her tires began to screech with protest and the rear end threatened to break lose, did she take her foot off the accelerator slightly. She handled the Ford like it was a European sports car and it rewarded her by staying glued to the road.

The sharp forty-five degree bend was just up ahead, and there was no guardrail between the road and the ravine below. Lydia jerked the wheel like it was Markiza's head, opened the door, and jumped out of the car.

She was dreaming her nightmare. Except she hadn't been driving a white van and, at the last second, was able to escape because no one had her locked in. Until now, Lydia hadn't understood that the reason she'd gone to the precipice in the dream was to save herself.

The Ford nose-dived and tumbled against rocks and trees. It rolled and jounced and finally disappeared into a mixture of burning gases that rose into the air like a volcanic eruption. The raging inferno jumped to trees and grasses. The hillside roared.

Lydia rolled several times until she crashed into a canopy of hardwood hammock. She slipped around the trees and ran down a skinny path. A hundred feet later she shimmied down the ridge until her head was even with the road. She pressed her body into hard earth and covered her ears. The explosions rumbled like cannon fire behind her, and Lydia almost didn't hear the Russians get out of their vehicles. She strained to hear their voices and thought she heard English but could not make out any of the words. When they took off in the vans again, she waited another five minutes before pulling out her cell phone.

Sans was quiet while Lydia filled him in. When she was finished he asked, "How badly are you hurt?"

"Best guess, a chipped elbow and a couple of broken ribs. It hurts to breathe. A bullet might have grazed my shoulder. Yeah, I think I popped an intestine. I'll tell you about that later. But right now you need to hear something else."

Lydia waited for Sans' intake of breath.

"There's something you didn't know about Sasha. This was his plan from the start. Back in Russia he didn't have to let Markiza take him. He chose to come to America."

She coughed and sputtered but forced herself to gain control. She had to make him understand.

"He came willingly to America with Markiza because no one would make the scumbag pay in Russia. He thought that in America someone would listen. Someone would help. Someone would put an end to the filth and horror.

"He found Andy. He found us. This was his dream, to stop Markiza once and for all. We're going to make it come true for him, Carlos," Lydia said.

"What do you have in mind?"

FIVE

In the still of the night, Port of Miami twinkled like a runaway carnival ride. Lit up cruise ships, container terminals, and giant cranes splashed the harbor in searchlight patterns of yellow, orange, and green. Inside a cramped office trailer across from the loading dock, a man watched Markiza go to the front window. He saw what the old man saw. The first patches of blue rupturing the eastern sky. He couldn't say how he knew exactly, but he was certain that the pre-dawn hour was Markiza's favorite time of day. After the stars had completely disappeared but before the sun rose to greet the world.

Tall and erect, hands clasped behind his back, the kingpin liked having one foot in a dark world where specters and conspiracies lurked, and the other in the new day alighting in so many possibilities. The man suspected Markiza actually believed that by leaning on the window, casting his countenance on the frontier, he could magically turn night into day. Another reason to fear him, and why he ruled the Florida underworld. The delusions only served to boost his power.

At 72, Markiza was an impressive example of manliness. He hadn't only retained a fine stature, but he also kept most of the muscle mass he'd earned from the wrestling days of his youth. Even his arms, though rippling with sinewy cords and thick veins, bulged under skin that was smooth and satiny. It was as if the skin had stopped aging long ago. Markiza looked exceptionally healthy.

But the man's nose sensed decay.

Even after a shower and a splash of expensive cologne, Markiza still emitted a sickly mixture of rotting garbage and piss-stained flesh. Odors that well scrubbed pores and creases could not hold back. A half century of turning people's lives into chaos and ruin had marked him with stink.

Whenever a new shipment was due, Markiza insisted that the man had to come and watch the arrival. He had said it was to show him what he was capable of. But it also occurred to the man that there might be another reason. He wasn't there just to watch Markiza gloat over his newest acquisitions. The older man was trying to fix him with the breadth of his influence. He wanted him scared. Hadn't too much time passed for the settling of old scores? Surely, but not if you were Markiza and suffered from obsessive-compulsive personality disorder.

The man had seen it more than once. Invading intrusive thoughts had brought the old man to his knees, paralyzing him. Those were memories of losing his family and how he'd been made powerless to stop the flight. Most obsessive-compulsives become preoccupied with hand washing or extensive hoarding. Markiza bought and sold young boys.

And the man knew why. Markiza had never truly wanted his family back. His only relief came through inflicting pain. For some reason he was also convinced that the man was partially responsible for his misfortune.

Unfortunately, besides the boys, he was the only one left Markiza could still punish.

As if suddenly disturbed by the man's orbiting thoughts, Markiza turned around and lobbed his meaty hand on his shoulder.

"You see how good it is to own your own ship. When there's a problem, you just detain the cargo until it's safe to move it.

"Of course, we almost blew it. Or should I say, *you* nearly cost me six million dollars." Markiza kept his arm on the man while turning back to gaze into the bleeding sky.

The man shrugged. "Don't blame me. I gave you Andy and, for ten whole months, your people could no more link him to any of the kids or the intelligence than the man on the moon."

"Andy was a partial piece of the big puzzle. It was the child that discovered the UPS driver and Sasha."

The Russian teenager's death had sickened the man. Since then, he had to work hard on burying that memory, as well as the picture of Lydia Angelova's last moments in a burning car. He had been told there would be no violence. No killings. He never learned. They always lied.

"It turns out that an eight-year-old has more brains and heart than you and all of my lieutenants put together." Markiza sniggered from deep inside his throat. He continued talking without any expression on his face.

"I'm quite fond of the little rascal. You should see all the pictures he draws for me. The boy's gifted and soon I'm going to put his talents to better use. You know, he's like the son I never had."

The words cut the man deeper than he would ever show. It wasn't in the old man to get attached. He hoped for the child's sake that hadn't changed.

Even though no sound reached them, the two men lifted their heads at the same time towards the distant ship. On the starboard side, a set of stairs began unfolding like an accordion. As delicate as shadows, the boys lowered themselves onto boats anchored to the ship. When the vessels reached the gangplank, they climbed up in pairs and began their first walk upon the shores of America. Like dogs in training, they followed their guides and snaked up across the dock and up a mesh-lined ramp. Two hundred boys ranging from five to fourteen years old—until a few minutes ago—all perfectly hidden in plain sight.

Soon after the organization got spooked, Markiza's cargo carrier reported a broken fuel line and, until today, sat waiting patiently for parts in the Atlantic bay. The boys had lived for almost two weeks aboard containers breathing air through vent holes. Their only visitors were guards who came twice a day to feed them and to empty the portable toilets.

"So that's what six million dollars looks like," said the man watching the perfectly choreographed march.

"And it's only the beginning. We have a new borderland before us; the prospects are staggering. Slowly but definitely, we'll be changing how things are done around here." Markiza said.

"That sounds reckless, even for you. Haven't you noticed? This isn't Russia."

The first of the boys climbed up into one of two tractor-trailers waiting for them at the end of the ramp.

"Don't I know it! When I was still in the motherland selling to the Baltics or Asia, all I could get was a measly two thousand per head. And those customers were predators. A bad lot, all of them. Here it's thirty thousand, and the boys have an opportunity to acquire a new trade," Markiza said.

The man howled. "A new trade? You mean like learning to scrub toilets and sew shirts and pants for ten hours a day? You're locking kids into servitude for life with no hope for freedom or dignity."

"Ah, but you see it from your lofty American arm chair. What they are really getting is a new start, a new chance at life. You would never understand this because you never knew hunger or disease. You were a spoiled child that always had someone to look after you. Someone you thought loved you." Markiza spoke the last word haltingly like the wrong pitch or tone might contain a poison.

"Those boys will be sold like slaves in the market. That doesn't sound like much of a life to me."

Men in starched blue-grey overalls shut the doors and locked them. Moments later, the trucks pulled away to head for the inter-coastal highway that would take them to a factory at the end of a sealed up, defunct industrial park.

"Don't you worry that one day these kids will grow up to rebel? That they'll run away and report their handlers? And you?"

Markiza finally lifted his hand from the man's shoulder and pretended to swat away the question, but decided in the end to answer. "They are smuggled goods who don't speak English or know anyone here. They depend on us for their most basic necessities. If not for us, they would die. I'm not worried."

Or if you were, you'd kill them, the man thought. "I suppose it doesn't hurt that you've told them if they try anything stupid, their families back home will be tortured or murdered."

Markiza shook his head lightly as if to say, no matter how hard I try, I can't make you see the light. "The times are changing. Your country is beginning to look more and more like all the other ones it tries to control. By the time these kids are grown, the United States will have become a two-tiered society. There will only be haves and have-nots."

Markiza moved to a shelf on the wall above where the man sat. Hovering over his companion, he pulled down a bottle of Jack Daniels. He found two glasses and poured in the whiskey. He handed the man his drink and swallowed hard.

"You know how politics work. After enough wheeling and dealing, mixed in with a few bribes, eventually the powerful will be able to buy the legality to own domestic servants. And they'll get tax credits for it too."

"You're dreaming. You can only go so far with this madness before you're caught. You know you're not invincible, don't you?"

"Is this what troubles you? That I might have feet of clay? No, I think you of all people knows better. As they like to say on the docks, 'you're just yanking my chain.'" Markiza wiped his hands sharply back and forth to make the point.

The commercial trucks had disappeared from sight. The sky lightened and waves crashed gently against the moorings. Seagulls squawked their first morning announcements and, in response, the sun poked its yellow head to begin the new day. A convoy of pick up trucks streamed down the inter-coastal highway towards the port, delivering stevedores to work. It appeared that the world was back in balance.

The man opened the door and let himself out. "Screen your buyers well," he cautioned over his shoulder. "Miami is the wealthiest city in the country. You're going to get a lot of bored people dripping with money. They'll pay top dollar but watch out, most of them are nuts," he said.

"Don't worry about me, just do your job. Watch the feds, ICE, and keep that cursed task force out my hair." Markiza slipped around the corner leaving the man absolutely alone, and more frightened than he'd ever been.

SIX

She counted 150 fish in the tank. More or less the same number Lydia came up with the last time she walked around the acrylic showpiece. If the directors of the clinic thought that placing a thousand-gallon, wrap-around aquarium in the middle of the waiting room was supposed to relieve a patient's anxiety and stress before surgery, well, they were right. It was like being in the middle of a luminescent dream or watching a Jacques Cousteau film. Lydia felt buoyant and carefree with so many beautiful combinations of colors and patterns twirling and twisting past her. Briefly, she wondered how often designers got their inspirations from nature.

The acrylic aquarium was filled with dozens of varieties of exotic fish, a kelp forest, decorative rock gardens and stones, and probably cost as much as an average house in southern Florida. Lydia calculated that twenty-five surgeries would have paid for it.

At this late hour the clinic was technically closed to patients. Full spectrum lighting inside the tank produced the only light in the waiting room. Sans used it to read his copy of Newsweek. Apparently another rebellion in the Arab world was sparking international attention. Lydia saw that her captain was only staring at the words.

"Carlos. It's okay. You can relax now. Look at *me*," Lydia pointed to her chest, "I'm not the least bit afraid or worried. So why don't you put that magazine down and talk to me."

"I've never known you to worry about anything. That's always been my job. I can't help thinking that if this wasn't the best plan in the world, it would be the worst," Sans said.

"Oh great. You know, you totally suck at this. It's supposed to be your job to keep me laughing with your long list of stupid blonde jokes or even some of those rookie cop stories you're always telling at the office. But no, suddenly you've turned into Mr. Serious. Very professional." Lydia grabbed her own magazine, rolled it up, and slapped it against her boss's arm.

Sans narrowed his eyes. "Maybe what we should be discussing is not my behavior but yours. Let's just call it the absence of behavior."

"What are you talking about Carlos?"

"I'm talking about your seemingly total lack of concern for others. Why don't you ever talk about the other detectives or Marla? They're supposed to be your friends and family. Yet what you've done and, what you're about to do, will devastate them. You know that, right? Don't you feel the least bit guilty?"

Lydia put her hand up in the air. "I can't think about that. If I did, then I couldn't go through with it. And I certainly wouldn't allow Miami's finest plastic surgeon cut me up like a slaughterhouse butcher." She laughed while Sans made wretching noises.

"But hell, when it's over, when Markiza's in bracelets, and the boys are freed, the shops closed, the buyers in front of grand juries—then we can tell them."

"What if it's too late? What if they hate you for what you made them go through?"

"It's a chance I'll have to take."

"You scare me. I figure you're either a sociopath, or just a gifted compartmentalizer. Either way, I'm glad you're on our side."

"Seriously, Carlos. We don't know who the mole is. If there is any chance that he's connected to Darryl or Andy or Marla, then they're better off not knowing the identity of Aunjanue Desmoné. One word, one look from them could give it all away."

Sans said, "You're right." Sans tugged at his shirtsleeve and nodded. "We all know how much the Russians love surprises. It's a lot safer if only you and I are in the loop, because the mole could be anyone. The pizza delivery guy, a mail carrier, or even a CI's mother's old boyfriend's first cousin."

"What about the feds?" Lydia asked.

The FBI is aware, or I should say the Deputy Director of Criminal Behavior, and he has received a sealed file written in code, along with instruction authorizing him to have it opened and deciphered in the event something happens to me."

"And what about the medical team?"

'Each one of them has signed a non-disclosure document. They don't even know our real names," Sans, said.

"Very cloak and dagger," she said.

"It's all down to you, Lydia. You really are our secret weapon."

"Nah, I just have a good imagination. Speaking of which, how was my funeral?"

Sans stifled a laugh and pulled his hand over his face. "The basilica looked like a flower farm. I bet five hundred people piled into St. Mary's. Cops, city and county folks, politicians, Senator Kastle. I counted ten judges and a whole sea of reporters."

"I'm sorry I missed it. I hope you took pictures."

When Sans took his hand off his face he looked tired.

"What do you think makes these gangsters tick? What are they made of? I can't find a code or any rules. Normally a syndicate has family, culture, or even religion at its roots. But not them."

"This monster was spawned under Soviet domination over eastern Europe. It's a new kind of institutionally organized crime. The politicians have been in bed with the criminals since the nineteen thirties," Lydia said.

"And most of those criminals met in prison? That's their bond? And now they seem unstoppable," Sans said.

He got up to stretch and peer at the fish. "But why the sudden exodus to the US?"

"Why stay in Russia? That country is experiencing record unemployment and corruption. The Russian mob is not stupid. They're moving to greener pastures," Lydia said.

Sans got up and walked slowly around the acrylic tank. He became mesmerized buy an orange-spotted hawk fish starting a fight with a slightly smaller version of itself. No, not a fight. A mating ritual. "Lydia, why does Markiza only pick boys?"

"When we arrest him, we'll ask him," Lydia said.

"You can still change your mind, you know. It's fine, we'll figure something else out."

"Carlos, what's eating you?"

"You know, the other thing you won't talk about."

"Geez, we've been over that. It's fine," Lydia said.

"I have to ask you one more time. What if you change your mind about the way you look? Will you go back to being Lydia?"

"Why would I want to get cut again? Besides, the doc's going to make me look beautiful." Lydia flashed him a smile even though he still hadn't turned around. And then he did.

"What if it becomes too hard to live with yourself?"

"You reminded me of Darryl just now," Lydia said.

"Sorry."

"Look, this is still my case. And I'm doing it for all the victims, past and present. And especially for Sasha," Lydia twisted her magazine. Then she unrolled it and looked at the cover.

"Was that your inspiration, Darryl's magazine?" Sans leaned in and studied the singer on the cover.

"Why did you pick that face? Of all the faces in the world, why that one?"

Lydia studied the cover of Essence Magazine for the hundredth time. The reggae diva from Barbados had a perfect heart-shaped face. There was something so alluring about wide cheeks that contrasted with a strong but narrow chin. Lydia already had the eyes and eyebrows, and skin color to look authentic. As soon as the surgeon inserted cheek implants, and cut the nasal spine to flatten her nose, she would pass for the real deal.

Lydia never told Sans that she long dreamed of becoming someone else. Starting over with a new identity was a common motif in books and movies. But to get to do it in real life—that was a chance at becoming fresh and innocent again. With a new persona she could observe everything in the world as if she were doing it for the first time. Like a child.

There could be no newness or possibility for discovery if her identity remained white. Lydia knew that world too well. But to walk a mile in a black woman's shoes, now that would be like piercing another dimension.

Lydia imagined Aunjanue Desmoné like a blindfolded child at party trying to pin the tail on the donkey. Dizzy and disoriented she would have to grope and struggle to make new friends and create experiences for herself. Whether she coped or even thrived in a racist world would depend as much on her choices as well the actions of others. Regardless, Lydia could not wait to shadow her new self through forbidden territory far from the reaches of her comfort zone.

"Look, here they come," Lydia said. The cheerful surgical team escorted the detective into the operating room. Ironically, Lydia didn't notice that the gabby nurse anesthetist was an African American woman.

After hugging Lydia and wishing her luck, Sans went back into the waiting room and tried reading again. He lifted his head towards the aquarium. Damn, watching fish *was* calming.

SEVEN

Tadzio was woken by flashes of light, shouting, and a slow burn in his stomach. He was used to the noise—guards yelled at the boys and each other, day and night. Everyone had cabin fever and was bored. Almost half the boys were gone already; most of them traded to the Chinese who lost a container of workers during an unexpected raid the month before. The remaining half lived in an uneasy truce with their handlers, the latter attempting to appease their charges with movies and video games.

And Tadzio knew why his stomach hurt. The day before Markiza threw a small party to celebrate his ninth birthday. Most of the guards and boys only watched from the sidelines while he and Markiza, ten selected slaves, and the man he brought around once in awhile, sat down to eat McDonald's burgers, fries, and beastly hunks of a multi-layered chocolate cake. It was like eating three meals at once.

But why was it lightening inside the building?

He slipped out of his bunk careful not to disturb the other young boys on his floor. He was being polite because it was in his nature. And not out of fear like before when Sasha was still alive and his only friend. Today he was no longer afraid of the other kids. Markiza took care of that a few weeks ago in the form of a very public rebuke and the slapping of a teen that had dared to poke fun of Tadzio for hanging around the big guy. He knew the kids still disliked him, but at least they were nicer. He padded over to the long steel tubular railing and squatted on his haunches to peer down into the cave below.

He saw the older boys lined up on either side of a crinkled grey backdrop. A guard was dragging one of them to stand in front of it. Another man took the boy's photograph. Every time he released the shutter on the camera, bright lights burst across the warehouse and then dimmed under two umbrella stands. Tadzio was temporarily blinded when he started his daily routine of counting how many boys were left. There were only forty-nine older ones; he had already counted the ones in the younger group, including himself, the night before. Total count: one hundred eleven. Soon there would be fewer. And after that, new ones would arrive. He discovered these things and more by hanging around with Markiza and his friend.

Whenever the man came around, Markiza always made a big production of asking Tadzio to join them. The man seemed nice, although he never talked to him. The boy realized if he also didn't speak, the two grownups would soon forget about him and start talking frecly. Mostly they spoke in English, but sometimes when he got excited or mad, Markiza would revert to Russian. Even though the man looked American, his responses in Russian were surprisingly good.

It was during those times that he missed Sasha the most. He wished he could ask him for his advice about the man. At night Tadzio prayed to his old friend and God to send him a sign that he could trust the man, the same way Sasha had trusted Andy.

None came, so far.

"Let's go downstairs and eat some oatmeal. It will help quiet the see-saw in your stomach," a voice behind him said. And now Tadzio realized that the old man had the power to see into his stomach. He would have to be very careful from now on.

Tadzio got up and put his hand in the kingpin's. "I see you are interested in photography. You know what, little cherub? I'm going to tell the guard to let you snap a few shots. I'm sure you could do as good a job as anybody here. Come on."

They were slowly climbing down the metal staircase when Tadzio halted. "Sir, can I get a picture taken of me?"

Markiza squinted his eyes and opened his mouth wide. "Boy, I already told you. You're not for sale. No, not like the other boys. You will stay with me forever. I have many things to teach you." He pointed at the line of boys on either side of the curtain. "They need their photos taken so the buyers will see that they are strong and healthy. You my dear one, don't have to worry about such things."

Still Tadzio didn't move. He looked up at his protector with wide unblinking eyes. He let his lips tremble a bit, the same way small children did in movies just before they got a big hug or treat from a grown up. "Sir, I just thought . . . I never had my very own photo."

Markiza scooped Tadzio into his arms and chuckled. "Well, why didn't you tell me before? Of course you can. When he's done with the others, I'll snap the photo myself."

EIGHT

Aunjanue Desmoné paced back and forth in front of a full-length mirror scanning her outfit, makeup, and hair. Today she had on pink cropped pants that hit right at the anklebone and a white sleeveless button-down blouse with tiny rose flowers. The clothes and Steve Madden Banglez sandals made her appear two inches shorter. She ran her fingers through soft, shoulder-length wavy black hair. Thanks to contact lenses, her eyes were hazel, bright in a kaleidoscope of shifting golds, greens, and browns. Pale red lipstick completed a retro look while setting off her flawless golden yellow complexion. She pulled on a knockoff Valentino shoulder purse and placed her hands firmly on her waist. Aunjanue twisted her hips side-to-side and smiled knowingly.

She was about to do something Lydia never could. Walk to work down the busy sidewalks of Miami as a black woman. She slipped on her large red shades and gripped the doorknob.

Aunjanue knew she had plenty of time to re-discover Biscayne Boulevard as Aunjanue, this time from the opposite direction, and still arrive at the station before Marla and the detectives. Sans, of course, would be waiting for her in his office eager to hear what she saw and encountered on the boardwalk. She stepped back from the door and mused that the excitement she felt would have been impossible to imagine three months ago.

_____

Sans had driven her home from the hospital to her swanky new apartment in upscale Brickell. He fixed her soup and later set out her meds and explained when and how many to take. After he left, she took a quick tour of the one bedroom unit. Everything was white: the walls, carpeting, appliances, and most of the furniture. The bedroom contained a queen-sized bed and small dresser; a sofa and an over-sized ottoman sat across from a flat screen television in the airy living room. A simple pub table with two stools separated the kitchen and living room. A big vase of fragrant Oriental Lilies covered most of it. Framed Jazz posters on the walls were the only other patches of color anywhere.

Her favorite was the new iPod with Bose speakers charging on the hall table—Sans had taken the time to download her entire song collection before throwing away her old mp3 player. He also tossed most of Lydia Angelova's belongings from the old apartment but saved a few personal possessions such as photo albums and jewelry, bank and checking account receipts, and a copy of a living will, all of which he stuffed inside a rented safety deposit box at a Fort Lauderdale bank.

Her new crib was on the seventeenth floor overlooking the mouth of Miami River and the ongoing hi-rise construction across the bay. She found the biggest surprise of all inside her closet. Almost as big as her old bedroom had been, it was crammed with dresses, skirts, and tops. She found labels belonging to Calvin Klein, Vera Wang, and a few Jones New York. The floor was layered with shoe racks: she counted 30 pairs of low-heeled shoes and sandals; not one pair of army boots in sight. Early on they had decided upon a trendy but elegant wardrobe makeover for her, but in this closet, Aunjanue had discovered what looked to be the long lost hoard of clothes and fashion accessories from Barbie Nation.

At first Sans came every day to check up on her. He usually brought groceries, mostly sandwiches from a nearby deli, and the newspaper. Sometimes he'd bring her magazines and movies. When she was up for it, they spent time cobbling the beginning stages of a new sting to bring down Markiza. When she asked for work gossip, the results were usually bittersweet. It was painful to realize how much she missed her job and her team members.

Everything was going according to Hoyle until the day they took off the bandages. After that she couldn't look at herself without breaking into a sweat. Sans had warned her and the surgeon told her to expect it. In the beginning the brain would not be able to recognize her new face. There would be a disconnect that might feel scary at first but eventually should dissipate into acceptance. But when that day arrived, Aunjanue wasn't just scared, she was terrified. And for a week she wouldn't let Sans back into the apartment.

She recalled that it wasn't just that Lydia had vanished, but no one had come to replace her. She could not make sense of what she was seeing because her mind refused to form a complete picture. She only saw parts, disparate pieces of flesh and bone that never quite fit together. The brain needed time to assimilate the new face, but six weeks later, even after most of the swelling had subsided, she still screamed whenever she passed a mirror. After that she covered them all up. While she washed and dressed without seeing her face, she felt almost human.

Aunjanue passed the time by matching outfits, practiced a languid walk and rehearsed saying her new name: *ä--jə-nü*, like ingénue, but keeping the first 'n' silent. She also trained to sound like she had a Minnesota accent by listening to voice CDs and even made Sans watch *Fargo* with her twice. One night she awoke thirsty. When she walked into the bathroom to get a drink of water the towel had slipped from the mirror, and she was staring into the face of a stranger who copied her every move.

Aunjanue put her hands over her face and then removed them. She played peek-a-boo with her image for a few minutes trying to figure out what the hell was wrong with her. She slumped down on the floor trying to control her hyperventilation. She had heard that people who got their vision back after decades of blindness never really grasped the three-dimensionality aspect of sight. *Just because the light's bright don't mean you can see.*

Her heart was hammering in her chest, and she shook uncontrollably when she made the call.

"I'm no doctor, but I think you are having a full-blown anxiety attack," Sans had said.

"Why is this happening?" Lydia cried.

"What are you thinking about? Talk to me."

"Carlos, I'm not here. I'm not in the mirror. Where, where did I go? Why can't I get used to her?"

"You mean your new face?" Sans waited a beat and said, "Imagine a child's building set or even one of those little girl's plastic jewelry making kits like my grand daughter plays with. A bucket of interlocking beads in all shapes, sizes, and colors. Think about spilling the contents on the floor and then very carefully snapping a few beads together. Eventually after some work, you'll end up with a finished necklace."

"CARLOS!! What the hell are you talking about? I'm ready for the funny farm, and you're giving me a lecture on plastic toys?"

"You can't trust your face because there's nothing written on it yet. No emotion, no history. That's why you can't see it. It's still in pieces inside the bucket waiting to be made, waiting to be loved. Now listen to me. Get out of the bathroom and go to your closet. Pick out a favorite outfit and then come back to the phone. Meanwhile, do not look at your face."

Aunjanue put down the phone and did as she was told. She tried on a few matched sets and settled on a yellow sundress and shawl before walking back into the bathroom. "Now what?"

"Put a towel over your face and only peek out of one eye. Look at your dress, look at your body. I'll hang on," Sans said.

She did as she was told. "Fine. I like this dress and I look good in it. That's what you wanted to hear, right? That I like something about myself?"

"Grab a hairbrush and comb and whatever product you need. Next, sit down at your vanity, and turn on the light-up mirror. Angle it so you can only see the top and sides of your hair. Play with your hair, work it up, make it your own."

Aunjanue really did like her hair and had already been doing what Sans was asking her to do now. Curling it with hot rollers, teasing the curls into place, spraying them with lacquer to preserve the style. But she humored him, tussled her hair a bit, and was surprised to find out she was breathing evenly again.

"This will be harder. Are you ready?" Sans asked.

"Oh, boy."

"Now angle the mirror so you can only see your forehead. You need to examine every square inch of it until you've memorized the contours. After that, you can do this either silently or out loud, tell your forehead how much you love it." Sans waited.

A few minutes later she said, "I hate you stupid forehead. Hate you, hate you."

Sans laughed. "Whatever gets you through the night. Let's work on your eyes. Put in the contacts first."

"You moonlighting as a shrink these days? Don't tell me the city doesn't pay enough to cover that lavish lifestyle of yours." Aunjanue was feeling better.

"I copied the home instructions the nurse put in your med bag. I'm guessing you didn't read them yet?"

Sans had stuck with her for hours that night until she was able to look at two major parts of her face at once without freaking out. She recalled how she tried saying "I love you" to her brow and eyes without laughing. Still she had gone to sleep quickly afterwards and felt more refreshed in the morning than she had in weeks. For a month she practiced loving her parts, separately and then together. And then it finally happened. Aunjanue Desmoné coalesced in mind, body, and face.

And today she was ready to take the new woman for a walk in the city.

NINE

On Biscayne Boulevard Aunjanue added a jaunty twist to her normal stride and painted a self-assured half-smile across her lips. Pendulous clouds canopied the air with dampness and, as ocean waves crashed and rolled, she breathed in fragrant breezes spiced with brine and marine life. Aunjanue felt goose bumps skitter across her back and arms even before the wind picked up sending chills through her thin clothes. For the first few blocks she reveled in feeling brand new and just like the ocean air—clean and fresh. Reassured by the familiar sounds of early morning traffic and the distant calls of south Atlantic birds, she was lulled into believing that her movements on the boardwalk were seamlessly entwining into the energetic morning tableau.

She thought again about how she looked just before she left the apartment. The woman who had stared back at her from the bathroom mirror appeared girlish and vulnerable. How could she have known that the innocence she cut in the mirror's reflection just minutes before would look like red meat to the outside pedestrian traffic?

The sidewalk was already crowding with men and women going to work or shopping. But here on the south side of Biscayne, the older Cuban men were better dressed; many wore light colored suits and carried attaché cases. Mostly bankers, they and their Anglo counterparts were headed to Brickell Key, Miami's financial district. When they saw Aunjanue they did not move aside but seemed to close in on her, swinging their heads and staring her down with impure thoughts. These were not the actions of romantic idealists hoping to recover memories but brazen attempts to show contempt and establish superiority. When it came, the solicitation froze Aunjanue's blood.

The man who accosted her had a bald waxed head, arms like timbers struggling to rip apart freshly starched shirtsleeves, and wet stains blotting his armpits. He was panting noticeably and she could see a line of perspiration across his forehead that threatened to drop into his eyes. Aunjanue was carrying and wished she could pull out the weapon from her pink bow-tie purse. But now was not the time to blow her cover. The behemoth stopped sharply in front of her, dark shiny eyes pricking hers, a fat roll of twenties squeezed between his thumb and forefinger.

Aunjanue used one hand to take off her sunglasses and showered the trick with a high wattage smile; that way he didn't have a chance to duck before she used her other hand to hit him in the face with her purse, heavy with the Beretta concealed inside.

The second time it happened, she was prepared. He was a short, fortiesh working class Hispanic whose eyes remained hidden under black Ray-Bans. He had recently slicked down his salt and pepper hair with oil, and his pencil-line mustache quivered when he spoke. This one she didn't have to hit; he smiled crookedly and strode off as soon as Aunjanue let out a stream of Spanish invectives.

The younger Cubans were no better. Block after block on her way to the station, Aunjanue was reminded of stories she had heard from women who traveled frequently to certain foreign countries. Just by being American they became fair game for any hormone-challenged male who wanted to score points with his buddies. They grabbed asses and brushed up against breasts without compunction. But for Aunjanue it was happening here in Miami at 7:30 in the morning. Young men in suit coats and ties sidled up to her, earnest grins plastered across their mugs while they pretended to run their hands across her backside.

The business pace of the boardwalk did not invite many young mothers with babes in strollers. But impeccably dressed-to-the-nines black and Latino women were also in large numbers hurrying to get to work. No diffident sideway glances from them this time. They shot her unabashed stares that culminated in expressions that seemed to say, *watch out! This is what the competition looks like*.

Black men of all ages were friendly and outspoken. They complimented her openly and smiled invitingly but rarely stepped into her personal space. Some waved and wanted to talk.

A half-mile from MAGS, Aunjanue's heart was racing. She reached into her purse and looked inside her money clip. There was a credit card and a thick wad of bills. The detective considered the difference between her jam-packed closet—filled with enough outer clothing to last a life—and the nearly empty underwear drawers of her roomy dresser. She could only assume modesty and embarrassment had held Sans back from purchasing too many of those delicate items. Yes, a little shopping might help calm her down before the adventure of facing the old crew. She should be safe in a lingerie shop.

Carmine's Curves was known as Miami's personal Victoria's Secret and boasted two large showrooms filled with robes, underwear, tanks and tees, and sexy summer dresses. Aunjanue worked her way down several aisles of panties until she found a display of bathrobes. She ran her hands dreamily down a silky French blue kimono when a voice startled her.

"He's been watching you since you walked in the door." A medium-skinned black woman with long straight hair in her forties cocked her head in the direction of a young Latino male pretending to adjust a sale sign over a bin of brassieres.

"Are you talking to me?" Although startled, the detective realized she was using her Midwest accent for the first time on a stranger.

"They caught some booster last week. Now they're checking out everyone who's black."

Aunjanue studied the man and then turned her head to see two clerks at the front cash registers exchange furtive looks with each other.

The older woman grabbed her purchases and brushed past Aunjanue. "Just make sure your numbers match your clothes items when you leave the dressing room."

Aunjanue grabbed bras and panties at random and strode toward the dressing room. She continued watching the manager who had moved to another aisle to straighten a row of camisoles, his hand lifting a radiophone from his belt.

A skinny, white, twenty-something attendant with short, dark hair counted Aunjanue's items slowly. She handed her a plastic number card and pointed to the rear of a narrow corridor. There, another young woman wearing gold hoop earrings and a tight green halter top, just like the one in the front window, shook her head and blocked her way to the dressing rooms. The detective shrugged and tried to give her the number card.

"Sorry, we have a policy against trying on underwear in the store," the attendant said.

Aunjanue scanned the walls and desk in front of the fitting room." I don't see no policy. Who in hell do you think you're scamming here?"

The young woman said, "Look it's not my fault, I'll get in trouble."

"You think I'm dirty? You actually believe that I'd stink up these clothes?" Aunjanue pulled the clothing items from her arm and threw them on the floor. "Happy? *Now* they're dirty."

The attendant frowned and was about to say something else, when an older plump white woman who looked like she woke up every morning smiling, came out of a stall holding up an armload of underwear. She stopped as if out of breath and pulled apart half the items and threw them inside a cart marked returns. They both watched her with mouths gaped open as she sped off smiling, all the way to the cashier's desk.

Outside the store with her heart racing and fresh adrenalin coursing through her veins, Aunjanue tried to focus, but she was too dizzy. It was as if in the blink of an eye she had somehow washed up on a remote island where everyone was a stranger, and she couldn't recognize any of the landmarks. This was a place where Lydia had never lived or visited. The land of in-your-face racism.

Aunjanue silently screamed. No matter how edgy or sexy she had looked, how irresponsibly she had acted, nobody but nobody had ever assumed Lydia to be a sex worker, nor had anyone ever tried to deny the white woman access to a fitting room.

She leaned against the store window, shading her eyes from the sun. If this was what it was like to be black when you're young, pretty, and female, imagine what fresh hell might be might be waiting for you if you were black and none of the other things. She turned around to stare at her reflection in the store's window making out the outline of someone who looked familiar. She didn't have to do it piece by piece this time. Her brain had identified the image in the glass as her own.

Aunjanue owned a face she loved. She knew she would care for it, protect it, and even go to battle if anyone tried to mess with it.

TEN

On the opposite side of town, in uppity Coral Gables—where else would a trolley run down a boulevard called Ponce de León—Andy sat on a cold bathroom floor, his legs wrapped around the base of the toilet, his arms cradling the toilet seat. He had one more round of puking left in him, so he waited while staring into murky water where chunks of yesterday's junk food clung to the sides of the bowl. When it came up he gagged on bitter bile and then it was over. He knew he should pull himself together and get ready for work. Because how would it look if he showed up late to meet Lydia's replacement on her first day.

If you asked him though, he would have gladly paid a million dollars (if he'd had it) to wipe out this day and all that it promised to shake loose from the calendar year.

Lydia used to harp that underneath his blithe mask, the Sunday afternoon football parties and all the liquor consumed, struggled a vulnerable man looking for salvation. Not those words exactly. But she had said that Andy had the capacity for change, to be better. Not any more. His chances evaporated the day Lydia's all too short life vanished into an abyss of fiery proportions. Right then, the last of his human parts froze over leaving his mind and heart to only imitate someone who was still alive.

When he tried to stand, his legs wobbled and his eyes refused to open. Pulling himself up to the sink, Andy opened the medicine cabinet and tore into a bottle of Excedrin. Next he took an eyelid hostage, forced it open but it snapped shut before he could coat the grit with eye drops. He stepped into the shower dragging his hangover and guilt. Slowly, the scene from the warehouse began to replay itself while shards of ice-cold water thumped his skin.

Lydia insisted that she had to meet with Sasha at the end of the day. And Andy had to make it happen. On that Friday morning almost three months ago, he arrived early at the warehouse and made a dramatic show of searching for a converter that could transfer older training audiotapes to a digital format. Not finding one, he got permission from the plant manager to order a new cable. After contacting the electronics store, he speed-dialed UPS to make the pickup. But Gregor, one of the line inspectors, ended the call.

"We don't use UPS no more," Gregor said in heavily accented English.

Andy feigned surprise although he had seen this coming. On his iPhone he pulled up a directory of delivery services and waited for the Russian to pick a company. The goon's finger landed on a picture of a reptile and without missing a beat Andy called Crocodile Couriers to place the order. The goon looked satisfied and so did Andy.

When he had explained what he needed, it was Marla at MAGS who took the order. Suspecting that the Russians might change up the delivery service, Andy reprogrammed his smart phone to be even smarter. By pressing the # key first, any and all numbers immediately rolled over to Marla's secure phone back at the police station.

Next, Andy had to coordinate with Sasha. He sent him an email instructing the boy to have his last cigarette promptly at ten o'clock.

I'm getting a cable delivered at the end of the day. After it gets here, I expect you to put in a couple hours transferring analog audiotapes. Work fast and you won't miss lunch.

That was their code. Saving or missing meals always meant Lydia was coming.

A few minutes to ten Sasha walked outside. Just as Andy settled down to create a log for the bogus tapes, Gregor came over to his desk and slapped him jovially on the back. The smile on the Russian's face stretched across his cheeks but his eyes remained flat and dull as mud.

"Come on, last cigarette break. Let's go outside."

Andy didn't like the sound of this but managed a smile. "That's okay, I don't smoke."

"No problem. Don't smoke. Come outside."

Andy shook his head. "Too hot out there. I like the air conditioning in here."

"We find you AC."

Gregor, Andy, and another guard, squeezed through a side door and made their way to the back of the parking lot. Gregor and Andy climbed into one van, the guard into another. This is where it all started to go wrong, but his own alcohol-clotted brain never made the connection. But later he realized, it should have.

Gregor lit up. Andy watched him inhale the unfiltered Russian cigarette. "Those things will kill you. And me, second-hand smoke," Andy said, pointing to the plumes that drifted across the dashboard.

Gregor said, "You can open a window but then don't complain about the heat."

A blue Escort traveling at normal speed stopped in front of Sasha and the delivery door. Andy stole a look around. Gregor was busy thumbing a girly magazine and talk radio blasted out of the other vehicle—the other guard was chuckling to himself.

When the redhead stepped out of the delivery car, most of her pregnant stomach obstructed Andy's view of Sasha. Almost ten minutes passed when he heard Gregor take a final drag of his smoke and toss it from the window. When the window snapped shut again, Andy watched the goon's eyes travel to the second-floor window above the stoop. But there was no one was there. Yet.

After a few minutes, Andy made to get out of the van but stopped when Gregor's phone vibrated. Or it must have, because the Russian pulled the soundless device out of his shirt pocket and put it to his ear. This time a large shadow spread itself across the window. A few minutes later, when a thick cloud slipped over the sun removing the glare, Andy saw Markiza and a boy. The old man had patted the small child like it was a cat.

"You always working on computers. Today I show you some fun." Gregor turned the key in the ignition and leaned into the windshield squinting his eyes. Markiza and Tadzio disappeared from the window and were replaced by a shorter stocky figure with a gun. Andy's window was completely down so he was able to hear the whiz of the silencer. The boy fell and the redhead scrambled to the ground throwing herself on top of him. Andy tried again to exit the vehicle but found his door was electronically latched. His head snapped up when he heard Lydia's car careening across the parking lot.

The two vans tore out of the parking lot clumsily, almost sideswiping each other before landing on the frontage road. Lydia was already out of sight and Andy didn't think they would be able to catch up to her. As reckless and daring as she might be about many things, including operating a two-ton vehicle, the detective was still the best driver he knew.

It was always here when his mind leapt to the next scene, that Andy would squeeze his eyes shut and search in vain for the rewind button. It wasn't like he and Lydia weren't aware that they might get caught someday, but what happened next seemed so wrong. Wrong like a gorilla falling out of the sky. What in the world had caused her to spin out and lose control of the stupid vehicle?

At first glance the road seemed safe enough. It was newly paved and lined with multiple yellow and black warning signs that alerted drivers to the sharp curves. All that changed when two underpowered, heavy metal machines traveling at high speeds chased down a small Ford car. Normally vans weren't built to turn on a dime but by some miracle, the two Russians had narrowly averted rolling their vehicles during several skids, righted themselves, and just kept on going. Andy recalled that as the Russian swept past the hairpin curves, Gregor guffawed like a deranged clown at an old-time circus. Maybe due to fear, but Andy thought those high-pitched sounds could just as easily have been the result of sadistic jubilation.

Andy had put all his money on Lydia that day. The Escort probably wasn't solid on cornering either, but she was so far ahead of them that Andy thought Lydia's chances of getting to the interstate and getting lost in traffic was worth the bet. He hadn't once considered his own safety. In some special place in his brain, he knew that if she got away, they would kill him on the spot. But the chase had reached euphoric heights and he couldn't recall ever having been afraid.

Finally the road widened and straightened. They saw the Escort a thousand feet ahead of them, barely visible, getting smaller by the second. And then like a kid's animated cartoon, the car steered itself sideways towards the shoulder and kept going until it completely disappeared.

Skid marks and deep ruts on the gravel–packed shoulder made the driver in front of them slow down. Gregor slammed on his breaks and screamed at Andy.

"Get out and see what you did."

Andy had been a corpse on ice waiting for a casket. When she plunged into the canyon, his status was instantly elevated to necessary live witness.

Andy joined Gregor and the guard at the precipice. Fifty feet below them the Escort clung to a narrow ledge by two wheels. He started down the hill when the car abruptly detached itself from the loamy surface and began to twist and spin against the steep ridge of the hillside.

Gregor kept yelling after him. "You see how weak you all are. You can't fool us. You can't beat us. Go back now and tell everyone that there will never be a victory over Markiza."

Andy felt the last explosion inside his lungs. His eyes stung and his ears were ringing. All around him the air was on fire; his skin felt like it was melting off his bones. He couldn't manage another step. Andy knelt down and beat his fists into the dirt. She was gone.

"Give up now or more people will die. Remember, we're watching you."

When he climbed back up the hill the goons were gone and he wept as he walked back to the parking lot and his car. While reaching for the door handle his orbiting thoughts landed solidly on one idea. It had been Tadzio who gave Lydia away. A better detective would have seen it earlier. Lydia would have known in a nanosecond. But then Lydia wasn't a drunk.

Andy remembered that Markiza had pushed Tadzio to the front of the window and placed one hand on the child's small head and the other on his shoulder. Andy formed a picture in his head. The kingpin acted like a scientist. He was monitoring subtle change. Feeling for a quickening in pulse or perhaps a small tick in the back of the neck. Something that might indicate awareness. While Tadzio took in Sasha's measure, Markiza was taking his. Whatever Tadzio gleaned from the encounter between his friend and the delivery woman, it had moved like a contagion, quietly but swiftly passing through his eyes, landing in his brain and then transferring the full betrayal through the surface of his skin— perhaps just a slight rise in temperature—where it was caught by the one that brooked no betrayals. Moments later Markiza had Sasha assassinated.

Andy was still shaking from adrenaline as he sped out of the parking lot. He had to find a phone fast so he could call Sans. His own was back at the factory, most likely already smashed into a hundred scattered pieces across the floor in front of his desk. He stopped at the first gas station and was about to say something to the attendant behind the plexiglass window, when a video screen filled with fire and smoke caught his attention. He listened to a female anchor reporting off screen.

EYEWITNESS NEWS 9 HAS JUST LEARNED OF A RAGING FIRE INSIDE LOS REYES CANYON IN THE NORTHEAST METRO AREA. BYSTANDERS WHO SEND US THESE IMAGES SAID THAT A SMALL CAR HAD LOST CONTROL ON THE HAIRPIN ROAD NEAR INTERSTATE 95, PITCHED INTO THE CANYON AND BURST INTO FLAMES. UNCONIRMED REPORTS CLAIM THAT THERE WERE NO SURVIVORS. EMERGENCY VEHICLES ARE ARRIVING AT THE SCENE...

The Russians with their camera phones had called in the story. He thought Sans would be watching the news so there was no further need to contact his superior. And he certainly wasn't about to deliver the Russians' threatening message. Because if he did, then he couldn't lie about where he'd been that morning.

Because how could he live with himself if his team found out that he had been forced to watch Lydia die? That he hadn't lifted a finger to save her.

ELEVEN

From where she stood Aunjanue could see a curtain of bunya-bunya trees hugging the boulevard next to a narrow brick path. Their coniferous limbs were so long, languid, and shapely, that they looked like they were dancing, swaying to music. The view from Sans' office allowed her to see past the tall trees into a small park framed in wrought iron benches and landscaped in ornamental foliage. Red and white ginger flowers stood erect above pinstriped leaves, while slightly shaded tight clumps of heliconia resembling lizards more than they did flowers, leaped ten-feet high in a display of cool peach and sunny yellow. A nearby pool lying thick with lily pads and leaping frogs, held in its center a two-tiered fountain with mermaids spouting high arcs of water.

A woman sat on one of the benches shading her eyes, and tried to look at a magazine. Two toddler-aged boys ran around the pool several times before leaping on top of their mother and putting an end to her momentary vacation from responsibility. It looked like an idyllic scene right out of *Parent* magazine, but it sent Aunjanue's mind racing with a stampede of questions. Was the woman really the mother or the nanny? Did the kids belong to her, or were they actors playing out roles for the promise of a 3-D movie and ice cream afterwards. For all she knew the trio were spies, placed in the edenic spot to look that much more innocent while they gathered information either electronically or through a trusted informant about the police department and its activities, only fifty feet away. Because that's how spies worked. Innocent-looking people that were really plants and, if not caught in time, could start city-wide panics, destroy governments, or make it impossible to catch a murderous human trafficker. In some cases, a well-placed mole could force a decorated detective to sacrifice everything she held near and dear, even renounce her identity.

It was time to face reality. The mole could be anyone in MAGS. It wrenched her insides to consider the main players on her team, but she'd be an idiot not to. Someone tried to kill her once, someone with a lot of information. Another attempt on her life, Aunjanue thought, did not hold a lot of appeal.

Darryl. One of Miami's most honored cops, thirty-two commendations in all: the first came just weeks after his rookie career began. Since then he made a dozen high-profile arrests, was shot and stabbed, and survived two deadly car chases. He had worked as co-liaison for the Southern Florida Anti-Gang Task Force, head of the local SWAT team, and led an anti-crime unit in South Beach before the neighborhood's gentrification. Over the years, departments—everyone from Special Victims to Homicide—used Darryl for their undercover operations because of his natural detective skills. He gave speeches at high schools and taught defense training courses at the police academy. Darryl had an unblemished career, got along well with his co-workers and, for the most part, did not run afoul of his superiors.

Andy. Plain-clothes, detail extraordinaire. In her book, he was the real actor in the group who could imitate anyone in the world. A drug dealer from Naples, a waiter in a four-star restaurant, a cyber hacker from Australia along with the accent. He was also the one you wanted when you needed a technician. Andy was a self-taught photographer, filmmaker, and recently, computer engineer. That he drank too much and had few close friends troubled some, but his work ethic was sterling and like Darryl, he worked collaboratively and his teams always produced results.

Marla. At the age of twenty-two, the ambitious Miami Dade College grad trundled her dual diplomas in Business Administration and Public Safety Management to the Miami Police Department and applied for a position in Human Services. After six years, she found herself in charge of managing the entire Miami police workforce. Her inventive organizational design and development models were implemented all over the state. And then a few years back Marla got bored. Again using her wiles and experience, the corporate manager talked certain officials, whose departments she helped turn around, into creating a new position just for her. One that was responsible for implementing strategies and policies used in the execution of specific and covert special operations. MAGS became her first undercover gig. It was up to Marla to makes sure that each member knew what the other was doing and that the assignments made sense logistically and financially. It was also up to her to track the whereabouts and functions of all outside liaisons, including local informants.

Her crew looked really good on paper. Just the kind of people that might surprise you. Because all people lied. About something.

A pop behind her made Aunjanue jump. She turned around slowly to see Sans crumpling paper, wadding it up, and throwing it into a metal wastebasket. Promptly he returned to what he'd been doing since she arrived. Scribbling notes on a yellow legal pad. The office looked different. Like the park below, the view into the room seemed strange and new. Like she'd never seen it before. Technically Aunjanue hadn't. And Lydia had only gone in and out to pick up reports or, as often, to listen to her boss reprimand her about some departmental infraction.

Nestled in between two long-angled windows that gave shape to part of the police station's structural chef's hat, the former detective, once called Lydia, began to study her boss's desk with a renewed enthusiasm. She felt like a sightseer.

It actually didn't look that much different from her own, old desk. Piles of both opened and closed reports sat on one end; a stack of photographs and caddies filled with pens, markers, batteries, Post-it notes, stapler, and scissors, cradled the other. Spread across the middle was a marked-up three-month calendar and above that lay her inspiration. Hidden among an assortment of communication devices sat a room-monitoring device she knew had never been used before. As soon as Sans stood up and walked over to a metal file cabinet, Aunjanue slipped behind the desk, eased her long lean torso into the wood bankers desk chair, and began swiveling from side to side like a child.

When Sans turned to look at her, she stopped moving suddenly and smiled up at him like the Cheshire cat. One long slender finger hung just above a black toggle switch in the middle of a matte-finished rectangular box.

"Don't you dare," Sans warned. But his eyes were glassy with mirth and she knew he would give in.

"Let's have some fun," Aunjanue said.

Sans looked at the closed door and whispered, "It wouldn't be right."

"Aw, come on. Be a sport. Let's hear what's on their minds before they have to pretend to like me. Besides, it will only be for a few minutes."

Sans pulled a disapproving mask onto his tired face, but he was in so deep now, why would he resist. When he gave the nod, Aunjanue's finger descended and the cubicles just outside his office door began jabbering with life.

"That's only the second time in six months that San shut that door. When do you suppose he's going to let her out?" Marla said. Aunjanue listened and imagined her old friend leaning over Darryl, shifting from foot to foot; the detective studiously ignoring her while surfing the internet.

But he surprised Aunjanue. "I sure hope as hell before that happens, Andy decides to show up. Where the hell is he anyway? He's never late. And today of all days."

"I do declare, you sound a little like nervous Nelly, Detective King."

"Aren't you nervous?"

In her mind Aunjanue was watching Marla moue a defiant 'no' between her lips, when she heard chimes, and then the elevator door must have released a body, because when the familiar MAGS pneumatic door whined open, she heard Andy say, "hey". Aunjanue felt her pounding heart leap into her ears. They would all be assembled now. Her best team, her best friends.

Darryl said, "Jesus, what the hell happened to you?"

Aunjanue heard the charge of spiky heels scrape across the tiled floor. "Get in the bathroom and comb your hair. And button your shirt right. You look like you slept on the railroad tracks last night." Marla was intent on getting Andy looking ship-shape.

A slap and then a chirp. Aunjanue looked over at Sans. He was trying hard not to laugh out loud. They had the same thought. Marla had cuffed the slovenly detective across the back, and he had recoiled in pain. That must be some hangover.

"Give me a break. I'm not feeling well," Andy said.

After a moment, Darryl started to whisper. Sans turned up the volume. "This is freaky. Sans said that she's some kind of fed and has a lot of Lydia's talents. Disguise for one. I don't know if I'm ready for this. I mean, she's—"

Marla said, "You mean you'd be more comfortable working with a man. But what about me? I'm stuck here all day long with you testosterone-bloated morons. It will be refreshing to work with another woman again."

Darryl said, "Did she just call me a moron?"

Andy said, pointing to the door. "She might quack like a duck, but she will never be our Lydia."

Sans switched off the monitor and said, "Let's get in there before it gets any more maudlin."

When Aunjanue got up, Sans eyed her up and down as if seeing her for the first time. "Hey . . . I think you look nice and those clothes will be perfect for the sting, but today, maybe you could have dressed more—"

"Don't turn all sexist bastard on me. You said I looked nice, and let's keep it there." She revolved the knob and slowly opened the door.

Expecting merely surprise or deferment, Sans and the woman who used to be Lydia were completely unprepared for the shocked looks the men and Marla gave Aunjanue and each other. But something surprised Aunjanue as well. While Darryl and Andy's attire looked normal, the former sporting a designer charcoal suit coat and Andy in his everyday rumpled look: clean but wrinkled khaki pants and black tee—it was obvious that Marla had dressed up that morning like she was playing for all the marbles. She wore an emerald green sateen shift dress with matching spiky heels and, highlighting the simple yet bright ensemble, was an array of peacock feathers sticking out of a beak-shaped hat on top of her perfectly corn-rolled do.

Aunjanue walked over to the tight knot of stunned co-workers and lit up with a reassuring smile.

"I'm so happy to finally meet all of you. You're exactly like the captain described. It will be an honor and a privilege to work with you. I know together we will bring down that mongrel Markiza and put an end to a lot of suffering. And I can't wait to get started."

No one spoke. No one moved.

"Umm . . . if you're wondering why I'm dressed like this . . ." Aunjanue turned her chin slightly towards Sans and gave them her best hang-dog look. "I had suggested coming on my first day wearing a suit, so of course you could take me seriously, but Captain convinced me to dress in the manner of my persona, the one I'm going to use to lure Markiza." She felt Sans' silent rebuke nipping at her heels.

No response. *Wow, what a tough crowd.*

Darryl asked, "Are you from Minnesota?"

Aunjanue laughed, "Why do you ask?"

"You sound like, no offense, Marge from *Fargo*."

"Aunjanue Desmoné is Senior Special Agent on loan to us from the Chicago field office. She comes from the National Security Branch specializing in counterintelligence," Sans said resurrecting a level of decorum.

"Don't worry, you sound great and you also look great," Darryl said, smiling a little too broadly.

Marla coughed. "You have to forgive these reptiles and their obvious lack of manners. Most of the time, they're really good detectives."

Reptiles. That's my girl. She not only dressed up for her, but by quoting Lydia, Marla had just passed the baton off and insured her admittance into the sacred bosom of MAGS. Marla had come through just as Aunjanue had hoped and prayed; the administrator would not judge. She was far too kind and open-minded, even if the new addition to the club looked half her age, dressed like a high-school girl lost at the mall and, to boot, was a butter-cream African American woman.

"Marla, that is some rad hat. I *Loove* it!" Marla clamped her hands lightly over her cheeks and tilted her head from side to side. Everyone laughed. Except Andy.

Something was happening to Andy. The longer Aunjanue stared, the worse he looked. Right in front of her, he started to resemble the man he might become twenty years from now, if only he lived that long. Andy might not make it to next year at the rate he was drinking. Couldn't anyone one but her see it? Sans? Why wasn't Marla dragging his behind to treatment? For the same reason Aunjanue couldn't punch every dirty rotten bigot she encountered. For them, putting Markiza behind bars would always be first.

TWELVE

They brought chairs into Sans' office and began chowing down on deli sandwiches and inhaling hot cups of coffee. Earlier, Marla had stopped off at the market. No more delivery food, no one was taking unnecessary chances. They all prattled pleasantly and ate quickly. Darryl was especially friendly. When he offered her his coleslaw and pickle, Aunjanue noticed he wore the same goofy grin he couldn't lose when they first started dating. One that spoke of many layers of crush, lust, and promise. But hadn't she also worn that look at one time and felt the same rush of hormonal heat? She fervently hoped her own slip wasn't showing.

Sans crumpled his lunch bag, tossed it in the trash, and wiped his mouth clean.

"Aunjanue specializes in deception and disguise. As you know, we've spent a lot of time and resources trying to find the mole the Russians wormed into our system. Now they are going to swallow some of their own bitter medicine."

While the captain detailed some of her fake accomplishments, Aunjanue watched Andy. Not once had he made eye contact. At the moment he didn't even appear to be listening, instead he stared out the window and, after a few moments, closed his eyes.

"We are going to set a trap by arranging a buy of human cargo. Aunjanue will play the role of an influential Colombian drug dealer's trophy girlfriend, and Darryl will be her mouthpiece." Sans said.

"Darryl looked around, "A what?""

The team looked up questioningly at the captain and Aunjanue.

Sans said, "Darryl will play the part of an attorney."

"Whose attorney?" the excited group asked all at once.

"Roman Delgado's."

Andy woke up. "What? I mean how? That Columbian drug dealer is doing life without parole at Sandstone."

Sans smiled and rubbed his hands together. "This is the good part. Delgado still wields enough power to control a large east coast drug operation. Even though he personally despises them, occasionally he does business with the Russians."

Marla squirmed like a little girl needing to go to the bathroom. Aunjanue laughed when the cherub-faced woman raised her hand. "He's no friend of ours. All of us . . . and Lydia, had a hand in putting him away. How are you going to get him to cooperate?"

Sans said, "That's what I love about this group, you always wait so patiently for the details." Marla responded by tapping her heel furiously.

"Okay, here's the scoop. Delgado doesn't know it yet, but he is about to have his Achilles heel bruised, and who better to provide the soothing balm? Yup, Miami's finest. MAGS."

Again, three bright faces beamed up at them. Aunjanue got up and walked around Sans' desk until her gaze squared with the team.

She said, "Delgado's only son, Francisco, is a first-year, premed student at Johns Hopkins. Last month he was caught with three ounces of pot. His court date is in two weeks."

"Oooh wee. I do declare, this is getting mighty good," Marla squealed. Even Andy managed a thin smile.

Aunjanue continued, "Even if he doesn't do time, if found guilty, the university will revoke his scholarship and expel him. It will break Daddy's heart because he's the child Delgado had such high hopes for."

Sans said, "The kid's not mobbed up. Just likes pot. We can make it go away. For a price." He got up and handed everyone a folder.

"It's everything you need to know about Roman. In a few days, Andy and Darryl will pay him a little visit. And now . . ." Sans handed another folder to each Aunjanue and Darryl. "I want you two to get started on rehearsing your roles. Inside is a script. Read it over carefully. Memorize your parts. You've got some time to get this right," Sans added.

Darryl said, "Like actors. God, I love this. This could be the role of my life. The jumpstart of something new. To the moon, Alice." All at once everyone faced Darryl and laughed from their guts. And just like that, the earlier strain and apprehension was gone, replaced by a fresh camaraderie.

"What can we do?" Marla pointed to herself and Andy.

"In the next couple of days you can help Aunjanue and Darryl prepare." Sans handed them copies of the script.

"But right now, your most important work is to keep hunting down the mole. If you need anything, just let me know."

Sans walked back to his desk and picked up four small pieces of notepaper. "Today is the last time we meet here. From now on we mix it up at our various safe houses. I've written down tomorrow's address. Memorize it and burn it. We meet at 11:00 a.m. Tell no one and that's an order."

They left Sans' office single file. Except for Aunjanue and Darryl. The pretend fed from Chicago stayed in the doorway and stared intently at Andy's back. Darryl stared at hers.

"You're barking up the wrong tree. He's cracked. Got a screw loose," Darryl said.

"Excuse me?"

"Ever since his girlfriend, ex-girlfriend, was . . . killed. You know, Lydia."

Aunjanue moved in slow motion toward the atrium. She saw Andy head for the bathroom.

"Since that day he's been, let's say, unsettled," Darryl said.

Something like a sharp rock lodged inside Aunjanue's throat. She stopped and turned around. "Why?"

"He's carrying around a boat load of guilt because they had words before she died."

Why did she continually fool herself into thinking everything would be easy from this moment on? She needed to face facts. From now on the ground would tilt on a dangerous axis. And she, the woman called Aunjanue, would have to remember not to tip over.

"Hard thing to get over, I guess. Hey, we have a little time. Want to grab some coffee?" Darryl said.

She didn't even look back at him, just walked out of MAGS and pushed the button for the elevator.

"Some other time, okay. I took the red eye last night and need a nap. To clear my head."

When the elevator doors closed she had her back to MAGS and Darryl. The tears came of their own accord.

THIRTEEN

The room was vacant except for the man sitting in the back corner, hunched over and clutching his queasy stomach. For months he hadn't experienced the daymare, but the images were back and he had to work hard to tamp down the rising bile. Vivid details scorched his eyelids, and he squeezed his eyes hard like a small child warding off the bogeyman. This monster, however, was an animated 3D movie that wouldn't bugger off.

In the dark, in the middle of nowhere, an empty roadway came to life. Picture frames stuffed with broken limbs and torn sinews spread over the tarmac like detritus. Wind picked up the disparate pieces and stained them with a thick red glaze. He always waited for them to either ascend to heaven or fall back to earth. Once upon a time, he believed that if the limbs tried hard enough, they could reconstitute themselves into a whole human being again. None of those things ever happened. The pieces always hovered in the air like zombie parts. Like they were in limbo.

He was in limbo too, and would remain there, unless he acted decisively. Time after time, the man promised himself he would stand up to Markiza and tell him to find another cheerleader. But he still hadn't. Fear always shriveled his resolve. Until now. Seeing the images again, he realized that the dread of dying was far worse than actually dying. The man had nothing to look forward to and everything to regret. No longer caring if he lived or died imbued him with an unexpected courage.

An insistent clunking of boots on linoleum snapped the man back to reality. He opened his eyes slowly and saw Markiza coming his way. Then the old man stopped suddenly. Both men turned their gazes toward the heavy metal doors. When they screeched open, young boys marching in single file, carrying trays, entered the lunchroom and took their seats. Moments later the reader approached the lectern and smiled tenderly at the group.

The reader was short, on the slightly paunchy side, with a full head of wooly grey hair. He looked like someone's cuddly grandfather. Maybe he was. Beneath half-moon glasses, twinkling blue eyes spoke of eternal optimism. His arms, constantly cradling the air around him as he spoke, seemed to summon joy and warmth. Stunned, the man realized that Markiza had outdone himself by hiring the consummate actor to brainwash children. The reader's looks along with his singsong voice had the power to melt steel.

"In each kitten roars the heart of a lion. You boys think you are still kittens, because you see yourselves as young and weak. But next time you pass a mirror, look really hard. What you see might surprise you.

"You might see, oh yes, a lion. Because thanks to the infinite generosity of the great Markiza, you now have the power to help yourselves and your families back in Russia. As long as you continue to work hard, all things will be possible. Don't ever forget that you, and only boys like you, were singled out to come to America. It's precisely because of your

exceptional strength of character and intelligence that you are here now . . ."

Markiza sat down next to the man and grinned. "What do you think? I've got three factories going 24/7. Two make officer uniforms for the Unites States military. This one grinds out the dress shoes. And I'm still left with more than a hundred boys that I can sell individually."

The man pointed to the reader. "Put a beard and fur hat on him, and he could pass for the Russian Grandfather Frost. I can just see him going around and dispensing gifts to poor Russian village children. Oh wait, that is what he's doing," the man said dryly.

"Brilliant, isn't it? Actually I borrowed the idea from Fidel's revolutionary Cuba. They say that the greatest cigars in the world are made in Cuba, their high quality no doubt the result of expert hands inspired by talented readers. That is what we have here. Inspiration, exhortation, and a clear means for ensuring efficiency," Markiza said.

"The Cuban readers go back to the 1830s. Back when men read to each other in prison. Later and long before the revolution, the Cubans brought readers into the cigar factories. But los lectores, as they were called, were artists who recited beloved poetry, classical novels, and informed the workers of important local and international news. Not even close.

"This is simply to keep them docile and obedient," the man said.

Markiza shifted uncomfortably. He was used to the man's barbs, but he did not like being corrected about history.

"Enough. Do you have news?"

"Not really. You already know that MAGS stopped operating out of the downtown station. Members show up from time to time on the streets to chat up their informants. But otherwise everything seems quiet."

"They're either gearing up to shut down completely, or they could be using safe houses. I'd feel better if I knew what they were up to," Markiza said.

"Why do they have to be up to something? They invested everything they had into the last sting. Now they have no leads, no links, or threads. You made sure of that," the man said.

"You're holding out on me, aren't you?"

Markiza knew. The man thought it was because his delivery was just a fraction too sharp and precise; the alternative, that the old man could read his mind, was unthinkable.

"I didn't think it was important, but if you must know. Even before MAGS officially left the station, we noticed that Sans stopped going there regularly weeks before. I wanted to know how he was spending his days, so I had a guy follow him for a while. After that, MAGS and Sans disappeared altogether," the man said.

Markiza rocked on his heels, hands clasped over his chest. In profile, the kingpin looked like a giant fossil. The man thought his exterior was as rigid and unbending as the empty heart inside. "Go on," the fossil croaked.

"For a few months, Sans paid daily visits to a Brickel apartment complex. Usually the captain stayed just under an hour. Once he was in there all day," the man said.

"Did your guy happen to get a look at the visitors' log?" Markiza asked.

"No. The place is up-market and filled with state-of-the-art security. You'd almost have to move in to find out what's going on."

"Was he having an affair?"

"That's what I thought at first. Except, one time his wife dropped him off, and then she came back and picked him up a few hours later," the man said.

"Sounds like scratches in the sand." Markiza sniffed the air and nodded at the reader. "I, on the other hand, have some remarkable news."

The man steeled himself. He wasn't ready for anything remarkable.

"In two weeks I will be cutting a historic deal with Delgado. In exchange for servants, he's promised me a small share inside his east coast operation. What do you think now?"

Now the man wished he could throw up at will. He had underestimated Markiza. The South Americans were supposed to hate the Russians. Steer clear of them. End of story. This was a game changer. What could possibly have caused one of Colombia's most powerful drug lords to go into business with Markiza?

"What does he need servants for? He's doing life without the possibility of parole. I know they can't be for his wife. Not after she testified against him."

"They're for his mistress. Someone who makes regular conjugal visits. He is simply, as the Americans say, mad about her. I'm going to need you on this. Fresh eyes and ears," Markiza said.

"You seem to be doing very well without my help."

Before the man could turn to leave, Markiza whispered into his ear.

"Son."

The man felt his own breath whipsaw inside his ears. He turned his face so Markiza could see the unmistakable mask of grimacing hatred. "Don't call me that. Don't ever call me that."

Even though the kingpin knew it was an act, Markiza shot up from his chair and backed away from outstretched fingers splayed like claws. If the man took a swing at him, Markiza would have to parry the blow with a knife or bullet. Otherwise, how could he live down an obvious display of public disrespect? But the man knew better than anyone that the last thing Markiza wanted was for his sidekick to die. Bereft of his greatest adversary, or his greatest joy, the kingpin would have no purpose in life.

"At one time, I would have gladly given you the keys to the kingdom. All of this could have been yours. Like other famous families, we could have built up a great father-son dynasty together."

The man choked back a giggle because he was reminded of Markiza's weakness. "You still think I'm responsible for what my mother did? For smuggling me out of Russia and giving me a new life?"

"You could have resisted her. Gone for help. I was your father and you never tried to find me again."

"I was four."

"She was a viper who poisoned you against me. My only regret is that she died before I could find her. Before I could tear her apart with my bare hands. I still dream about it sometimes."

So do I. "Dream about this old man. Guess how many *apparatchicks* my mother had to sleep with until one fell hopelessly in love with her and then did anything she asked?"

Markiza looked away, allowing the man to close in on him.

"The answer is five. Five government officials that she fucked for years, until she got what she wanted. Herself and me away from you. The last one, before he helped us get on the boat, asked if he should put you down like a dog. Even after all of the beatings, the woman still spared your life.

"I wish I could have watched your smug face crumple when you came home to find us gone. I bet you shit on the spot when you realized she'd won."

Markiza stood still for so long, the man thought he'd suffered a stroke. When his father spoke finally, the words rained on him harder than any actual physical weapon. Once again, the man's abiding shame threatened to grind his resolve to ashes.

"My son the genius. You had everything, didn't you? Good and loyal friends, dinners at fancy restaurants. The best education, a fine job in your chosen field.

"Oh, and how you wore your impeccable character so smartly. That was your mother's doing. Teaching you, or should I say paying others to teach you values, morals, and leading you down the righteous path. Afterwards, you not only did well in school, you volunteered service to help the less fortunate. Two tours in the Peace Corps. Another year in Vista. You were a strong, capable man with solid bearings.

"So tell me, what happened to you? Where did you lose your way? And tell me also, how long did it take before you bent like a twig for me? Describe the moment when you realized you were about to give up everything you treasured in your life, for me.

"Your mother. Your cursed whore mother. Face it, son. She failed."

The man relaxed for the first time that day. This was their ritual. This is what they always did. Piercing each other with hateful barbs was meant more to excite than to punish or humiliate. But how long, he wondered, could they go on like this?

"While you're finishing up your meal and getting ready to go back to work, I want to leave you with one last piece of advice. In today's news, I have learned that all over this great land, boys, just like you, are working hard to provide industry and military with the best products human hands have to offer. You know what this means, don't you? One day, by staying the course, using your skills, you all will have enough experience and money to start businesses. Young men like you will rise to top and then there will be nothing in heaven or earth to stop you from doing and achieving anything you want. One of you can even grow up to be CEO of your own company someday. Be patient lads, because it all begins with the small things—"

FOURTEEN

Aunjanue parked her compact rental in the middle of the high-rise parking lot and watched the traffic stream in and out of the lobby. Darryl and Andy had arrived early in separate cars. Marla's cab would be late, and Sans had spent the night. There was nothing to link the MAGS team members to this second safe house location, but she watched anyway for anything unusual in and around the lot and front doors. When Marla finished paying the cabbie, Aunjanue waited another five minutes before going in. She walked up to the metal tablet in the entryway, punched in three numbers, and waited for the buzzer.

The elevator held an old-fashioned bench seat covered in rose brocade damask. Aunjanue sat down and straightened the folds of her dress. It would be a slow ride to the apartment on the thirty-third floor. She took a book out of her satchel and pretended to read; if anyone joined her going up, they wouldn't be able to see her face.

No one did, and she took the time to think about Andy. He was always polite enough but still avoiding talking to her at all costs. Unless they were rehearsing their lines, Andy left any room she entered. That he was terribly uncomfortable around her wasn't a surprise. That she still hadn't angled herself into his good graces yet, did. She'd have to work on that.

————————————

Sans handed Aunjanue a bottle of water and sat down next to Andy and Marla on an L-shaped sofa, while she and Darryl faced off in the middle of the living room.

"I don't care what you think you heard Roman say. If he was here right now, he'd let me have as many as I want," Aunjanue paced agitatedly as she read from the script.

"Look Felicia, you're not buying towels or sheets. These are human beings, and they cost a lot of money." Darryl knew his lines by heart. He stood in the middle of the living room with his arms relaxed at his sides, appearing serious and resolved. Like an authoritative lawyer from a top-notch firm.

"Do you realize the amount of work it takes to run my house?"

"Oh, you can stop right there, little missy." Marla marched up to Aunjanue and looked her up and down severely.

"What? What's wrong, Marla?' Aunjanue asked.

Today Marla was wearing a lavender tracksuit; the only nod to her usual smart and stylish grooming was a matching lavender scarf, wrapped around her forehead. That and a pair of round, wireless reading glasses made her look hippy-esque. Andy's job was to coach Darryl, but he rarely interrupted the actor. Marla, on the other hand, stopped Aunjanue every chance she got, signaling that the actress, who would be Delgado's girlfriend, had a long way to go before she was believable.

"You're all wrong. You sound namby-pamby. No matter how fair-skinned and comely you think you might be, you've still got to act like you know yourself, like you have a spine. Like you're black. Right now, you sound like a peevish prissy white girl."

"Marla. Cut her some slack. Does it really matter how she does it? Because I hear her saying it's her way or the highway. And who really cares, she's got Delgado's purse strings. Markiza'll know that," Darryl said.

Marla slapped the surface of a low coffee table so hard that it rattled all five sets of keys strewn on top of it. She threw her hands up, "Who cares? You're telling me, it's more important that we don't offend our Chicago fed here, than pull down the heavens and all the stars, and anything else it takes to catch the prize? I give up."

Aunjanue glanced at Sans. He was studying the floor. Aunjanue looked back at her script and felt conflicted. Of course she wanted to bring Markiza down. That and black coffee were the only things that kept her going most days. But at that moment more than anything, she wanted to please Marla. Marla was family. And most days, Aunjanue mused, she was who she was, even though they might not know it, because she felt like she belonged. To them.

"Help me. Show me how you would do it," Aunjanue walked over and placed her hand gently but firmly on Marla's heaving shoulder, just like Lydia used to. She felt it rather than saw it. Marla completely softened under her touch and slowly turned around.

"First off, start moving your body. You can have your way with men using attitude, not facts. Sit down, watch, and learn," Marla said.

The administrator sashayed around the living room several times peering through slitty eyes at each of them but just for a second. With one hand firmly hitched on her hip, Marla stopped in front of Darryl and waggled two fingers just inches below his nose.

"Oh no, you didn't! No! No! No! You did not just say that to me." Marla then made a big show of dismissing Darryl and turned to face Sans, who was playing the part of Markiza. "You know what I want. Now show me the merchandize."

Aunjanue got up and looked over her script. She threw it down on a chair and smiled at the group. "I get it. Seize and pounce. Thanks, Marla."

They worked all day, barely breaking for lunch. At three o'clock, Sans shut down the show. "Good job everyone. Go home now, and have a life for a few minutes. Tomorrow morning we'll pick up where we stopped. We're almost there. Just a few more days of this."

While everyone else was collecting their belongings, getting ready to leave, Aunjanue noticed Andy go into the kitchen with his computer. He set it down on a small table overfilled with multi-colored files and plugged it in. Several boxes with more files sat on the floor. She followed him.

"Can I help you with these?" Aunjanue knew he would be cross-checking and backing up files on informants and then doing individual background checks on everyone that had ever been connected with the undercover sting on Markiza.

"No, thanks. I can handle it."

She walked around table and faced the detective so he would have to look at her when she spoke. He didn't.

"I'm free the rest of the day, and I love research. I have my laptop here so I could help you organize and collate some of these—"

"I'm good. Thanks, anyway."

"Look, I know how hard it must be for you to see me in Lydia's place. I wish things were different; I don't want to replace her. I just want to be useful."

This time Andy did look at her. "If you don't mind, I need to focus here."

Back in the living room, Aunjanue saw Darryl and Marla exchange glances.

"I told you," Darryl said.

"Yeah," Aunjanue sighed.

"So, how about that coffee?" he asked.

"What?"

"You drink coffee, don't you?"

"How about a rain check. I've got to be someplace," Aunjanue started for the door.

"Really, because I just heard you tell Andy that you didn't have to be anywhere," Darryl said.

"I forgot."

"It's only coffee, no booster shot required," he said.

Aunjanue had her keys and satchel and was half way out the door. When she heard his words she stopped abruptly and so did Marla, who was right behind her. Then she felt her old friend brush quickly past her.

Aunjanue turned around and faced Darryl. He had his arms outstretched, palms turned up. She cocked her head, stuck her tongue firmly in her cheek, and rested both hands on her hips.

"Well, why didn't you say so in the first place?" Her old lover squirmed slightly under her gaze. Marla's lessons were paying off already.

"Shall we take my car?" On the way to the elevator, Darryl sounded less confident.

"Oh, yeah," Aunjanue stuck a fingernail into the down button.

"So what do you like? Café au Lait? Mocha Latte with skim? Black? There's a great neighborhood coffee shop about a mile down the road," he said.

"I've got news for you. We're not getting coffee," Aunjanue said.

"Then, what?"

The elevator opened, but Aunjanue didn't get in. She held the door open with her foot and fixed him with her eyes.

"If you're going to embarrass me like that in front of the entire unit, you'll have to do better than coffee, "she said, and stepped inside.

"I don't understand," Darryl said, holding the doors open like he was afraid to be alone with her.

"I want a big dinner. At a really nice restaurant. An eight-course meal with all the trimmings. Do you get that?"

Darryl laughed. He wanted to say something, she knew. But instead he just shook his head.

"What, cat got your tongue?"

"Damn, I hardly know you."

"Do you realize how much take-out I've ordered in my career? Or how many sandwiches filled with processed lunchmeat and soggy pickles squeezed inside two pieces of moldy bread I've eaten. I'm starving. I mean really starving. I want good food and lots of it." They rode down in the elevator in an uneasy silence.

Outside it was like walking into an open oven. The mid-day sun, still high in the sky, made everything in the parking lot shimmer. When they arrived at his car, Darryl stopped and looked around. "Aunjanue, I know a place. But you'll have to wait one more night. Do you mind?"

She looked at his crooked self-deprecating smile and wanted the rewind button. For a whole week she had skillfully sidestepped his come-ons and one-liners. All of Darryl's not-so-subtle attempts *to get to know her better*. She had avoided him just like Andy was avoiding her. But succumbing to Darryl's seduction had always been a foregone conclusion. In spite of everything, their history, having above-average intelligence, and above all, sitting at the brink of the most important bust of her life—just like her former self—Aunjanue was still in love with the man who didn't know Lydia was alive.

"I guess not. I'll just save my appetite."

"It will be worth it, you'll see."

"This place you're taking me. What do I wear?"

He shielded his eyes from the sun and grinned. "By all means, dress up."

FIFTEEN

Andy turned up the air conditioning and settled in to read medical reports on his team members. He could waste time feeling bad about it, or he could continue scrutinizing every detail available to him. Thank god he hadn't let Aunjanue stay. She made him too anxious. Aunjanue thought it was because she had replaced Lydia. But that wasn't it at all. Someone would have eventually. So what. The truth was she scared the crap out of him. In some creepy, Frankenstein horror-movie way, to Andy, she was more Lydia than Lydia had ever been.

She did so many of the things his former partner had. Barging into a room because she thought she owned it. Cocking her head back and forth while arching one eyebrow. And the walk. Even though she was a little shorter than Lydia, Aunjanue had that same lumbering gait. The two of them could have been twins separated at birth. Didn't anybody else see it?

That wasn't even the worse part. When she looked at him, it felt like Aunjanue was seeing straight into his heart. It terrified Andy to think that if she kept on him, one day he would crack. And tell her and then the whole world what really happened on that morning. He wasn't ready for that. Lydia had died in front of his eyes and, as long as he lived, he would never stop feeling responsible. But maybe there was a way to redeem himself.

Andy shoved the medical files aside and closed his eyes. He had been entertaining a hunch for a while. While everyone else searched for the mole by digging into the motive angle, Andy thought that careful examination of opportunity and means might get him closer to the rat. In less than a week, Darryl and Aunjanue would be confronting Markiza. He had to make damn sure their covers stayed airtight.

But where to start? His thoughts always flitted back to the workday inside the factory just before the failed sting. He was almost positive that the Russians were still completely clueless in the early morning. Nothing in the email chatter pointed to discovery. The wiretaps revealed no leaks. The boys didn't display any unusual behavior nor did their handlers. But later, something did change. Recognition passed through him like a shudder.

After lunch, the normally loud guards and supervisors had been silent vanguards anticipating a breech. Rather than perfunctorily shouting at the kids or each other, they walked in straight lines back and forth, as if in a trance. Sometime in between late morning and lunch, by way of a freaky accident or an unexpected alignment in the stars, the mole must have stumbled onto classified information. And he either showed up in person or used a disposable burner to tell them about the operation. Otherwise why would have Markiza suddenly suspended the delivery of 200 smuggled boys into the factory?

Andy decided to call a CI he'd known for years. The informant was a known drug dealer to gay bars. One of his steady customers was Gregor, a man who normally displayed the persona of a straight-white-Russian goon. The goon that took him on Lydia's car chase.

"You're asking me to remember what some ugly Rusky might have said three months ago? Kidding right?" the CI snorted.

"Let me refresh your memory. The Marlins creamed the Twins. It was still raging hot, and a kid got beat up real bad during tailgating. It's still an open case, and now they're calling it a hate crime," Andy said and waited.

"I remember. Gay kid, still in high school. Brain damaged, right? Wait. That day was also Gregor's birthday. He was going to celebrate at the Winslow and wanted me to bring him a quarter weed stash. Because it was a special occasion, I got there early and even threw in an extra bud."

"What happened when he picked it up?" Andy asked.

"That's just it. He never showed. Not until a few days later. And then he acted like it was Christmas day. He wanted to pay me extra, do you believe that? These guys are normally stoic, even morose. And not usually generous with pocket money. They don't ever show emotion. But, that night, he was positively giddy. Said something about a bonus."

Andy knew why. Saving Markiza 200 boys would definitely earn you something extra. Finding out how he was able to do that was the key.

"Thanks," Andy hung up the phone and got up to stretch. Something else niggled at him. Tadzio.

What exactly had prompted the little boy to stop hanging around Sasha and become a favorite of Markiza's? Was it the same day?

Sans padded quickly across his thick living room carpet over to the bay window. At least he hadn't been in the middle of cooking dinner when the senator called to say he was coming over. The quiet time he looked forward to spending with his wife would have to keep a little longer.

He opened the blinds and let in the bleak early evening. Rain streaked the glass, and the storm painted the sky like a bad watercolor: depressing charcoal in the east and an eerie green in the south. A thunderclap sounded like it came from inside the house causing Sans to jump back from the glass. He looked outside again and tried to make out the street. The mature mango trees almost completely shaded the lawn from the steady rush hour traffic. And then he caught the spray of headlights as the conversion van made its way up the slight incline into his driveway. The driver stepped out holding an umbrella and waited for the platform to roll to a stop. Kastle rode out of the vehicle in his motorized wheelchair and, when he was halfway up the walkway, Sans opened the door for him. After making sure that the senator was able to negotiate the low stoop, the driver nodded and returned to the vehicle.

Kastle turned his motorized chair so he could face the chintz sofa and motioned for Sans to sit down. "I flew down here right after the committee meeting because I wanted to tell you in person."

Sans scanned the younger man's even features and thought he saw a muscle twitch below one slate blue eye. He owed this politician more than he could ever repay. If it weren't for the senator, there would be no stringent anti-trafficking laws on the books. Florida's citizenry would still not know that Port of Miami had become the biggest and most porous gateway to human slavery in the world, and without Kastle—MAGS wouldn't exist. But today it was clear that the senator hadn't stopped by to deliver good news.

Sans asked, "That bad?"

"They want a progress report. ASAP."

Sans folded his hands and forced himself to sit still. "We need more time."

"How much time?" Kastle asked, but his tone was clear: Sans' answer would never be good enough.

The captain gave it all he had. "Senator, please. We need a month. Four weeks, to get this absolutely right. We've worked too hard to abandon ship now."

"You've got until next Wednesday. If you can pull it off, whatever it is—in one week—then MAGS might have a future. If not, the funds disappear," Kastle said.

"No." Now Sans was up and pacing around the sofa. One hand reached into his hair and pulled thick strands over a deeply creased forehead, while the other hand sat clamped over his mouth like it was trying to stop him from screaming.

"This can't be happening. What's going on?"

"Calm down Carlos. You always knew that the fund was discretionary. When things were good, the faucet ran without interruption. But things aren't good anymore. The economy is in the toilet and my friends on the other side of the aisle are calling in *everything*. You've got to know that I fought this tooth and nail."

It wasn't the Senator's fault. There was nothing more either of them wanted to say, so they went outside together into the rain, this time Sans covering Kastle with his own umbrella. When the van doors closed and the driver pulled away, the captain walked to the edge of his driveway searching the street for signs of a tail. Without the trees in his way, he could see clearly for blocks in either direction, and across the nearby intersection where traffic remained steady but light. The tan four-door he had spotted a few times was nowhere in sight, and Sans was certain that he had not been followed in more than a week. He walked back into his house and locked the door behind him.

Sans pulled out his mobile and willed it to ring. One part of his brain hovered over an irrational plane where he kept a glimmer of hope alive that Kastle would call back with *gotcha*, saying that it all had been just a big bad joke.

That never happened. So Sans returned to Kastle's last words. "I have faith in you, captain. And I have a gut feeling that you are more ready than even you believe. Go get 'em."

Sans knew what he had meant. Go get Markiza. Get it over with. At his desk, he started a list. When his wife came in to ask about dinner, she took one look at her husband's expression, rolled her eyes, and walked out of the room without saying a word.

Sans scribbled his thoughts down on paper for more than an hour. He scratched out words and erased sentences, revising the order of the list several times. But no matter how he tossed it, Delgado's name flipped back to the top. He fired up his laptop and made reservations for Darryl and Andy to fly into the Duluth International Airport. Only sixty miles from the federal penitentiary, there would be a rental car waiting for them to drive to Sandstone, Minnesota. He needed to put in a date. Sans would have preferred yesterday, but knew he had to have two more days. Sunday. The detectives wouldn't like it, but they'd go. The only problem was—when they got there—would Delgado agree to the new plan?

He'd have to.

Sans lost his taste for cooking and told his wife to set the table and uncork a good bottle of wine, because he was going out for Chinese. He promised he would be back soon.

But they would not see each other again that night.

SIXTEEN

Aunjanue leaned against a pillar in the bowels of Miracle Mile's parking ramp, waiting for Darryl. They were still being careful about being followed and seen together and, as was her style, she arrived early to act as lookout. When he pulled up in his vintage car, Aunjanue was struck by the first of two invasions into her new identity that day. Like in a dream, not only were the busy rooms of her consciousness, with all of their beliefs and attitudes, closing the doors, they began pushing off into the distance beyond her reach. And she didn't much care.

While Darryl held the car door open, Aunjanue leaned in and inhaled the musky interior air. She eased herself slowly into the seat and as soon as she buckled up, lost track of the contours of her body as they melted and dissolved into the soft plush leather seats. It was like being wrapped up in a creamsicle cake. She recalled that Darryl had bought the Audi at a county auction soon after they had started dating, and the only thing he restored was the interior. *For Lydia.* Inside the confines of the car's chamber, Aunjanue felt lightheaded with the rapture of being alive. She sank in as deep as she could and savored the sensation.

After they'd driven for a few minutes, she felt Darryl's eyes upon her. "What are you thinking about?" he asked.

"That this seat is unbelievably comfortable," she said with her eyes closed.

"Before you got in, it looked like you had something on your mind," he said.

Aunjanue didn't relish coming to, but she remembered with a start that earlier her new persona had been perched to ask him a question. It seemed that Darryl was keenly observant this evening. He might regret that. She was about to play a game with him precisely because she knew who he was, and he mistakenly believed he didn't know her.

"Not sure how to ask this without sounding judgmental."

"Be honest. I can take it," Darryl said.

"How do you guys do it? I mean, how do you get away with breaking the rules?" Aunjanue sat up and talked to his surprised profile. "I'm talking about dating co-workers. Sans told me about you and Lydia, and Lydia and Andy. Now, we're going out to dinner."

"Since when is there a law against sharing a meal?" he asked.

"Seriously. Aren't you afraid that one day these shenanigans could cost you your jobs?"

Darryl shrugged. "There are things about me, about the unit, that are well, just different. We're sort of special. Because we're not beholden to the same regimen as police who work out of well-established divisions. See, Lydia and I originally came from vice, Andy was a homicide detective for eleven years, and Marla—HR extraordinaire."

"So you should know better." Aunjanue was enjoying herself immensely.

"That's just it. One day when we were minding our own business, doing good police work, the stars started to align in a really weird pattern. A few years back, southern Florida county commissioners and the city council, in conjunction with other civil-sided entities, all had a come-to-Jesus moment. They came up with the same goal: keep crime low in bustling tourist areas. And what better way to ensure peace and tranquility in The Magic City, than to poach some of Miami-Dade's finest to do their troubleshooting. They handpicked various police and assigned them to task forces, neighborhood street patrol, and temporary stings like MAGS. Every few years, some combination of this unit gets brought in to work special cases."

"So, you made 'fooling around with whomever you please' a work benefit because of . . . what is it? Uncertainty regarding your work detail?"

"Actually, you hit the nail on the head. It comes naturally with the territory. We risk more than most, and the higher-ups turn a blind eye. Just think of us as free lancers, add a mixture of humanity and hormones, and VOILA," Darryl said.

On Coral Way, the sky had turned dark and large drops of rain splattered the windshield. Darryl turned on the wipers.

"Don't worry, we'll be driving away from the storm." Darryl said.

Aunjanue hadn't noticed the sudden change in weather because she was thinking that Lydia had had the same discussion with Darryl years before. Back then, her former self agreed with him, and that made Aunjanue realize she might be teetering on a slippery slope bringing up the subject. What if Darryl remembered that conversation and got suspicious? But Aunjanue couldn't stop herself; she was having way too much fun. She decided to ramp it up.

"Can you talk to me about Lydia? No one else will."

Whatever she had expected didn't come within a screaming distance of Darryl's full-on smile or what he did next. He pointed to his suit coat pocket, which was pulled tight under his seat belt. Aunjanue reached in and lifted his wallet.

"Go ahead, look on the other side of the money flap."

She found several photos of a couple with small children—his sister's family—and one of his mom and grandmother with Darryl at his police academy graduation. The last one was of Lydia. She was so startled to see her old face that she opened her mouth and couldn't close it again. "She was so beautiful; I didn't realize . . ." Aunjanue stammered.

She hadn't meant to say that. But after seeing a likeness of her former self, in, of all places, Darryl's wallet—she didn't think even her own parents carried her picture—she had to say something. Otherwise Darryl'd think his date was jealous, or worse, crazy.

"Lydia was one in a million. I really fell for her," Darryl said.

Aunjanue felt envy. What an odd feeling to find you jealous of *yourself*, she thought. Here was yet another strange and painful moment she would have to scale in order to graduate to the next one, and the one after that. But shit, they were talking about her. Her old self. What if he said things that she wasn't ready to hear?

"In so many ways Lydia broke the mold. She was bright, intuitive, very athletic, and not afraid of anything or anyone. Like a superhero. Everyone who met her, either fell in love, or was in awe. I couldn't believe she chose me." Darryl said.

"Why did you two break up?" Even though she asked, Aunjanue didn't want to listen to his rehearsed answer. Again he surprised her.

"Beats the hell out of me. It certainly wasn't anything Lydia did. I was always crazy about her. I just didn't think I could . . . hell, I didn't really think." She watched Darryl hesitate and it was agony. He seemed to be searching for just the right words that would make sense, to him and to her. "No, I did know. I was sure I couldn't measure up."

"To what? Was she so demanding of you emotionally that you got scared away?"

Darryl shook his head. "Nothing like that. I just wasn't ready to take the next step. I think I was afraid of something else. I can't believe I'm telling you this."

Aunjanue drove it home. "Of commitment?"

"I didn't think I would be good enough. I thought I would drag her down."

"You broke up with her?" She watched him nod. "Love terrified you that much?"

"I had been married before. To a junkie. In the beginning, Karen, my ex-wife, hardly even drank. But a few months after we were married she met a guy at work who got her on crack; she got hooked so fast. And it got real bad. She lost her job, didn't eat, even emptied our bank account. She almost killed me when she learned I switched banks. I put her through treatment. Twice.

"Karen got better, got worse. I couldn't help her. Finally, I stopped loving her. I failed as a husband."

"You divorced?"

He nodded. "After twelve years, I just gave up. And I wasn't about to do that to anyone else again."

"But it sounds like you tried everything in your power to help your wife. You stayed longer than most would."

"But don't you see, it still didn't work."

Aunjanue mused that Darryl had rarely talked about Karen to Lydia. And he had never admitted failure around his marriage. Either Aunjanue was easier to talk to, or Darryl was mellowing.

They drove in silence for the next few minutes. "Okay, you've got to let the cat out of the bag sometime. Where is it exactly, that you are taking me for this dinner extravaganza? You owe me." She shrugged. "I even dressed up like you asked."

Darryl turned his head and eyed her with approval. Her little black dress was simple but stylish. A matte jersey, one-shoulder design with a smocked empire waist. She wore no earrings, but for accent had put on an old-fashioned two-strand crystal beaded necklace and matching bracelet. Her flat shoes were black with white tips. A large rose-petalled barrette swept the hair off one side of her face, and the clutch that lay on her lap looked like it came from the same showroom as her shoes. Inside, she kept a neatly folded light chiffon wrap, in case the restaurant got too cold.

"You look very pretty, Aunjanue."

"Thank you. Now answer my question."

"Here's the thing." Darryl actually leaned over and patted her hand like she was a small child. "You are going to think this is a little weird. But on the last Friday of each month, friends and family get together at my Mom's house in—"

"Coconut Grove. We're about 20 minutes away. The reason I didn't tell you before is because I thought you might say no. And you still can. I will turn this car around and we'll find something else. But please hear me out first.

"It's no ordinary dinner. My mother prepares like the royals might show up. She hires help and together they cook and clean for two days. They bring out the family china and linen; the wood is polished; the floors get waxed. Before we eat we go outside on the porch and sit on swings, while my cousin Laura and uncle Charles serve up mint juleps, and gin and tonics. The limes are picked fresh from mom's small orchard.

"When we're called, we all go into the formal dining room where we sit down to eat and don't get up for hours. Because there really are eight courses. We eat, laugh, joke, and gossip. The kids tell stories, These are stories they've written themselves, sometimes they recite poems. After dinner it's customary to finish up with apéritifs—at mom's, that's a wine-based drink mixed with blueberry liqueur she ferments inside a cedar closet. Then we walk around the yard and inspect the gardens. Each month there are new flowers, fruit. You name it.

"And the last thing. We go back inside one more time for the pièce de résistance. For a little while we all sing. We sing our hearts out. Everything from smoky jazz licks to rock and roll. It's as if—"

Even though Darryl was doing the actual talking, nonetheless, each syllable flowed out of Aunjanue's head like she'd written the narrative. Because Lydia had memorized that speech long ago. Aunjanue, formerly someone else, had just been clobbered by the second invasion. OMG!

How was she supposed to get through the next four hours with Darryl's formidable mother, Anita? This was taking GUESS WHO'S COMING TO DINNER? to a whole new level.

SEVENTEEN

Sans' head throbbed like Hades. Because he had stupidly allowed his emotions to get the better of him—hadn't he always lectured Lydia about that—he exchanged cooking his and his wife Liset's favorite meal, enchiladas Suizas, for picking up Chinese takeout. But when he got to the restaurant he found that the joint was closed due to a burst pipe. He went next door and ordered a pizza with everything because he didn't ever order pizza, and had no idea what they were supposed to have on them. Now on the way home, he discovered he was being followed. Why didn't he see the tail earlier? Had he even bothered to look?

When you're police for thirty-two years, you develop a sixth sense for scoping out your surroundings whenever you leave home. Too many arrests and too many almosts to take chances. And for him there was the very real fact of actually having been followed in recent weeks. But he'd done that, right? He just didn't see.

The captain had scanned his streets for a tan sedan and failed to notice a white van. Was it because his brain was so addled with thoughts of Markiza that he could no longer function like a good cop? Was he more upset about the schedule change than he cared to admit? The news had thrown him for a loop, and he worried justifiably about what would happen to the sting now that Mr. Money Bags, Senator Lex Kastle, had decided to close the door to the bank. He could have kicked himself for not saying or doing something to persuade Kastle to give them more time. But a kind of dullness in the younger man's eyes convinced him that it would be worse than useless to try to pursue that course. Still he was mad at himself for failing to put up any kind of fight at all. Just took it like a chump. Like a public-servant-working-stiff-chump.

All along, Sans knew that none of that mattered. They were as ready as they would ever be. Often, working without a parachute produced the best results. If they could pull this off quickly, even unexpectedly, Aunjanue and Darryl would not come off as over rehearsed, or over confidant. Thinking on your feet doesn't allow for second-guessing. You just fly out of the gate with blinders and head for the finish line. To win.

The real worry was Delgado. The man in prison must have hated the position he found himself in: helping cops take down a career criminal. But what else could he do? His beloved son was in trouble, and the only way out of it was through MAGS. Not that there had ever been any love lost between the Colombian drug lord and the Russian human trafficker, but Delgado would tell you it was the principle that mattered. And soon, Darryl and Andy would have to cajole Delgado into acting early. Sans was sure Delgado would push back. He'd want something more in addition to charges being dropped against Francisco, and the whole arrest hushed up. Something else that they just didn't have time to negotiate.

Sans' brain changed gears when he spotted the second van. Where did it come from?

After he left Augustino's Pizzaria, he had spotted the first one. The driver of the dirty white vehicle didn't seem very good at surveillance because he stayed close behind and turned everywhere Sans did. Wasn't even trying to be discreet. That could have been a really good thing or a really bad thing. Sans decided to turn into the municipal parking ramp and find out which it was.

Sans wished he could call someone. But whom? Darryl and Aunjanue were on a date, supposedly, at Anita's. That left Andy. He might be drunk by now. Sans had, after all, given everyone two days off. Crap.

The captain drove up the ramp to the third floor, the place you went if you were planning on seeing a film at the independent theater complex. He looked in the rearview mirror, the van was still with him. Sans pulled into the first empty spot and unbuckled his seat belt. He reached into the back seat, grabbed an old newspaper, and made a big show of checking his watch while he scanned the movie section. It occurred to him then, that he didn't have his gun.

Sans was parked right next to the elevators and had a clear view of all the vehicles coming and going behind him. He was sure the driver of the van had parked a few stalls ahead, but when he turned around to put the newspaper back he didn't expect to see another white van blocking him. Oh yeah, there were really two of them.

What Sans did next, he would never remember. Because in order to create memories out of events, you have to stay conscious for a period of time following whatever it was that happened. Events come and go, but if you don't store them properly, you will never get the chance to recall them. That's just how the brain works.

He had no gun and no back up, but Sans was running on adrenaline and experience. His car, a 2009 Passat, was as powerful as an Indy stock car, and when he rammed it into reverse, the impact hit and crumpled the van behind him like it was a sardine can.

A van, unless it is properly loaded, is nothing more than a metal box filled with air. A gusty wind could push it off the road, while a full-on smash into the rear quarter panel would send it sailing into the next row of cars. Next, Sans pulled forward and then back again, angling out of the tight spot. He heard clomping footsteps. The Russian from the wrecked van was running towards him with his gun drawn. In the side view mirror Sans caught the lights of the first van as it moved to block him. He gripped the wheel, turned hard and aimed for the exit lane. The pillar was in the way. He ground the gears into reverse and ducked as the first bullet struck his windshield. He didn't dare raise his head and just aimed for the lane as he slipped into drive. Sans felt the wheel slip out of his grip. The collision crumpled the concrete pillar like it had been hit with the full force of a detonated car bomb. Moments later a riot of cracks heaved the low ceiling into large boulders, vaporizing everything in their path.

EIGHTEEN

Darryl eased into a spot recently vacated by a compact car. They sat across from his mother's house and casually surveilled both sides of the street. It was easy to do because they were on a narrow lane that ended 300 feet ahead of them. Every car that came by either parked on the street or turned into a driveway. When they were satisfied that they had not been tailed, Aunjanue rolled down her window, placed her arms on the windowsill, and rested her chin. If Darryl thought this was strange, he didn't say a word. Instead, he got out and waited patiently by the passenger door.

In the past when arriving for these dinners, Lydia had always gotten butterflies in her stomach. She had loved looking at the palm and banyan trees, a thick lush botanical feast as far as the eye could see. The heavenly scents of bougainvillea and jasmine that filled her nostrils had made her want to weep with joy. But none of that ever changed the fact that beyond the urban forest lay a love/hate relationship with a house that belonged to a woman who seemed to belong to no one.

The temperature was going down quickly along with the orange sun. Evening breezes carried spicy earthen smells despite the low humidity. Aunjanue climbed out of the car, and together they walked into the front yard. When they were less than twenty feet from the cracker-style structure, Aunjanue stopped and dug out painful facts and memories.

In front of her stood a house that paid homage to the simple one-story wooden cabins built by Florida and Georgia settlers in the late eighteen hundreds. Darryl's childhood home however, had two stories, an attached closed-in porch in the back, and multiple decorative gable-fronted dormers. She especially appreciated the nostalgic feel of the dandelion-painted rough-hewn vertical siding that contrasted stylishly with a steep-pitched roof covered in chestnut-colored shingles. Recently, cracker-style houses had become all the rage in southern Florida. With cross-breeze windows that allowed for old-fashioned air conditioning, and stone chimneys that kept the houses warm in the cooler months, they were models for state-of-the-art energy efficiency.

But Darryl's father had this one built in the late 1970s right after becoming an associate professor at University of Miami, because it reminded him of the large estate house in the middle of the poor Jamaican village where he'd grown up. Seven years later, after the house was paid off, Oliver King left it in the trusty hands of Anita and his children. Then he stealthily made his way back to his ancestral home and was never heard from again.

Even before they had made their way around the wide verandas, Aunjanue could hear the soothing sounds of water cascading over rocks. Tiny pebbles wove a meandering path that sloped gently towards a long multi-tiered waterfall. At the bottom, a woman dressed in a flower-patterned sleeveless shift was kneeling down and staring into a heart-shaped pool where the newest tenants, glistening koi—were making happy laps. Aunjanue would have known Michelle, even if she had been covered in an abaya.

"Aunjanue, I want you to meet my favorite sister, Michelle. Michelle, Aunjanue," Darryl said.

Aunjanue would remember later that when Darryl's sister rose to her feet, it wasn't the woman's hesitation or the lack of words that made her stiffen. It was what Michelle was doing with her hands—clenching them, and then jutting her neck forward like a puppet's, while her eyes watered and then narrowed with disapproval.

"Oh my god. Darryl, when you said you were bringing someone, I immediately thought of Lydia. Crazy, huh? But a few minutes ago I saw you two atop, and from the back, I believed you did bring Lydia. But that couldn't be. Because Lydia is dead. So she can't be Lydia," Michelle said.

Aunjanue and Michelle stared at each other while Darryl shifted his gaze wildly, first from Michelle to Aunjanue, and then back to Michelle. He didn't bother to conceal his irritation. "Aunjanue, please excuse us. My sister's having a stroke."

Darryl took Michelle firmly by the arm and led her through a vine-covered pergola into the back gardens. Completely on her own, Aunjanue supposed she should mingle and not try to follow them.

She waited until the waiter brought her a cocktail and then walked past a group of teenagers, smiled at them and said hello. She stopped to look up at the flowering wisteria entwining the pergola, glanced once behind her, and slipped through the opening. She followed another rocky path that circled a trio of utility sheds. When she heard voices,

Aunjanue stopped and then gingerly made her way to the back of one of the little brick buildings.

Darryl's voice was stentorian. "Have you lost your mind? Or do you just hate me that much? What were you thinking, Michelle?"

There was a pause and Aunjanue thought Michelle must have backed up or in some way was trying to escape Darryl's reach. "Darryl, you never brought anybody here but Lydia. Even when you were married, Karen hardly ever came. I think I got confused."

"Are you kidding me? This is all I get? You embarrass me in front of a colleague, someone I respect—"

"Maybe even someone you like a lot, I know. But you have to understand, something in that woman triggered memories. I just kept seeing *her*."

"You mean triggered insanity," Darryl was beginning to calm down. Another pause and the detective heard a soft crinkling sound. Fabric against fabric. That could only mean Darryl had walked up to his sister and put her arms around her, because Aunjanue heard Michelle begin to cry softly. "I miss her."

A small, cool hand pressed into her arm. Aunjanue turned around startled, because she found herself staring into the warm, gentle eyes of Darryl's grandmother. The diminutive septuagenarian whispered, "I'm Allison Green, Darryl and Michelle's grandmother. Anita is my daughter. You must have not met her yet, because if you had, you'd know she doesn't let just anyone wander back here, where. . ." Allison waved her hands over the air, "it's not completely finished yet. Come on, let's get out of here, before anyone else finds out you were eavesdropping."

Maybe MAGS should hire Allison for their surveillance work.

As they walked back up the path, Allison Green said, "We grieve for our dead, I'm afraid. That never stops. Darryl obviously was the most affected by Lydia's passing, but it's my daughter and Michelle that don't know how to deal with the loss. Michelle cries too much and Anita doesn't know how."

That about summed it up, thought Aunjanue. Michelle was a sweet woman to whom high drama and tears flowed like a natural stream of water. On the other hand, Anita was the original ice princess. Always coiffed to the nines, perfectionist in all things she tackled, Darryl's mother wasn't just reserved and aloof, she eschewed intimacy and kept most relationships at a detached and distant-proof level. Yet here, Aunjanue was being told that underneath Anita's frozen exterior, lay unresolved sorrow and something akin to compassion.

Aunjanue walked behind the thin wiry woman through the pergola and up another hill towards the back of the house. "Mrs. Green, how did you know we were back there?"

"Please, everyone calls me nana. I'm afraid people here are terribly curious to know about the woman Darryl brought to the dinner. That included me. I love my grandson, and I loved Lydia. But don't worry about that. He's obviously crazy about you. Even if you can't tell, I can." The older woman stopped suddenly and whispered in low conspiratorial voice. "I heard what Michelle said and watched where you all went. You could say that I pay attention."

Nana had admitted spying on them. Aunjanue found that adorable.

At the top of the hill, she counted a dozen adults standing around on the stone-tiled patio, and five children playing in the kidney shaped pool. Darryl and Michelle were already up there and walking over to them.

Darryl said, "I see you've met my nana." He gave his grandmother a loud smooch on the cheek. Nana clasped his face in her hands and smiled broadly. "My Darryl."

Michelle took the moment to whisk Aunjanue to far end of the pool. "Darryl might be the smart one in the family, but I'm definitely the theatrical sibling. I'm sorry about my earlier outburst. Most of the time I'm pretty normal, honest. Here, I want you to meet my twins. Marissa, Jordan! Come on out of the pool. It's almost time for dinner."

Two big-eyed nine-year-olds climbed out of the pool in a show of exaggerated exasperation and grabbed towels. They ran up to their mother spraying water on both Michelle and Aunjanue. "Hey, hey, watch yourselves. I want you to meet Darryl's friend, Aunjanue. Tonight you get to have a new audience member for your stories. Say hello."

Marissa held out her hand and in a very serious voice said, "I'm Marissa, and I'm happy to meet you. You have a pretty flower in your hair."

Justin looked up shyly at Aunjanue, stuck out his hand and said, "Hi, I'm Jordan."

"Okay, get showered and dressed, or you'll be late for the first course," their mother said.

Michelle touched Aunjanue's arm and pointed towards the French doors. "Would you like a tour? It's not a big house but we all love it. Come on, I'll show you around."

At that moment Aunjanue looked over at Darryl and saw a partial smile freeze on his handsome face. Then his eyes began tracing something or someone behind her. Everyone else appeared to be craning their necks to look in the same direction.

As if on cue, the sun descended, spreading a golden haze over the entranced faces of the guests. Fairy lights switched on in the trees and bushes, and Aunjanue noticed someone had lit the Tiki torches around the pool, because their little flames were waving and sputtering like messengers proclaiming important news. The air stilled or maybe everyone had stopped breathing.

It happened so quickly. A precise clicking of heels marching across stone, a kiss planted gently on a son's cheek, and the rustling of a gypsy skirt trimmed in mirror beads turning around to face the new guest. Aunjanue watched the upturned corners of Anita's mouth form a genuine smile and sleek car eyes welcome her.

Aunjanue wondered if something had happened since her last visit to transform everyone's personality. Or was she the one who had changed? Had she always been wrong about Anita, Michelle, all of them? But how could that be? She knew better than try to analyze a situation that was still playing itself out. She would examine these things later.

"Aunjanue, I'm Anita Green." Anita extended her arm and then embraced the detective lightly. "I'm so happy you could come and join us tonight. We have a lot going on, and I want you to feel like you fit right in. Why don't I start by giving you a tour of the house?"

Anita was already turning Aunjanue around when Michelle's grabbed her arm. "Mom, I was going to do that."

The mother stared down her daughter until she let go and walked away. Aunjanue also thought she saw Darryl start in their direction, but when she looked around he was gone too. Okay, so not everything about Anita had changed.

They went upstairs, where two identical sunny bedrooms filled with handcrafted teak furniture, were separated by a large loft space that looked out at most of the first floor. They stood under the cathedral ceiling and admired the breathtaking expanse of contemporary and island design. A multitude of windows let in light and cast shadows simultaneously. Back on the first level Anita introduced Aunjanue to the cook she had hired to help her with the occasion. The smells coming out of simmering pots and pans made Aunjanue's mouth water and she said so. Anita looked pleased and led the detective past glass-encrusted countertops and appliances that blended with the wood-planked walls into the dining room. She pointed to Aunjanue's seat, and said Darryl would sit on her left. The last room looked identical to the dining room but contained a grand piano and a long mahogany bureau laden with silver framed photos. Some, she knew, dated back to the late 1900s.

Anita picked out a large horizontal frame and pointed to various faces. "This is my great grandfather Harold and his second wife Roxie. His first wife, Annabelle, died in childbirth." The next photo was gruesome. It was Annabelle lying in her coffin, with the baby infant on her dead chest. Anita explained that was customary back then. To take a photo of a dead mother holding a live baby, so the child would always know how much she had been loved.

"These are some of my aunts and uncles." There were at least a dozen. "And here I am with my own brothers and sisters. There were fourteen of us. Eleven survived. And eight are still alive. But they're scattered all over the country, and it is hard to stay in touch. They have their own families and busy lives," Anita said.

Nana walked into the room and put her hand on her daughter's. "Honey, Clara says it's time. She needs you in the kitchen."

"Excuse me, Aunjanue, I have to go. We'll be serving the first course in just a few minutes. Mom, can you finish telling our guest about our family history? Nothing too sordid, okay?" Anita winked at the detective.

Winks, hugs, and smiles. Aunjanue couldn't believe how good it made her feel. It made her realize how completely bereft and parched she had been, starving for family. For love. But how long could it last?

Nana took down a photograph Aunjanue knew well and not at all. Looking again at Oliver King was like staring into the face of Darryl. They could have been brothers. But in reality, they were estranged father and son.

"Darryl's father was a wonderful man. Learned, generous, hard working. I think he had a terrible secret deep inside that he never shared with anyone one else. Something so dark and troublesome that it caused him to leave his family." She raised her arms and waived them around as she exclaimed, "You know he built this house for his family. Then suddenly one day he must have woken up and said to himself, 'today I must go'. We don't even know if he's still alive," Nana said with tears starting to form in her eyes.

"What's wrong?" Aunjanue asked, alarmed.

"It's my poor Darryl. If you only see his good looks and big smile, you might think everything was fine. But you only have to look just a little harder to see that he's as troubled as his father. Oh, and not for the same reasons as Oliver. Whatever those were.

"But the guilt, it colors everything that man does. He thinks because his father failed his family, he will too. He's afraid he's like him. Darryl doesn't want to take chances on love. But I know him. He's not what he's afraid of. He has so much to give. I wish there was someone who could convince him." Nana fixed Aunjanue with a questioning look that was too hard to return and answer. She was glad when the kids came bursting into the room.

"It's time! It's time!" Jordan and Marissa squealed with two laughing toddlers taking up the rear.

Everyone took their places. Aunjanue sat next to Darryl and across from Anita. Michelle and her husband sat on either side of Anita, the kids next to their dad. Uncles and aunts, cousins and neighbors, all held their glasses of sparkling wine high, clinked and dived into the first course: vichyssoise soup with bread and olive oil. Time passed dreamily as platters were set on stands, served, and bussed. Aunjanue consumed shrimp jambalaya, crispy broiled catfish, southern pan fried chicken, creamy potato mash, fried okra, and black eyed peas over mixed greens.

After professing to Darryl that she couldn't eat one more thing, she found herself greedily sampling all of the desserts; corn griddlecakes, coconut layer cake, apple brown betty, and red velvet cake.

After the dishes were cleared and the table cleaned off, everyone waddled into the next room. Marissa read her essay comparing Florida's migrant orange workers to a new wave of slavery in post-modern United States. Jordan followed by reciting a poem he wrote about Lebron James.

When everyone stopped clapping, uncle Charles opened his guitar case and began strumming some blues riffs. Nana sat down on the piano and tried to follow his improvisational style. After a final, *Make Me a Pallet on Your Floor*, all the kids made a line and began singing Usher's *DJ Got Us Falling in Love Again*.

———————————

Darryl pulled alongside Aunjanue's car. Once again they were sitting quietly in the parking ramp, looking around for anything out of sorts, before getting out. Aunjanue unlocked the door to her car but did not open the door. When she turned around to say good night to Darryl, she saw him leaning on the trunk of her car. She walked over and placed her hand on his arm.

"I have to admit, it's hard to see the evening end. I was in dithers when we arrived at your mom's, but I can't remember having a better time in a very long while. Thank you for everything."

"The evening doesn't have to end now," Darryl said.

"If it were up to me, it wouldn't. But it's not up to me."

"Then who?"

Aunjanue felt herself heading towards the demarcation line between two strata. Between using her head and doing what her heart wanted. She knew that once she crossed over the checkpoint there could be no turning back. She wasn't just risking the sting; she now owned the power to tear this man emotionally into shreds. She hugged Darryl and pecked him on the cheek.

Darryl embraced her gently and leaned his head into her hair. He murmured something that sounded like *mmmm*, or was it *yummm*?

Quickly, she pulled away and opened the car door. When she sat down in the driver's seat, Aunjanue looked in the rear view mirror and saw Darryl repositioning his behind against the trunk. She turned on the engine and let it idle. He didn't move. Some things you just don't want to control. She shut the car off and slipped back into his embrace.

"What took you so long?" Darryl said.

"Don't take this the wrong way, but I've been seriously craving human contact. It's been some time, if you must know."

"Take all the time you want." Darryl lifted her face and kissed her gently on the lips. He kissed her again and she pressed into him. Her entire perception of self shifted as the left hemisphere of her brain began to shut down. She no longer felt apart, separate, and restricted from life around her. Suddenly she was connected to every part of everything, and understood that all things in the universe were fluid and possible.

Just for a second, Aunjanue wondered why Darryl's persona had also morphed from wound and controlled, to something as amorphous as a jar of melting honey. Because with Lydia, it had taken weeks before he could completely let go. Completely trust her. With Aunjanue, it had been instant. Was it because her body felt familiar? Did it feel like home? What would happen if he thought about it? How much like Lydia's, this body was. It was a good thing then that Darryl was definitely past the thinking stage.

As one, they saw the last of their conscious pixels give way to a soft vibration, a delicate dance through time, completely removed from study and judgment. It would be okay, everything would turn out fine. Something that felt this good could never be . . .

A phone started ringing. It was coming from the Audi.

Darryl kept kissing her even as he talked. "That's mine. I better check. I left it inside the car the whole time at mom's."

Aunjanue watched Darryl in resignation as he yanked his car door open and pulled a mobile from the back seat. He put it to his ear and listened. Once he asked a short question that she couldn't make out. Or didn't want to. When he turned around, he looked sick and bewildered.

"That was Andy. He's at Cedars Medical Center. Sans just had emergency open-heart surgery."

NINETEEN

"Aunj! Aunjanue. Are you all right?" Darryl hovered only six inches from her, cradling her face in his hands as he spoke, but the words echoed around in her brain like marbles trying to pass through molten metal. *Sans? In Emergency? Undergoing surgery?* Darryl had said more. Something about a collision, and a car being buried in a parking ramp. None of it was good, Aunjanue thought. If Sans died, then everything they had set up together would be for nothing. If he died, the unit would lose Markiza. If he died, she'd lose the man who believed in her. If he died . . .

"Pull yourself together. Come on, I'll drive. It's going to be okay."

Aunjanue snapped. "It's going to be okay? What the hell do you know? Sans might die on the operating table." Oh god, oh god. Darryl was right, she wasn't thinking straight. Just get in his car and something will occur to you she promised her shell-shocked, doubtful self.

Darryl drove out of the ramp onto Coral Way and headed east towards the hospital. He kept turning to look at her every few minutes, but she had retreated to a secret place and only stared straight ahead.

He said, "I'm sorry, if I sounded flippant back there. I'm all torn up about this too. Sans is like a father figure to me. I love the guy. I can't imagine what I would do if he . . . but this is no time to freak out. I mean . . . is there something I should know? You're taking this really hard, and you barely know the man."

If I told you what you should know, it just might kill you, she growled inside. Now, certainly wasn't the time to explain how she and Sans had concocted her disguise so Aunjanue could remain on the case without anyone figuring out that Lydia hadn't really died. But if Sans didn't make it, she knew that the FBI deputy director would step in and take charge. Then what? Would her new boss have the authority to allow preparations for the sting to continue? If he did, would he give the operation his seal of approval? What did it matter, really? If Sans died, the higher ups would have to reveal Aunjanue's identity.

Shit. Unmasking Aunjanue might have worse consequences for Sans than even for Aunjanue. If the others learned Aunjanue was Lydia and Sans died, those poor bastards wouldn't even have time to grieve for the man, but for the resentment that they would surely start to feel. If they believed that their fearless leader had not trusted them with the truth, they would be crushed. Dead or not, Sans was a devout Catholic, and she was certain guilt would start turning him in his grave if he even suspected his actions had caused the others to feel turmoil. Oh, she herself could explain until the cows came home about security factors and safety issues, and all the other things that went into keeping Darryl, Andy, and Marla in the dark, but it would never ring true and sincere, unless they heard it from the man himself. He better live, damn it.

She had always excelled at compartmentalizing emotions and, now, with considerable effort, Aunjanue managed to wall off her blooming panic attack and said, "Look, I'm upset because he's a good man. It's unfair. I'm also freaked out about what this might do to our case. All of our work. And fucking Markiza."

She turned to look at Darryl. "You understand that I'm not authorized to operate on my own. I was put directly under Sans' supervision and, if he can't function as lead on this, I don't know what will happen. I have to call my boss."

"He already knows," Darryl said.

"What? Deputy Director Nelson? What are you talking about?"

"Sans' emergency contacts were the FBI and his wife. Andy got the call from your Nelson and was told that the whole thing got hushed up in a nanosecond. As far as anyone knows, the guy that crashed inside the parking ramp was someone called Arturo Gonzáles. A realtor from Jacksonville on vacation with his wife, Soraida. According to the report, he'd suffered a heart attack just before crashing into a pillar. I guess it's good we're coming dressed up like jet setters, and not like working cops."

Aunjanue could not hide the incredulity out of her voice when she asked, "Why did Nelson call Andy?"

"I don't know, maybe he did try to reach you. Where's your phone?"

At the bottom of my clutch with the ringer turned off.

Aunjanue thought that having your sun-burnt skin scrubbed with rubbing alcohol was preferable to sitting in hospital emergency rooms. Not because they were places where you might go to right before dying, or that the folks who survived them first had to endure a great deal of unbearable pain and suffering. No, it was because she knew them to be labyrinthine bureaucracies filled with interminable paperwork and ungodly compliance litmus tests. Once, she had come in with swelling from an unknown bite after vacationing in Key West. After an hour of filling out page after page of pointless questionnaires, most likely designed to protect the company who compiled the butt-wipes, she stopped writing and said to the intake nurse, "no, I do not remember the exact date when I got that last pimple on my butt, but do you think I might be seen anyway, because my arm is starting to kill me?" The nurse never cracked a smile, never saw the point of the joke. Another hour later, Lydia received a shot in her arm along with a script for steroid cream, and an admonition to stay out of the ocean for the next two weeks.

Now, the pretending Mrs. Soraida Gonzáles was doing the same thing. Bent over a clipboard not designed to accommodate an inch-thick stack of forms, she dutifully filled in the blanks—pink page after blue page after orange. Andy was beside her crouched on the floor carefully picking up fallen sheets, when Aunjanue and Darryl strode through the glass doors. He brightened when he saw them, got up, and so did the very real Mrs. Liset Sans. She dropped the paperwork onto her chair and let Darryl wrap his arms around her, while she began sobbing earnestly into his chest.

Aunjanue watched the pretty, slim woman, appearing ten years younger than her fifty years, with a mixture of sadness and bewilderment. She felt cornered by an adversary that she could not scale or remove. Her new identity. It prevented her from showing the same kind of love and sympathy that Darryl could, because Liset wasn't supposed to know her. It was another lifetime ago when Aunjanue had played Texas Holdem' with Liset, Sans, and Darryl, cleaning up every stinking nickel from the unsuspecting trio. How they had all laughed back then, pouring back beers while pretending to solve the problems of the world and the universe beyond. Now she couldn't even say 'hey' to her distressed friend. Unfortunately, Aunjanue knew, this frustration was small potatoes compared to what lay in store for her.

"Oh, honey," Darryl led Liset back to her chair and handed the clipboard to Andy, who looked pleased to take it.

"Darryl, he's in a coma and they're operating on his heart. My low-cholesterol, plaque-free husband apparently suffered cardiac arrest because he wasn't wearing his seat belt when he crashed into the concrete pillar. The impact cracked his chest wall and caused a coronary artery to burst. The EMTs saved his life once, now the surgeons are trying again. Oh, God in heaven."

Darryl introduced Aunjanue, but Liset was still looking at Daryl when she said, "My husband has spoken very highly of you."

Darryl asked, "Liset, do you have any idea why Carlos would go to the mall tonight. Why do you think he was on that parking level in the first place?"

Liset said, "There's an easy entrance to the independent theater up there. Years ago we used park up there because we liked to see foreign films. But tonight Carlos only went out for take out. And he promised to be right back."

Darryl almost jumped out of his seat. "Carlos? Take out? I thought he had a rule about that?"

"He does. But he was so upset after the senator left, he didn't want to cook. I think the only reason he went out at all was because he loves me and didn't want me to go hungry." Liset said.

"Wait, Lex Kastle was at your house today?" Darryl shook his head and looked at Andy who shrugged.

"Yes, the senator came over around dinner time, stayed for about a half hour and when he left, my husband was fit to be tied. When I walked into his study to ask him a question, he looked someone possessed. I mean, his eyes—bulged from inside his head." Liset stuck her fingers under her own eyeballs and pushed, to indicate madness. "You should have seen his face, it was red, and he was muttering. There were maps and notes laid out all over his neat desk. You know how anal he is about his desk. Everything in place, usually. I did not want to stick around there. After I walked away, I'm sure I heard him pounding his fist into something hard, and then he started clicking that mouse like it was his mortal enemy. He came out later looking a little better, and said he was going out for Chinese.

"He was gone so long, I got worried. I went to his computer and everything was still a mess. But an organized mess. He had made a calendar out of blank copy paper, and the next five days were laid out neatly on the floor. There were smaller notes posted on the monitor and around the desk, and I found two airline tickets taped to the printer."

Andy asked, "Was there anything written on those calendar pages?"

Liset said, "Your names."

Aunjanue asked, "Anything else?"

This time Liset looked squarely at Aunjanue and said, "On one of the sheets, he had written in red marker, Wednesday, Strike Zone, Aunjanue and Darryl."

Andy shot up suddenly letting the forms he had neatly collated earlier scatter once more to the floor. Darryl whistled softly. But Aunjanue kept her eyes locked on Liset's.

Darryl broke the spell, "Liset, would you mind if we went to your house and took a look at Carlos' desk. We could get a better understanding of what he was working on, and what might have happened earlier between him and the senator.

Aunjanue watched Darryl hug Liset once more before accepting her key to the house. She felt her arms start to reach out towards Sans' wife, and quickly retracted them, but not before catching the older woman's eyes flash something cryptic in her direction.

TWENTY

The key turned smoothly, but when the bolt lock slid back, Darryl didn't move. He was rooted to the threshold, to all of his dark thoughts. Ever since the drive over from the hospital, he had been seized by a disturbing premonition of how things might play out if they all went in together. But what choice did he have?

After saying goodbye to Liset, Andy, Aunjanue, and Darryl had walked over somberly into the parking lot and piled into Darryl's Audi. For most of the ride over to Sans' house, Andy had sat like a statue in the front passenger seat and stared intently at something in the road, distant and invisible to everyone else. Aunjanue, on the other hand, had squirmed in the back seat like a two-year-old and muttered to herself. Darryl had caught a few escaping explicatives and other random words: ramp, set up, followed, Russians, don't die. Darryl recalled that Lydia used to do that. While trying to deepen the breadth of a criminal investigation, she would spin what-ifs inside her big brain, making new neural connections, trying to find the answers. Eventually her mind would land on a few plausible solutions. Then like a lightening bolt, one of them would plant itself in front of the others—the gold shot. Darryl wondered if all women did that. Pairing up dozens of neurons, firing up possible connections, eliminating the duds, clarifying the best input.

To Darryl's astonishment, after Aunjanue settled down, he had strangely felt Andy's own negative stream of silence explode like firecrackers in the already claustrophobic space. Why did he dislike her so much, Darryl wondered. Was it because Andy somehow blamed Aunjanue for the captain's accident? Perhaps his on-and-off partner for the last dozen years had finally lost his mind to the carnal ravishes of alcoholism, and thereby his self-control. Was Andy no longer fit for the job?

There was also another terrible, unbidden thought that he could not tamp down. Andy's behavior mimicked a cop, who, for whatever reason, had personal knowledge of a crime or a person's involvement in a crime, but was not allowed to question the suspect because of a direct order by a superior. *Andy did not trust Aunjanue.*

Darryl's brooding was cut short by the sound of squealing tires zooming up the driveway and skidding to a stop next to the Audi. He stepped off the threshold and folded his arms over his head. In any other instance, Darryl and the other detectives would have reacted offensively, even drawn guns, especially after what had just happened to Sans. But in this case, they only looked relieved—even Andy—because Marla was the only one they knew that drove with her brights on when she was in a hurry, and always managed to park a little cock-eyed.

Marla stepped out of a small red SUV wearing a tracksuit, this one was grey and white, and there were hair-curlers under a brightly-colored paisley scarf. Darryl also noticed Marla's eyes were puffy and her cheeks, ashy.

"When Andy called me, I was helping my daughter with her homework. I got to the hospital as soon as I could and stayed with Liset for a while, before hurrying on here. Marla reached inside the car to pull out her keys and turn off the lights. "Liset told me you all were going to search Sans' office." She looked them up and down and grunted. "So, why are you just standing around? Go on in."

The living room was aglow with string lights badging the archway, a few were spread delicately over two tall dragonfly plants. Someone turned on an overhead light and they marched down a narrow hallway to Sans' study.

Rather than an office, the room resembled a tropical library you might find in the West Indies. Three windows were covered in wide-slotted burnt-orange bamboo shades. The floor was also bamboo, lighter and satin-finished, with colorful fiber rugs scattered haphazardly. African violets dotted almost every visible surface, and waxy-green philodendrons draped floor-to-ceiling bookshelves. But it was what was in the center of the room that interested Darryl.

Sans' desk, identical to the one in his office, usually only held a large iMac on one end and a bowl of fruit on the other. Today it was laden with piles of paper; some had spilled onto the antique banker's chair. Darryl's eyes, just like Andy's, turned to the floor below the desk. Five yellow, legal-sized sheets lay in a straight row—the mysterious calendar that Liset had referred to earlier.

Darryl and Andy crouched on the floor and began looking from one sheet to the other. Aunjanue stood nearby at a bank of windows reading a crumpled piece of paper, when she heard Andy's long, slow whistle. Reflexively she glanced once over at the detectives but quickly looked away to continue reading.

Darryl and Andy were frozen in place. They were afraid to touch the calendar, as if by doing so, they might contaminate a crime scene. "Can't be," Andy croaked. "Because according to this, we fly out of here day after tomorrow to meet with Delgado, and Christ . . . four days later, you and Aunjanue are supposed to meet with Markiza. It's too little time. What happened to our month?" He stood and stretched his back.

When both Andy and Darryl were up and out of her way, Marla slipped into the banker's chair, punched the computer to life, and typed in a password. Everyone stood mesmerized as she scanned document after document in a folder called, All Hell Breaks Lose. "Kids, it's all here, in between the cussing and the typos. He was sure in a mighty hurry, our captain. But Sans wrote a kind of log. It's super detailed, like he intentionally wanted to document every thought he had between 6:00 p.m., right after Senator Kastle's departure, and 8:30 p.m., when he finally left the house."

Marla swiveled her chair around to face the detectives. "Looks like MAGS has a new agenda and so go all of our assignments." The men didn't disagree so she turned back to the computer. "Y'all can read it, if you want. I'll even print out a copy for each of you. But it boils down to one thing: the money for MAGS has run out. That's why we don't have a month to corral Markiza anymore. See, because of ruthless strong-arming by some very conservative ideologues, we, and the whole state of Florida, are on a strict budget, and now we have to prove ourselves. In other words, the operation has exactly six days left to its name. If we produce something by then . . . oh, for instance, capture and hogtie Markiza and then free all of his stashed slaves, well maybe then we'll get our meager allowances back."

Darryl said, "Six days? What the fresh hell! We're not ready. How are we supposed to get everything done in less than a week?'

"According to this," Marla pointed back to the screen, "Sans thinks you are ready. Exact words: 'they were born ready'."

Darryl and Andy stood stone-faced, angry; they didn't want to believe her.

"Look, Sans was going to send everyone texts, informing us where to meet up in the morning for an emergency pow-wow. But he never got the chance, ok."

Still, the men did not move.

Marla searched and pulled up a new document. "First point of order is for Darryl and Andy to finesse the strategy for dealing with Delgado. It looks like Sans printed out the e-tickets and they should be—"

"Right here," Darryl said. He had been reading over her shoulder and peeled the Delta coach tickets from the side of the computer.

As he looked at the tickets, Darryl felt dazed. To him, suddenly, Sans was like a schoolteacher, and that colliding with a pillar in a mall parking ramp and suffering a heart attack afterwards, was a fait accompli. In order to head off any unpleasantness that his absence may have caused in the future, Sans had left a step-by-step manual the students could use to teach themselves.

"This is so wrong." Andy was no longer wandering quietly inside his own world but up front and personal in everyone's face. He paced hard and his face reddened. He said, "Haven't you all noticed something here? Something missing? Like our fearless leader? We can't go anywhere, or do anything without him. We certainly can't think about taking down the Russian, because we have don't have authority. We'd have to go through the FBI, and then a judge, and we can't do that and take down the kingpin in just six days."

The dread that Darryl felt earlier was making another appearance. Andy was right. Something really was wrong. But it was with Aunjanue. He had almost forgotten about her, because until this minute, the newest member of the tribe had been so quiet that she had turned invisible. Now, a soft susurrus of fingers sliding paper into an envelope brought his head up sharply. Suddenly he saw the pieces firing together and became afraid.

Darryl recalled with alacrity that as they were leaving the emergency room, and right before she reached the emergency clinic doors, Aunjanue had excused herself, saying she needed a minute. He had assumed she had gone back inside to go to use the bathroom. The rest headed for his car and waited. But she had gone back to Liset. *Because they'd had that weird intense, non-verbal exchange.* Liset had told her something with her eyes, and Aunjanue seemed to understand. Aunjanue had gone back inside to retrieve from Sans' wife the envelope she was now holding and waving in her hand. Andy's eyes were glowing and glued on her.

"Actually, we do have authority," Aunjanue said. She handed the envelope and its contents to Marla. "It seems Sans' final act was to write an executive order, witnessed by Liset. He must have been pumped so full of angry energy that he just couldn't bear not to turn over every stone. Address every eventuality."

She had spoken the words haltingly, as if they were sewing needles whose sharp tips pressed dangerously against her vocal chords. She looked exhausted, bereft. Aunjanue found a chair and sat down before continuing.

"I'll cut to the chase. And you're not going to like this. Personally, I hate it. Sans wrote that if anything happened to him, I should take his place. He put me in charge. There. I've said it."

"You? Andy strode towards her with a rhythm and speed that would not allow him to stop in time before colliding with her chair. Only two things seemed possible to Darryl: either Andy would miraculously float up into the air at the last possible second, or he'd end up in Aunjanue's lap.

Neither happened and Aunjanue didn't flinch when Andy stopped suddenly and bent down to stare into her face. "What the fuck? Are you sleeping with him? Is that it?" He straightened and turned sharply around. "I should have known."

Darryl would recall later that he had wanted to say, "slow down dude, calm yourself. Come on, let's see what's in the letter". But he never got to. His reptilian brain snapped and he found himself moving across the room like an escaped animal. One minute Darryl was at the desk standing next to Marla—the next—he'd had Andy by the throat and was shoving him into a wall clear across the room.

Darryl never got a chance to do more because Marla swooped over him like a mother pouncing on a toddler. She pulled him off Andy and made him sit down on a stool next to the door. As she hovered over Darryl, she turned slightly to look at Andy who was shaking his head and rubbing his throat.

"You two lose your fucking minds? You see what's happening, here?" Marla circled the air with both hands, and then when she was absolutely sure that the two men would not start anew—that Andy would not open his mouth again, and Darryl would not try to kill Andy—she walked over to stand by Aunjanue.

Marla said, "There are a lot of moving parts here. And we're about to find out what they are. Yet, I bet you my salary, that Sans put the newbie in charge because he knew exactly what would happen if he left the reins to you two pathetic morons. And he sure as hell knew I wouldn't want the job." Marla put her hands on her hips and dared anyone to speak.

After awhile, they all went over to the computer to read Sans' log in entirety. They took notes, asked questions, and devised strategies. No one brought up the tussle, and no one questioned Aunjanue's authority. Probably because she had said, "I might be in charge, but I want what you all want. Markiza. So, come up with best plan, and we'll do it."

After midnight, as they were getting up to leave, Darryl asked Aunjanue, "Do you think one of us should call Kastle and tell him what happened?"

For an instant, Aunjanue brightened and flashed an old version of herself. "Hell no. As far as I'm concerned, he's the reason Sans is in the hospital. Let's make the senator wait until hell freezes over."

TWENTY ONE

Andy was glad it had been an uneventful flight. It gave him a chance to ease into being with Darryl again. He had not forgotten what happened the night before and had no regrets but one. Andy knew that his actions had gotten under Darryl's skin, and now he worried that he may have permanently lost his partner's respect or, more importantly, his friendship.

They had arrived at the airport separately, boarded at different times and were assigned seats ten rows apart. They didn't talk once until they were inside their rental car, well after pulling out of the airport-parking ramp. What followed was mostly superficial chatter about directions to the prison. After disengaging the GPS, they used a paper map, so as not to leave a fingerprint of their whereabouts in Minnesota. While Andy drove, Darryl navigated.

Andy was also glad he was not hung over today. The night before, he only drank flavored water and went to bed early. He could do that sometimes. Remain stone cold sober for a few days while working on an assignment. That's because he knew he could binge-drink afterwards. That would be his reward.

After twenty minutes, they stopped for gas and coffee. Getting back into the car, Andy found his voice. "Any news about the van?"

The look on Darryl's face said he was grateful for the opening. "The crime lab hasn't put any real teeth into forensics testing yet because they still think it's the strange case of a tourist having a heart attack in the mall. But we got lucky despite that. Mostly, because the mall owners are putting pressure on the lab to find fault with the tourist. There's been talk already about pre-existing cracks in the concrete columns. So the insurance companies want someone else to take the financial heat for all of that metal carnage. I heard more than thirty cars bit the dust."

"Wow, the captain lies on his death bed while the vultures circle," Andy said. "So tell me about the break."

Darryl said, "I know a technician at the crime lab and called him myself. He went out there and told me he saw a weird tear in the back seat. The kind of tear a bullet might make if it grazed upholstery fabric. A team had gone in preliminarily, but he wants to go back to see if he can uncover a bullet, or casing. Finding anything in that concrete haystack would be nothing short of a miracle."

"It's possible that someone tried to shoot him? Maybe we'll just have to wait for the captain to wake up and tell us what really happened," Andy said.

After that, it was another five minutes before Andy spoke again. "I think Sans was followed and he detoured into that ramp to ambush the stalker. But then something went wrong."

"What gives you that idea?" Darryl asked.

"Process of elimination. We all know the captain. He is one practical guy. If he's going out for take out, then that's what he'll do. He'll order it, throw it in the car, and head back home. And remember, he had just been pummeled with some damn bad news. So even though he got a lot accomplished before he left, you just know he was itching to get back to his notes and stuff. He wasn't distracted.

"Someone else did it for him. Either he saw a suspicious vehicle go into that mall, in which case he followed it. Or *he* was followed and tried to shake off the stalker. You heard Liset. His heart attack happened after he smashed into the pillar."

They could talk about Sans all the way to Sandstone, but it wouldn't make things better between them. Why was talking to another guy, so difficult? No, why was talking to Darryl about Aunjanue, so difficult?

"About last night." Andy started.

"Forget it," Darryl said.

Andy took a breath. "I was out of line."

"You're not the only one," Darryl said.

"Look, I think it's like Marla said. There's so much going on here and only time will shine a light on all of it. But I just don't get Aunjanue. It's like she fell out the sky. And no one questions it. Don't tell me you weren't a little shook up when she announced she was taking over the case? Slick as snot." He looked over at Darryl who merely shrugged his shoulders.

"And you fall for her like someone hypnotized you. Dude, I met you way back at the academy. The Darryl King I've known for all of these years does not move that fast."

"What are you talking about?" Darryl sounded irritated.

Andy knew he was wading in murky waters. But the genie was out of the bottle, and he continued. "I just gotta say it, man."

"No," Darryl almost whispered the word.

"Is it only me? Have you noticed how much Aunjanue acts like Lydia? Is that why you're with her? Because she reminds you of Lydia? You're not like in love or something?" Andy said.

Darryl leaned his head back and cleared his throat. Andy didn't think he would lunge at him again, but he felt the condescension dripping even before he heard it. "Andy, come on. She's nice. She's hot. But how can I love someone I don't even know." But there it was. Darryl had also asked the question. And as if in reply to himself, he said, "It's weird, though, how comfortable I am when I'm around her. I don't think I ever felt anything like that before."

Darryl turned to stare at Andy and this time he did not look away. "What about you? When you're around Aunjanue, you act like she's the plague. What in the hell did she do to piss you off, anyway?"

"This might sound nuts and I know you're going to chalk it up to me feeling guilt because I didn't make amends before Lydia died. And god knows, maybe that's part of it. Still, well . . . I get a feeling that Aunjanue is not who she says she is. Like maybe someone trained her to act like a cop. It's more than that. Like someone trained her to act like Lydia. You have to admit, there's something to what I'm saying."

"Maybe Aunjanue studied Lydia's profile, and some of her personality rubbed off." Suddenly Darryl sat up straight and said, "What do you mean you don't think she is who she says?"

"I mean, what if she's not FBI?"

"What about Sans? He brought her into MAGS. And where do you suppose he found her? Hollywood stunt double school? Yeah, only one problem, Andy. Have you noticed she's a colored girl?"

"I just can't put it into words. Sometimes, I have this gift. I know what someone will say before they say it. Like I know that Delgado will want a bonus added to the deal we're giving his son. I figure these things out because I run all the possible scenarios first. It's like having a thousand fishing reels all at once with little itty, bitty fish dangling on the hooks. And then you see the big catch. Way out there splashing against all that shimmering water.

"But with Aunjanue, I don't know have to try to figure out what she's going to say beforehand, because in my head, she's already said it. Mark my words, friend. Very soon, we will want Aunjanue's real story."

For the rest of the trip to Sandstone, Darryl had kept quiet. Andy was pretty sure Darryl was no longer mad at him. He was pulling his own reels now, turning them over, examining the lines, and worrying about what the supposed fed from Chicago was up to. And they were both thinking about Sans, and what he might have neglected to tell them.

As they got closer to the building, instead of coming into sharp focus, Sandstone Federal Penitentiary loomed blurry and unsettled. From the parking lot, the prison looked deserted, like a shuttered high school might after many years of neglect. The two-toned brick facade needed painting and repair, and the expansive lawn in front of the parking lot, now mainly composed of deeply-toothed dandelions and clumps of creeping charlie, added to its insignificance. The weird animal-monuments in front of the low security facility made the detectives want to laugh.

Where was everyone, Andy wondered? He looked up, expecting to see guards with high-powered rifles and razor wire, instead satellite dishes dotted the flat roof of the main building. Somehow the punishment and human desolation that most jails emitted, even behind closed doors, were missing here. The detective was reminded of the television series, *Prison Break*. In Season Three, the main characters find themselves at the Panamanian prison, La Penitenticaría Federal de Sona, a prison run by the inmates and guarded only from the outside. But here there wasn't even a soul outside.

"Delgado will want more," Andy said suddenly.

"We've talked about this ad nauseum. He gets one thing and one thing only. Charges dropped against his son for marijuana possession. That's it."

"Still, he will want something else. Whatever it is, we better be prepared to give it to him," Andy said.

"Aunjanue said to use our best judgment. As long as he doesn't ask for a reduced sentence for himself or any of his cronies, I suppose we can hear him out." Darryl said.

"It's going to come from left field," Andy said, as he eyed the little elephant monument in front of the car. He looked back at Darryl and saw his partner nodding.

———————————

Andy and Darryl were met by the deputy warden who led them past several corridors of two-tiered cellblocks and into the back courtyard. Outside again, they walked down a narrow brick path and when they reached the west campus, they waited inside the first set of doors until a guard let them in.

They were ushered into what looked like a small lunchroom. All the tables but one had been collapsed and set against a wall. Clean, industrial-sized pots sat on a metal shelf next to stacks of plates and spoons. The walls were white, the floor spotless and gleaming. A man with thinning, dyed black hair, dressed in khakis and a pale-blue polo shirt, sat rocking back and forth in a chair, arms folded over his massive chest.

"You're late and I'm going to miss my poker game. I was down last week and need to win back my losses. I'd appreciate it if we could get this over with, fast," Delgado said.

The deputy director nodded and smiled at the inmate who smiled back. Andy decided the other inmates would wait for this man before they started the card game. Here, probably not much got started or stopped, unless Delgado approved.

Darryl wasn't impressed. He sat down across from the Columbian drug lord and slapped his brief case on top of the table. He unlatched it and took out a cell phone. He began pushing numbers and then listened as a series of bells chimed and stopped.

Andy took the cell and handed it Delgado. "We've programmed in Markiza's number. Just press the arrow and talk. It won't be Markiza, of course. Just like before, one of his hired hands will pass on your message. Just tell him you changed the date. Say your girl is in a hell-fire hurry, and that he better make sure she gets what she wants. You could remind him of the juicy little cut into your action that you promised him earlier. Whatever. Just sound natural."

Delgado cradled the phone in his hands, looked at it quizzically, and then laid it down gently on the table as if it were made of the finest china. He closed his eyes, leaned his head back, and sniffed. "You said a month, and now it's a few days. I sense desperation, boys." He straightened and opened his eyes into obsidian slits.

Andy said, "What's it to you? Same deal as before, just shuffling things around. Something unexpected came up and we need to close this sooner. That's all."

"It makes me very sad, that you come in here with no respect. Just demands, like I was a piece of shit. No, you are treating me even worse than a piece of shit. Because with a piece of shit, you always acknowledge it first before you flush the toilet. You act like I don't exist. Yet, you expect me to cooperate." Delgado rose slowly and smacked his fists on the table. The sound reverberated for what seemed like minutes, across the room. Andy and Darryl assumed poker faces; Delgado smirked and folded himself back into his chair.

"We're getting all charges dropped against Francisco. He will be able to finish medical school and become the dream boy you always hoped for. We can't do anything else for you. We're just working stiffs. *Entiendes?*" By addressing the inmate with the familiar form of you in Spanish, instead of the formal, more respectful, entiende, Darryl was showing Delgado that he was not intimidated. And that he did think the drug lord was a piece of shit.

"What I want for helping you get out of whatever mess you're in now is so tiny. Very miniscule." Delgado pronounced the word with much sibilance, a rebuke to Darryl's rudeness. "And you will do it for me. Or you all can all rot in hell."

"If he has to, Francisco will go to Spain and finish his education. It doesn't matter. He just wants to be a doctor. He's even thinking of duplicating Che Guevara's trek across South America, so he can work with poor indigenous people. It is his dream to help them, heal them. That's what kind of son I have. So don't tell me you can't. You can and you will."

Delgado got up and turned his back to the detectives. He sighed deeply. Andy scraped his chair back hard like something had bitten him beneath the table.

"I knew it. You don't just want the charges dropped. You want an apology, don't you?" Andy said. "And not just any old apology. You want the cops, no, the Baltimore chief of police, dressed in full uniform attire, to apologize to your son. Better yet, apologize to the kid in front of the entire Johns Hopkins board of Regents. You are a fucking son of a bitch."

Delgado turned around and spread his arms out like Jesus. "Now that you're awake, give me that phone."

TWENTY TWO

Uncertainty did not sit well with Darryl. Since that moment on the drive down to Sandstone when Andy echoed his own doubts about Aunjanue, Darryl had felt his senses attacking him. His skin was hot and prickling—sounds from the road, and especially Andy's voice—were too loud, too conspicuous. And his eyes had started playing tricks on him because whenever he glanced out, he thought he saw shapes forming, trying to break free from the bare rural landscape. Time to change things up, and this time he was in the driver's seat.

Instead of heading back to Duluth, they were driving south on interstate 35W towards the Twin Cities. The last flight to Miami from Duluth had already left, but Sans booked their return flight out of the Minneapolis/St.Paul International airport. If they maintained interstate speed, the detectives would be there in another hour and still have more than three hours to kill. That gave Darryl an idea that might help clear the air and at the same time vindicate Aunjanue. Or not.

Thirty miles before the airport, Darryl left the interstate and headed into northeast Minneapolis, towards Edison High School.

"We're making a mistake, dude. Just because I have some questions, doesn't mean you should start investigating her childhood. Maybe there is a good reason she hasn't fully disclosed everything about herself." Andy said.

"Like what?"

"What if Aunjanue had been a covert operative and somehow her identity got compromised. It's creepy, spying on our . . . our . . . so-called boss." Andy said.

"You're just saying that because you feel more comfortable behind a computer screen where no one can see you when you hack into people's lives. There you can feel safe and insulated.

"Besides, I have another reason. I'd like to know if Aunjanue grew up to be prom queen. She's the type, don't you think? Smart, beautiful, ambitious," Darryl said with more bravado than he felt. He and Andy both knew what happens when you start tearing apart a person's life. As you spend more and more time digging out the past, pulling fine threads of history and information, the more you want to know. But you can never pull enough threads to understand everything; to do that you would have to walk in the person's shoes for a long time. In between what you know and don't know, lays a sea of blank pages begging for you to create your own work of fiction. Even if he wanted to, Darryl couldn't very well turn back now because the carnival ride had begun, and the promise of untold thrills was intoxicating.

"How did you find out where she went to high school?" Andy asked.

"Oh, I got a couple things out of her on the way back from dinner at my mom's. Relax. We've got time, and I'm dying to see what she looked like when she was eighteen." It was only a half lie.

Darryl parked in front of the school. They sat a while watching throngs of teenagers rush the front doors and fly down the steps. Lunchtime. Darryl was surprised to sea a mix of black, Hispanic, and white students. He read somewhere that out of all of the neighborhoods in the Twin Cities, northeast Minneapolis had been the last hold out during the school desegregation era of the 1960's. How quickly things change. Or maybe not quickly enough.

They walked inside and showed their IDs. At the front desk, Darryl asked to see the 1995-2001 class yearbooks. The administrative assistant cocked her head like she wanted a reason. Darryl said, "I just came up for a family reunion, and have never met half of my relatives. I could get a good jumpstart on family jokes and teasing if I had an idea what my cousins looked like when they were young. The woman smiled warmly up at him but shook her head to and fro, like he was one of her naive students. After a moment she got up to collect the books. As soon as Darryl began thumbing through the first one he understood the woman's earlier reluctance. Nearly twenty years ago, almost every student at Edison high school was white.

"Would you look at these clothes, not much better than the eighties," Darryl chuckled. He picked up another yearbook and scanned senior photos quickly, pausing on the Ds, for Desmoné.

"Does this tell you anything?" Andy asked as he slowly turned pages.

"Should it?"

"These kids look like babies. We're getting old," Andy said.

Darryl wanted Andy to think he was unconcerned about what he might find, so kept up a stream of jokes and comments while pointing out dated fashions and hairstyles. Twenty minutes later, Andy closed the 1995 yearbook and said, "I think she sold you a bill of goods. This is the last one, and there's nothing here."

Darryl took the yearbook from Andy and slowly scanned the photos in the senior columns. He willed Aunjanue's face to appear and was rewarded with a crushing blow to his diaphragm. He stopped breathing. Sweat broke out on his brow and, at last, Darryl understood what people meant when they said their hearts were breaking. His had just split in two.

Andy moved towards him in slow motion, a big question mark across his eyes. Darryl saw his partner's arms reach out suddenly, and then he felt gentle fingers pry something out of his hands.

Darryl watched Andy scan the page and thought he was taking way too long to find her. Probably because he was still looking for a photo of Aunjanue. When realization came, it struck Andy almost as hard as it did Darryl.

"Oh, shit. Jesus, Darryl. This somebody's idea of a joke?"

TWENTY THREE

The moon was almost full. Big and orange, like a sleepy sun in a sleeping sky. Aunjanue never looked up. She strode in the darkness, stepping over cracks, avoiding the trash piling up on the sidewalk. Faceless men and women darted back and forth, some ducking into shops, others leaving bars after imbibing one too many cocktails, heading for home. She ignored them. Her mind was on betrayal. Darryl and Andy had been back at least two hours from their trip to Sandstone, and neither one had picked up the phone to call her.

Aunjanue wasn't miffed because of her newfound status. She didn't expect her partners and friends to be at her beckoned call just because of an inherited, unsolicited title. She was angry because her team members, no, her closest friends, didn't take the time to tell her what was going on. They hadn't bothered to keep her in the loop about Delgado. This had never happened to Lydia.

Her feelings of dejection were magnified by obsessive thoughts of Sasha. Of course, she thought of him everyday, replaying the ambush events down to the millisecond before Sasha was killed. Trying to figure out how it could have gone so wrong. And what she had missed. But Aunjanue usually managed to plaster over her true feelings of devastation and sorrow with visions of the end of Markiza. She was all about the plan, the strategy. For her, even creating a new identity was like forging a new, stronger, and sharper weapon. She lived for the moment when they arrested or killed the kingpin—either was acceptable—with all five of her keen senses. It's all she thought about. In her mind, the bastard had been dead for weeks, killed a dozen different delicious ways, always suffering prolonged, unrelenting pain, before he croaked. These pictures and a scene of freeing untold numbers of bedraggled young boys from bondage, nurtured and sustained her. And kept the grief underground. Until last night.

Last night, Aunjanue had been undone by dreams. In the first one, Sasha looked exactly the same, but she knew he was much younger. And she was still Lydia. Together they walked along an endless stretch of white sandy beach. Their feet sank gently into something that felt like cool flour. When the waves came, they towered above them for a moment before spreading themselves over the sand, over their feet, bequeathing the land thousands of tiny sparkling shells. Sasha picked up a handful of shells and let them scatter back to ocean. Then he began to run. Lydia put up her hand and shielded her eyes from the sun's blistering glow to watch his exquisite youth, breathless and free. As he ran he yelled, "Back home the shells were all broken. I'm glad you're my mother now because, wherever we go, there will always be sun and sand, and beautiful, perfect shells." Aunjanue woke up inconsolable. The sheets were wet and sticky from sweat and her face was drenched in tears. Once, Sasha would have been her son. And now, her lovely boy was really gone. How was she supposed to abide?

When she could, she sat up and looked at her phone. It was 7 a.m. She pulled the curtain on her emotions and tried to concentrate. Darryl and Andy were just boarding their plane. She hoped they didn't kill each other before meeting with Delgado. How she wished she could have gone with them. Without Sans and without the guys, she was bereft. Marla was not available either. She had gone to school to meet with one of her daughter's teachers.

Aunjanue remembered another dream and ducked under the covers.

She and Sasha walked down a long corridor at his school, looking for an office. Whenever they got to the end of a hall, it managed to clone itself into a replica hall. Each time they started anew, somewhere a metal door clang open on rusty hinges, followed by a squeaky rolling that stopped when the door slammed shut again. They walked for what seemed like miles searching for someone who had summoned them. Whoever it was, Aunjanue knew they had to find him or her, or they would live out their lives wandering the maze. Once she almost got a glimpse of a figure in the distance, but it disappeared and another, empty hall morphed in its place.

Aunjanue stopped in front of a very real and heavy door. She opened it and squinted as she surveyed the noisy bar's interior. She looked fretfully for Darryl and found Andy instead. It was too late to cut and run because he had her in his sights and was maniacally waving his hands in her direction.

Andy, friendly. Shit, that could only mean one thing. He must already be drunk and well on his way to becoming passed-out-on-the-floor wasted. Aunjanue walked over to the bar and experienced a rush of excitement when she saw a familiar cocktail shaker in the bartender's grasp. She allowed herself a long moment to imagine an icy martini numbing her lips, coursing down her throat, slowly beginning to coat her blood stream and raw nerves with color and song. Oh, to be Lydia again. She grimaced inwardly as she ordered a domestic beer for Andy, and a glass of house red wine for Aunjanue.

Andy's companion tonight was the racist whose car Lydia once nearly trashed.

"Get up old man. That seat's mine," Aunjanue said.

The old man grunted and looked like he was going to do a lot more to *show her*, but Andy pointed to the glint of blue metal peeking out of Aunjanue's jacket flap, and motioned him off.

Aunjanue sat down and slid Andy his beer, "I was hoping to find Darryl in here. Find out how it went with Delgado. You'll have to do, I guess." She gulped her wine.

"Oh, classy dame. You must not be a wine *carnerseur*. Try taking smaller *ssips*." Andy hiccupped and smiled rakishly.

Polishing off her glass, she said, "Look who's talking. I feel like I slipped into a courtside seat just in time to watch your brains slip out of your head, one and then the other one."

"Why are you so bitter?" Andy raised his hand, and out of nowhere a waitress appeared. "Get my friend here a good bottle of red wine. But when you come back, set it down gently. See, she's crabby."

Andy cast around for something more to say, but froze suddenly. His mouth was left slightly opened, but his eyes were fluttering shut when he began sliding down the booth.

"Oh, crap! Andy, are you having a black out? Snap out of it. Talk to me about Delgado."

When the waitress came back with a bottle of wine, Aunjanue waved it away and said, "Just bring us some ice-waters. And one strong cup of coffee."

When the waitress returned, Aunjanue took one of the glasses of water and poured it down Andy's shirt. "Shit, stop. Shit." he cried. "For god's sakes, I sent you a text. It said Delgado made the call. Now stop."

When Andy straightened, defiance and hurt creased his eyes and sagged his mouth. To her, he looked a bit like a street urchin out of the movie, *Newsies*.

"I'm worried about you. Truth is, everyone is. Hard to understand why night after night, you willfully throw your life away. You give it up to booze and oblivion, when you could choose a completely different road. Isn't there anything more you want from life than this?"

"Aunj-an, Aunjan, Auj," Andy gave up on completing her name, leaned over and laced his fingers around hers. "You're arrright. Mebbe I was wrong about you."

"What the hell are you mumbling about?" Aunjanue asked.

"I have a secret. I can't tell anyone. Cuz it's a secret." Andy pretended to button his lip and winked. And then he started to cry.

"Andy. Come on, let me take you home," Aunjanue said, and got up. When she tried to hoist him up, Andy was dead weight. She sat back down.

He put his head in his hands and rubbed his eyes. Just when Aunjanue thought he was going to zone out again, Andy said, "I was there. I saw her die."

The space across the booth that used to separate them began to vibrate with an electrical charge. Aunjanue felt dizzy. Andy's anguish became her anguish. She gently placed her hands on his face and turned it towards her. In it she saw a gaze filled with fear and loathing, and then recognized that what was in his eyes could only be a reflection of her own crumbling countenance.

"Andy, be careful. You don't know me."

"I'm going crazy, Aunj. It hurts so much. Everyday my head swells up, feels like it's going to explode into millions of pieces. I don't want to live like this anymore. But I'm not sure how to end it, either. I'm a coward. But you could help me."

It was then that Aunjanue knew it was over. But how long exactly had it been over? What happened? What did he know? And what was she supposed to do about it? The last thing she had expected from this night was Andy showing suicide ideation.

Andy drank his coffee, wiped his mouth, but the tears just ran faster. "I saw the car explode.

"I wasn't supposed to be at the warehouse that day. You didn't know her, but, when Lydia wanted to do something, no one could stop her. She asked me to pretend that one of my projects needed patchwork. So I went back there, to the warehouse." Andy's arm flew backwards, whopping his hand against the back of the wooden booth. When it boomeranged to the front again Aunjanue saw that his knuckles were raw, on the verge of bleeding.

"I wasn't supposed to work that morning, but came in and ordered a bogus part from a bogus manufacturer. Something that Lydia, in her newest disguise, would deliver to me a few hours later. See, she wanted an excuse to come by and talk to her boy Sasha. To find out why things got so screwed up in the first place, and to say she was sorry that she hadn't taken him out yet.

"I don't know how or why, but the Russians were waiting for her. They knew. And about me, too. They made me go outside and sit in a truck with them. When Lydia pulled up, I don't know, it happened so fast . . . I heard gunshots, Sasha was down. She held him in her arms. Then, miracle of miracles, Lydia got away from them. In that tin can of a car. We started to pursue.

"She was so far ahead of us, she should have made it to the interstate. Instead—"

"No more, Andy," Aunjanue said. She was crying too. Had he noticed?

"She did this weird thing with the car. It still doesn't make sense to me. It sort of leapfrogged to the right, like a cartoon bouncy-car, and then disappeared from sight.

"But when we got there, the car was rolling in the canyon, on fire. I saw her die. Burn to death."

Listening to him was like watching Andy go up in flames. The man was going to self-immolate, and she was the only one who had the power to extinguish the fire.

"We're going now, Andy. Get up."

"My truck," he said.

"We can pick it up in the morning. I'll take you home in my car."

Andy quickly passed out in the back seat. While she drove, Aunjanue tried to focus on the road and ignore the growing screams inside her head.

The next morning, Aunjanue walked around Andy's house taking in the walls and furniture, finally settling in the kitchen. If one of the purposes of a home was to provide self-expression for the owner, Andy's residence was a continent in contradictions. Every room was it's own gallery hung with bright lucid art. Cuban José Fuster's impressionistic watercolors of his homeland lived happily next to Minnesota's Bill Dietrichson's fey, Ibsenesque portraits of jesters and fairies. German amber paintings shared space with Steve Palmer glass vases.

The kitchen was her favorite. It held light-wood cabinetry that reached almost to the top of ten-foot ceilings, an oval, black and white granite breakfast island, and a blue-green glass mosaic splash board that surrounded a stainless steel sink and black stovetop. Small glass and metal canisters filled with spices and herbs were attached to a brushed metal wallboard. Stylishly framed photos of his family and friends covered a narrow wall between the refrigerator and the wide arch that opened into living room. The design and decorations were a friendly mix of modern and earthy. The kitchen along with the rest of the house was also neat as a pin. Unless you had known Andy as long as Aunjanue had, you would never guess that the house was owned and maintained by a certified alcoholic who managed to make a mess out of almost every other part of his life.

"Get out here, your coffee's getting cold." Aunjanue yelled at the closed bathroom door. When she heard the shower shut off suddenly, she padded back to her seat at the island.

Andy came into the kitchen wearing a white bathrobe and looked surprised when he saw juice, cereal, toast, and coffee waiting for him. He jumped up on one of the black bubble stools and put his still-damp hands around a gleaming white coffee mug. They ate in silence. When Andy was done, he got up scraping his stool back into position. "I'll get dressed and we can go," he said.

Aunjanue poured more coffee in each of their cups. She pointed to the empty stool, and Andy reluctantly hoisted himself back on to it.

"Andy, we don't have to go in yet. I have something to tell you. And I want you to promise me that you won't say a word until I've finished."

Andy couldn't wait that long.

"What's wrong with your voice?" he asked. "Wait, what happened to the Minnesota accent?"

Aunjanue waited patiently until Andy's clotted brains reshaped their thoughts and adjusted his belief system.

When realization struck, Andy blinked rapidly and allowed himself a thin smile. Which grew and grew until he was laughing unrestrainedly. Aunjanue joined him, and soon two old friends were howling like demented wolves. When exhaustion finally overtook them, all they could do was sit and stare at each other.

Andy said, "I knew it. I knew it. Damn, I knew it." And then the cackling started over again.

Darryl had just missed Andy at the bar the night before. The bartender told him that the detective had left with a woman only minutes earlier. After a restless night, in the morning, Darryl started the usual drive towards MAGS, but found himself turning in another direction, headed for Andy's. He wanted to ask him a question before facing Aunjanue. Still shaken by seeing Lydia's senior photo in the Edison High School yearbook, Darryl wasn't sure if he should confront her or not. Maybe, it was just like Andy had said. Aunjanue might be a true cop's cop, and was forced through circumstance to protect her real identity. It wasn't like they had been buds for years and that she was supposed to unconditionally trust MAGS members, even if they were lawmen. But he would never understand why she told him she had gone to the same school as the dead woman she replaced. If she had to lie, why pick Edison High School? Maybe Andy could put things in perspective for him.

Or maybe not.

Darryl hoped he was hallucinating. He had parked across the street from Andy's house and had a clear view of a car that looked just like Aunjanue's rental vehicle. Was he at the wrong house? He stared hard at the bungalow and even though he hadn't been here but twice before, Darryl recognized the copper rain collector hanging from the eaves. A souvenir that Darryl had him brought back from Japan years ago.

He wouldn't be sure about the car without seeing the license plate. Because there had to be a million grey Chevy Cobalts in Miami. He craned his neck, drove in reverse, and got out his binoculars. Bingo, rental plate.

If yesterday's epinephrine rush after seeing Lydia's young face had left him shaky and weak, today's surge spinning out of his adrenal glands only served to energize and focus his anger.

Fuck them to hell. Fuck both of them.

Just concentrate on the case. Three more days. And you never have to see her again. Never have to work with Andy again. His cell phone beeped once.

Darryl looked down and saw a missed text. He touched the screen and read a message from his ex-wife.

Call me. We need to talk about Aunjanue.

TWENTY FOUR

Darryl loved a small, crowded cafe. All that whirring and grinding, it was like being cocooned in sensory heaven. Sometimes, tucked inside the aroma of wafting, freshly-ground coffee, he could just make out the scent of a newly-opened pack of cigarettes. And then, Darryl had to remind himself that he no longer smoked. Instead, he drank more coffee in order to tamp down the urge to light up. For Darryl, it was always more than just the coffee taste, or even the kick-me-up-to-wake-me-up stir it created in his brain. His favorite part was cupping cold hands around a hot heavy mug and watching the liquid swirl while he blew on it, trying to cool it down. Today, this ritual also helped reduce Karen's monologue down to a reasonable drone. But she was on to him.

"Darryl. Come back from that faraway world you go to whenever I try to tell you something important. And this is important."

"It's been a crazy week. I have work on my mind," he said.

"I know that. You always do. But try to focus. Because what I am about to tell you will blow your mind," she said.

"Sorry, you've got my full attention." Sorry, shit. Being with Karen always made Darryl feel really bad about himself because it turned him into a hypocrite and a liar. He wasn't sorry and he didn't want to be here. For the millionth time, Darryl wondered why people couldn't just shed their social filters and be real with each other. If he could be honest with his ex-wife, say what he really thought of her, maybe then he might dislike her a little bit less.

He looked directly at Karen. She looked older but hadn't changed much. If possible, she had gotten even prettier, more angular in the face. Same big round gleaming eyes, her hair: an asymmetrical short bob, the longer side partially covering one eye. Today she wore skinny jeans with a shimmery, molded-to-the-bodice silver top that brought stares from twenty-feet away. His stomach clenched. While Karen sipped her mocha latte with sprinkles and infinitely licked her lips, smiled her simpering smile, he knew exactly why he couldn't be truthful with the most irritating woman in the world. If he told her what really lay at the bottom of his heart, that kind of darkness might destroy her. One soul slayer in the family—ex-family—was enough.

He turned his head and watched a barista slide a lemon-poppy muffin out of a gleaming acrylic case onto a white plate. She handed the muffin along with a cup of tea to a waiting customer, while another employee rang up the order on an old-fashioned cash register that pinged and whistled every time the drawer opened. Darryl wondered how he could have once fallen in love with a woman that he could barely stand now. While he day-tripped into the past, he was careful to catch every other word Karen spewed—she had just started talking about her back-stabbing cousins—in case she decided to test his retention level. That latest family saga should take up at least five minutes, he thought, giving him plenty of time to contemplate the origin and collapse of their marriage.

Darryl was certain that, in the beginning, it was purely raw sex that drew them together. Such great sex could make any man blind to the truth. But he was also young and infatuated with Karen's persona; she'd had that vulnerable, damsel-in-distress look. And a perfect, petite body to go with it. When they started going out, Karen could not do enough for him. Every minute that she was not at work, his ex lavished him with attention and consideration. There had been gifts, surprise picnics, and epicurean dinners. She took care of the small things, too: ironed his shirts, cleaned his apartment, and shopped for groceries and toiletries. It didn't hurt that she consistently flattered him, and kept them both entertained in bed.

But it didn't take long for the young cop to sniff out a rat. Before the drug abuse, before the bitter divorce, the signs had been everywhere. The problem was that he always looked away. Truth was that Karen was a phony with a big P. She honestly didn't give a shit about anyone else but herself. As a matter of fact, he recalled, she had been the worst kind of narcissist. By taking very careful steps to make sure his life had been comfortable and secure, Karen had carved out the very existence she had envisioned for herself. And by the time they were married, she'd gotten what she wanted: expensive furniture, trips to the Caribbean, and of course, party time with the right sort of Miami crowd, with the perfect man at her side. How many times had he been in a room with a dozen or more people who went out of their way to show that they did not care one iota about what anyone else thought or did?

He remembered them as fatuous carbon copies of each other. All just like Karen. And, he was also certain that he had never heard her compliment another human unless she was also fixing to extract a favor from that person. She had been competitive and catty; to Karen, other people's failures were tantamount to her own personal success.

Still, he had to admit she had been successful in her own right. Karen's parents practically sold the farm to put their only child through a nurse anesthetist program, a niche field that earned her as much money as some family-practice doctors, and often brought in more prestige. All of that came to a screeching halt the day she got arrested for soliciting crack cocaine. Then after several failed stints in treatment, Karen eventually stopped using altogether. After three years of sobriety, she also got her nursing license back, along with a new lucrative job at Miami-Dade Plastic Surgery Clinic.

Karen had moved on to prattling about celebrity clients—never actually saying their names out loud, but dropping enough hints to identify tabloid icons. Darryl smiled and smirked during the appropriate pauses. This way he could let his mind continue wandering; this time he considered what really bothered him. Andy and Aunjanue.

Only yesterday, Andy had Aunjanue pegged as an unscrupulous undercover agent with enough secrets to provide juicy material for a daytime soap opera. Then four hours ago, he had spotted the same Aunjanue-wary Andy at his kitchen window, drinking coffee and laughing with the enemy. At 7:30 in the morning!

What had she been doing at his house? Had Aunjanue really spent the night? Were they both gaming him? Now he felt sick all over and wondered if, just this once, he could unleash a gallon of disgusting bile on Karen and feel better, if even, for a moment. She hadn't noticed the change in him, the belligerence in his eyes or the fisted hands, because she had segued to travel-tales about a doctor she had been seeing for awhile. Darryl had had enough.

"Mother of God, get to the fucking point." Darryl inhaled hot coffee, burned his tongue, and did feel slightly better.

"Darryl, I'm sorry if talking about my new guy makes you angry. We both know nothing can ever replace what we once had, but Andrew is a fine man. I mean, I don't want to marry him, I just—"

"I just have got to get to work."

"Give me a minute to explain, I need to set it up."

"Why?" Darryl asked.

"I don't want you to misunderstand my motives for what I am about to reveal. I am not doing this out of spite. Can I help that it just fell into my lap? You of all people have to understand how much it hurts to tell someone the truth, even if it's horribly unpleasant. I mean you were brutally honest with me when I was down and out. You were real, told me just how it was. No sugar coating. Well, that's what I'm trying to do now.

"Look, when we got divorced, it felt as bad as if I'd lost an arm or a leg. I know it was like that for you, too, at least in the beginning. But you moved on and so did I. I have myself a really fine man, a great new job—"

"I want to kill you. Kill you dead. Happy now? I'm out of here. Have a nice life." Darryl stood up, spilling coffee across the table. He scraped his chair back with so much force that it drowned out the rest of the café's sounds, leaving several people at nearby tables to stare agape at them.

Karen moved before she got splattered. She looked around her and quickly placed one hand on his arm, and with the other, began to blot the rolling liquid with a napkin. Something other than appearance was on her mind today. "Sit down. Darryl, for your own good, you need to let me finish."

Darryl stood stock-still and glared at the ceiling. He lowered his gaze and slid back in his chair when he heard her next words.

"I saw Anita a couple of days ago. I've been sitting on this, but I realize for your own safety—"

"You went to Mom's? Why?"

"She said it was a peace offering. The week before she had called inviting me to Friday night dinner. Anita said it had been too long since I attended one of her events and that after all of this time you would not mind. She claimed everyone wanted to see me again. She emphasized that I was still a part of the family," Karen said.

Darryl knew that was a lie. Most likely, Karen had been calling his mother for months, inkling for an invitation. Mom had given in.

"But then she called me back to say that it was a bad idea, as Michelle had just told her you were bringing a date, and my Andrew was out of town. And wouldn't you know it, a few days later, Anita called me again. This time to invite me for afternoon tea. I think she felt bad."

No, you wanted to know all about my date, so you made her feel bad. Here he was, Darryl thought, waiting interminably for the other shoe—any shoe—to drop.

"We small-talked for a bit. She asked me about my family and I told her about Andrew."

"Karen, speed it up," Darryl said.

"I hope you're ready." Karen tried to pin him with her wide-eyed innocent stare. She succeeded. "Then I asked about Michelle and her family. Anita said that they were doing fine, and that the kids had really grown. She said she'd show me. We went into the great room where Anita pointed to a few photos she had developed that morning. I saw this eight by ten of Jordan and Marissa. They were leading a sing-along, I guess some hip-hop song. They really, really looked great. Jordan so handsome, Marissa, just as pretty as picture. Time goes by quickly, doesn't it Darryl?"

Why settle for chaos when there could be a cataclysm right around the corner? When Darryl was sure he couldn't stand to hear one more insipid syllable, Karen surprised him.

"I took the photo from Anita and really stared hard because I thought I recognized the woman standing in the back."

"Aunjanue," Darryl whispered. He hoped Karen had brought an extra cyanide tablet.

"I asked, 'Darryl's date?' Then she showed me another photo, a close-up of you two. This time I froze because I knew I had seen her someplace before. But when it hit me, I almost fell to my knees. Of course, I didn't say anything to your mom. I'm sure by the look on my face she guessed I was in shock. But I swear, it wasn't because of jealousy."

"Then, what?" Darryl pressed.

"I told you how we get these celeb athletes and their wives coming into the clinic. Everything, all hush-hush. But awhile back, I caught a really strange case. And I hadn't even been scheduled to work that night. At least I shouldn't have been because I was the junior nurse anesthetist. Alicia, that's the senior one, preps all the classified situations, so to speak. But wouldn't luck have it, her water broke and she had her baby earlier in the day.

"So, right before my shift ended, the surgeon told me to go home, said to eat a nice meal and return around nine. Nine! He was doing something so secretive and late in the day I guessed it was going to be an identity change for a person in a witness protection program. I came back and before scrubbing in, asked to look at the patient's chart. The surgeon said it was off limits. Top-secret; even he hadn't read most of the file.

"The operation went well, although it took more than five grueling hours. This client had extensive work done. And I mean extensive."

"How long ago was this?" Darryl asked.

"Three months, maybe more. Afterwards, we transported her in a limo—one retrofitted to serve as an ambulance inside—to a boutique Fort Lauderdale hospital, where she recuperated for a few days. A week later she came back for a follow-up. It's late evening and once again, just me and the surgeon. At that point, she's still super swollen and black and blue and purple. She came back twice more. The last time, she looked almost like she does now. And a lot like that pop singer you see on all the talk shows. Her hair was a shorter and lighter, and I know she was wearing dark foundation.

"Next time I see her is at your mom's. In the photo with you. Your date, Aunjanue. The same, hush-hush, top secret woman who got cut into the middle of the night."

"Karen, you know this is wrong. You signed a confidentiality agreement. You should have never told me. Don't you understand that there are reasons? Revealing people's identities can get them killed. I'm serious, if a word of this gets out to anyone else, I'll have to arrest you."

"Baby, believe me, you will never have to worry. Because I know better than anyone that for a woman to do what she did, there must have been a terrible, terrible trauma in her past. So unspeakable, that the only way she could get through the rest of life was by changing races."

Someone in India could have heard the explosion in Darryl's head. He had to know. A dying man gets a last request, right?

"What was she before?"

TWENTY FIVE

Aunjanue felt jubilant and numb all at the same time. This was the day of retribution. For Sasha and voiceless children all over the world. After months of planning, rehearsing, and sweating bullets, she and Darryl were finally going to give the Russian mob a taste of Florida justice. That was the jubilant part of her brain. Another part hovered on simmer where she tried not to think about Marla or Darryl. Or what she was concealing from them.

Andy had been crossed off her list, but she had put up with his changeling self the last couple days. He smiled and joked and didn't drink. The Mr. Pollyanna act made Marla cringe and Darryl speechless. She knew why he was happy, but she was sick of it. Thinking about Marla brought a mist to her eyes. When this was over and they could all go back to their former lives, she, Aunjanue, would confess that she had no life to go back to, unless they accepted what she had done. Would they? Could they ever understand? Selfishly, she needed Sans to open his eyes and make the case for her. Convince them she was still one of the gang. Marla might understand. Darryl might not.

Andy had told her about going to Edison High and Darryl's reaction to the yearbook photo. Aunjanue had a feeling that was only the tip of the iceberg. When Darryl finally would know the full extent of it, that she had changed races to insure her part in the capture of Markiza and the release of the boys, Darryl would be inconsolable. She flashed on an impression of what that might look like in real life and instantly turned the simmer in her brain to off.

They were gathered at one of the safe houses. Marla, Andy, and the deputy director, Stacy Nelson, watched Aunjanue and Darryl rehearse for the last time. When they finished, the detectives paraded in front of their rapt audience for a few minutes and then bowed graciously. That got a lot of hoots and hollers and whistles from Andy and Nelson. Marla jumped up and down in place and clapped. She announced, "Today, you two could fool God."

It had taken them days to decide on a look for Aunjanue when she met with the Russians. *What does one wear to go shopping for human slaves?* Finally, everyone agreed on a pink-and-white strapless number that emphasized the detective's toned shoulders and arms, and suggested, rather than revealed, an ample bust. Although the cocktail dress was knee-length, white-spiked heels made her legs look like she had been doing runway work all of her life. Aunjanue's hair was fashioned into loose cornrows and long-beaded earrings crackled when she moved. She looked like America's sweetheart. She walked like a mythical Greek temptress. Just what you would expect of Delgado's moll.

Next to Aunjanue, Darryl looked serious and staid. But his white, Ralph Lauren shirt with thin maroon stripes under an Italian-made charcoal suit, screamed large and top-honored Miami law firm. The matching maroon-and-white, striped-on-the-bias tie ensured an anal-retentive personality necessary to contrast and tamp down his client's impulsive nature.

Markiza, Russian child trafficker, meet Alan Treadwell, partner and founder of Treadwell and Lewis. And this is the one and only Felicia Brown, number-one girlfriend to imprisoned Colombian drug lord, Roman Delgado.

While they waited for the Russians to call, Aunjanue stood in front of the full-length mirror and played with her hair.

"Hands down, Aunjanue. You don't want the wire to fall out," Andy said.

Aunjanue asked, "How sensitive is this recorder?"

Nelson said, "It can pick up voice transmission as far away as two blocks. But we'll be right across the street above the barbershop. Just make sure you don't stray too far."

"How sure are you that their detectors won't pick up the wire?" Marla asked.

"State of the art. It's our newest gadget and you will not find any information about it on the Internet, yet. Instead of plastic, the wire is encased in nylon, which can't be found by conventional detectors. The technology is heat sensitive so you don't need a lead cord to your neck or wrist, where it would normally detect a pulse. All you need is body heat for it to work. It will even register the thin skin on your head. Nothing to worry about. We'll wait for your signal, and then we'll come in."

Darryl said, "How quickly can you get your agents to the drop?"

"As soon the Russians call Darryl and we know where you're meeting, three SWAT teams stationed in various parts of Miami will deploy to surround the location. Some will get there faster than others. Also, there will be a car following you discretely from a distance. Now listen, I don't care how it's done, just get Markiza to talk about the buy, set an asking price, and produce the boys. I promise we won't do anything until you give us the signal."

Aunjanue asked, "What if he stiffs us?"

"Not this again." Darryl said.

"Every time I ask this question, I get ignored. I'm just posing a what-if scenario. Seriously, *what if*?"

"Really, two hours before the sting, you ask," Darryl said.

"I've been asking and asking. I read the reports. We . . . you got screwed last time you attempted this. And you did not have a back-up agenda. I'm just saying, it might have helped. Let's all agree on what to do if there are no boys. Do we negotiate another trade date and leave? Take them down without the kids? Or can someone suggest an alternative?"

They stared vacantly at her and then jumped when a cell phone rang. It was Nelson's. A minor family crisis.

Aunjanue shook off the dismissal and went back to looking in the mirror. Mainly she wanted to get out of range of Darryl's glare.

Andy followed her. "Look, it's normal to have last minute jitters. We all know something can go wrong at any time. Best laid plans and all of that. But this deal is sealed. It's Markiza's chance at the big time: the American drug market. He'd have to be crazy to pass on the Colombian's offer. Kid, I have a great feeling about this."

Go feel great someplace else, Aunjanue thought. She picked up a crossword puzzle, found a sharp pencil, and ripped into the newspaper while she waited for the call.

They walked into the afternoon light without talking. Darryl touched the keyless lock on the rented Continental and got in the car. Aunjanue waited for him to unlock her side and slid in silently. They didn't say a word until they got to the restaurant. Not because they were mad each other. They were trying to stay focused. Just like in the old days, Aunjanue thought.

It was a long, narrow bistro with fine dining on two levels. Half of the tables were filled with animated patrons and it sounded like everyone was talking at once. The ambient noise was deafening because it reverberated between the two open floors like backfire. Back and forth. The kitchen sputtered with clanging metal pots, sizzling griddles, chefs barking reprimands, and ancient waitresses hollering out lunch orders. A man at the end of the serving line, about ninety, hit a bell every time a plate flew onto the stainless steel warming counter.

Darryl and Aunjanue informed the hostess they had a lunch meeting with Mick Altamont. The woman smiled warmly and led them to a back stairway, pointed down and said, "Second door on the left. Ring the bell twice."

Aunjanue and Darryl knew immediately that this location was what cops called a ghost-staging center. The restaurant was too out-in-the-open to be a regular hub for conducting illegal business. These traffickers would never do business here again. Aunjanue looked over at Darryl, "Shit." They were both thinking the same thing. It would be impossible to contain more than a handful of boys here. The first bad omen.

The second came when a man called Stefan, told them Markiza would not be attending the meeting.

The Russian opened the door and showed them to a short sofa where they stood while another Russian ran a scanner over them. Satisfied, the goon walked over to join three other men who stood at a long rectangular steel table that held no chairs but one. They were all large and muscular and they scowled. Stefan insinuated himself between them and sat down in the chair. Darryl introduced himself and Felicia. Seeing that no one wanted to shake hands, the detective set down his briefcase and Aunjanue took off her sunglasses. She was sure she heard two, no three, audible gasps. Russians were such dweebs when it came to women of color. For people who literally believed only lily-white skin represented purity and goodness, they would inevitably experience something akin to heart failure whenever they stumbled upon a good-looking black woman. Dweebs. But she could use that.

Stefan stood nodding and began examining Aunjanue from head to toe like she might be the one for sale. After a beat, she and Darryl sat down.

"Felicia Brown and Alan Treadwell." Stefan had a slight accent. "You come highly recommended by Delgado."

Aunjanue crossed and uncrossed her legs. She leaned forward and said, "It doesn't get any higher than him. Delgado is my boyfriend."

Stefan chuckled, leaned to his left and right to look up at his goons. They didn't speak English and had no idea why he was laughing. They kept their frowns.

"We know who you are, honey. But would you mind telling me why you want boys. Young boys. You enjoy the kinky stuff, Felicia?"

Marla flew into her head and Aunjanue snapped her head towards Alan. "Can he talk to me like that?"

Darryl pulled an apologetic grin and said, "Felicia is high strung and . . . hmm, how to put this? She's always had a little trouble getting along with her own gender—"

"That's because females are a lot of trouble. They don't know how to listen. And they're lazy. I know because I used to run my house with all Latinas. And it was simply a disaster. I told Roman, only boys from now on."

Aunjanue got up and straightened her dress. She turned sideways and looked down to momentarily inspect her hose. Then she turned back and walked slowly, brushing her body along the long table, long nails clicking here and there. She smiled at the Russian goons and, again, three out of four smiled back.

Stefan asked, "How many do you want?"

"To buy?" Aunjanue gave Stefan her most ingenuous look. "Why six, of course. Three older ones to do the heavy lifting and three little ones who will become my personal little attendants." With a smirk she added, "Hey, Alan, I just realized I'm a black person buying slaves. Oh, my gosh, what a trip."

She heard two sounds pop simultaneously. A muffled intake of breath from Darryl, and a louder, guttural expression from Stefan. "Are you joking?" the Russian asked. "You know the deal was three boys."

Felicia hoisted one hip onto the edge of the table and shook a long manicured finger at Stefan. The goons watched, hypnotized. "Let's be honest, Steve. That's what," she twisted her other hand to point backward at Darryl, "you and my attorney agreed on. Here's the thing, though. Roman told me I could have as many as I want. You seem to understand English pretty well. So understand this. Show me six boys."

After a moment, Stefan shrugged and reached for a cell phone. Darryl motioned him to put it down.

"Felicia, Roman okayed three. Not six. Three," Darryl said. His look told her not to challenge him. Good, she thought, she could use this too.

"Really. Has it come to this? Why don't you just call him then?"

Darryl appeared speechless, Stefan amused, and all four goons were now smiling in unison.

"You can't just change your mind like this. These kids cost a lot of money."

Darryl said.

Felicia sank back into her chair with a thud, as if dealing with mere mortals was completely exhausting.

"Look, Darryl, there's plenty of money in there."

"What are you talking about?" he asked.

"Don't you know about the false bottom? Roman wired me another forty-five thou, just in case. Go ahead, check."

Darryl got up from his chair and said, "Stefan, give me a moment to confer with my client." They walked over to a corner and huddled.

From across the room, Stefan addressed the goons. Felicia shushed Darryl and listened. She was moving her head as if she was talking, but instead, she was dead quiet and listening to the Russian.

*("Посмотрите на них. Черных. Низкий класс,
независимо от того, сколько денег у них есть.")*

"Look at them. Blacks. Low class, no matter how
much money they have."

Finally, Darryl said, "Seriously, false bottom?"

"I'm improvising. That's not Markiza. We need him,
not just some lowly lieutenant. All or nothing. I want it all."

"Maybe you can't have it all," Darryl said.

"Just follow my lead. Trust me on this." Aunjanue
thought she saw a wave of skepticism crease Darryl's eyes
and, just like that, it vanished.

Aunjanue walked back to the table and spread her
arms wide. "Gentlemen, we've reached an agreement. Six."
She prayed they didn't have six.

Stefan got up dialing his cell phone and pushed open a
skinny wooden door. When he came back, he snapped his
fingers at two of the goons. They lumbered through the same
door and when they came back, the Russians were pulling
along six boys. They were teenagers ranging between fourteen
and sixteen years old. The boys wore tan shirts and navy
pants, and stood ramrod straight with their eyes firmly glued
to the floor.

"Oh, for god sakes! If I had wanted malnourished,
dog-faced children I would have hired ordinary illegals. And
are you deaf? I asked for three little ones."

The goons stiffened; the black woman was yelling.
Stefan remained expressionless, although Aunjanue felt the
table move. She suspected his legs had started to shake
against the side of the chair.

Darryl stood. "She's right. At fifteen-thousand a pop,
Felicia should have what she wants."

Stefan said, "These are all what we have here. We can negotiate a price."

Darryl picked up his briefcase, latched each side, straightened his tie, and gave his elbow to Aunjanue. "Let's go Felicia, we can call Roman from the car."

Stefan groaned and then stood. "Treadwell, stop. We can do business. But not here and not today."

TWENTY SIX

The weather was unseasonably hot, even for Miami. Only mid-February and it had hit 90 degrees two days in a row. Too hot to be outside. Unless there was something to do. Which there never was ever since they transferred the last of the fit-to-be-sold boys. Now you couldn't even run around and play football. Or what the Americans called soccer. Nothing at all to do but sit on the stoop. And that just made Tadzio lonely for Sasha.

It wasn't any better inside because most days the air-conditioning was on too high. Then he shivered even when wearing two sweaters. Without bodies, there was no assembly work, no new deliveries, so nothing to shred or clean up. Before they took the boys away, when the factory was still making widgets, Tadzio had been promoted to janitor—earning a measure of respect by moving a big dust mop down the aisles. Twice a day he cleaned those floors. Now nothing.

The few boys left were deemed by Markiza unsuitable to play with. True, Tadzio knew, they were slow and, in his opinion, sickly looking—but for all that, they were really nice. Never picked on him or called him names. Not like the old days. A few times, Tadzio tried to engage the two younger ones in a card game called Go Fish. Something Sasha had taught him. Tadzio had explained the rules, made them practice, and let them win most of the time. That ended abruptly when one of the goons reported that he was spending more time playing with idiots than making new drawings.

Once when Markiza was standing around with a couple of other men, Tadzio worked up the courage to ask to go to school. The men barked with laughter, but he had seen a strange light go on in the old man's eyes. That week Markiza brought him a dozen new DVDs and as many books. They were small books with pictures, but he couldn't read the words because they were in English. He guessed he was supposed to teach himself. He tried. He used a translation program to look up each word, then a dictionary website to learn how to pronounce them. It had taken him two whole weeks to discover the world was coming to an end in *Henny Penny*. But he knew better than anyone, that to really understand and enjoy the rest of the books, he would have to go to a regular school or at least work with a tutor. If Sasha had lived, he would have helped him.

The movies he watched painted beautiful worlds where good guys triumphed, bad guys went to jail, and little boys were loved and cared for. But inside the warehouses where Tadzio existed, life ceased to mean anything. The days and weeks rolled into each other like a grey rubbery pigment. He had long ago stopped fantasizing about escape and no longer believed in surprises. So, he wasn't expecting a sudden alteration in the daily routine.

As usual, Tadzio had sat with Markiza in the big lunchroom preparing to eat. These days, the old guy liked to brag about a future investment into something called drug trafficking. Markiza made it sound dangerous and moneymaking at the same time. Afterwards, he always asked

Tadzio's opinion on various things he had talked about. Tadzio knew the only way to stay safe was to politely agree with all of Markiza's decisions, flatter him and, occasionally, state that he wished to be a helper when he started his new business.

Tadzio was about to bite into a sardine and mustard sandwich when one of the lieutenants barged in, flailing a cell phone in his hand like it was on fire. Phone calls and messages were strictly forbidden when they ate lunch or dinner together, but the goon, sweating and turning red, promised on his life that the person on the other end said it was an emergency.

It must have been because Markiza grabbed the cell, listened, and grimaced, and finally threw the phone back at the messenger.

After that everything went topsy-turvy. Markiza slammed the table, threw away his lunch and told Tadzio to go to his quarters. A handful of lieutenants ran around the warehouse cussing, one pulled out a set of keys and ran out the door. Tadzio slowly packed up his lunch and, as he walked away, he heard Markiza say, "I know you've been bored and lonely. Wait until tonight. We're going to have ourselves a spectacular show."

As Tadzio clambered up the stairs, one of the goons came up behind him and kicked him lightly on the calf.

"You know what this means, my young friend? Finally, another big sale. Maybe this time, we will put you on the auction block." He laughed dementedly.

Another man came to stand by his tormentor. "What do you think this healthy little Polish boy would fetch?

Perhaps a vacation in Siberia." Both men laughed and slapped their thighs.

Tadzio pushed against the men and wound his way up to the dormitory. He sat on his bed and lifted his sketchbook. He used to be afraid that he might indeed be sold, but now he welcomed the idea. How bad could it be? Anything had to trump continuing to rot in this dark empty cold cavern.

Tadzio jumped off the bed with the sketchbook under his arm, grabbed a couple pencils and the sandwich, and made his way to the window bench in the stairwell. It was his favorite place to sit and draw. He liked the perspective from up high. Drawn in foreshortened perspective, people and vehicles always looked more animated. Like they were actually moving. So much more fun to look at than something drawn at eye-level. It was from here that he had sketched Sasha for the last time.

All of a sudden Tadzio lost the energy to draw. He wanted to cry. He wouldn't be seen doing that here. It was dangerous to cry in front of Markiza or any other adult. He had seen what happened when one of the slow kids cried. He got beat and then he cried more.

When Tadzio cried, it was for his dead parents and for Sasha. Sometimes he cried for Lydia. Today the tears wouldn't come. But the sadness that sat on his stomach hurt like someone had punched him. That icky feeling was back. Once he had described it to Sasha.

"I get scared and then hot bubbles burn in my stomach. It feels likes something is alive and moving in there, and I want to hit it to stop."

Sasha said, "That's from always worrying and missing your homeland. When it happens again, you should think about change coming, and you will feel better. Remember, it won't be long."

Tadzio asked, "How will I know when change is here?"

Sasha said, "You'll know because change will bring freedom. Close your eyes, Tadzio, and try to remember freedom. Think back to living on the farm, when your parents were still alive. In the morning, right after breakfast, you always went out to feed the chickens. First you ran at them, to scare them a little—remember how fun it was to see them scatter—and when they calmed down, you strewed the feed. And as soon as you were done, you threw the pail and started to run. You ran as fast as you could. Through the tall grasses, across the rocks, and down to the pond. You ran and ran like there was nothing or no one else in the world. And no one to stop you. But when you finally did stop, you fell on the ground and just stared up at the sky. You could hardly breathe or get up again, but you knew absolutely, that nothing could ever beat that feeling, That feeling of freedom."

Tadzio spread open his sketchbook and took out his sharpest pencil. He focused on a colorful bird that had perched on a nearby, yellowed palm, but it fluttered away. He was staring hard into the distance trying to find where the bird flew that, at first, he didn't notice the vehicle. There hadn't been a courier car or package delivery truck in weeks. But when the squeal of brakes on the gravelly tarmac finally reached his ears, he looked down and saw it.

Change had come.

The UPS truck was parked in the same crooked way that Lydia used to park. He couldn't see the driver but he heard the door below clatter open. It was a heavy pneumatic door that if pushed open all the way, took forever to close. He grabbed his things and ran soundlessly down the stairs and out into the sun-scorched day.

Tadzio ducked inside the truck through the driver's side and snaked his way to back. He hid under the packing shelves and remembered his sandwich and how hungry he was. He'd only taken a couple of bites when the driver returned. Tadzio peered over the boxes and was disappointed to see that it wasn't Lydia. No matter, he was inside a UPS truck and it would surely take him to her. *She* at least had survived. He knew that because when she roared off in her little blue car, she had left the vans in the dust. She must have gotten away.

When the truck reached the interstate, it was going so fast it felt like they were flying.

TWENTY SEVEN

Marla ambled, making a circuit of the MAGS offices. When she got to Andy's cubicle, she pushed the cheaters down on her nose and glared at him with narrowed eyes.

"What?" Andy said smiling.

"Something's not right." Marla said.

"With?"

"You! You're happy."

"What's wrong with that?"

"It doesn't look right on you." She pushed her glasses back up and started to walk away. "And I don't like it one bit. Sooner or later, I'm going to find out what you did with the old curmudgeon I used to fear and loathe."

"Maybe this old miserable dog finally realized there's a big beautiful world out there. Look around us Marla. So many dreams to dream and opportunities to seize."

Marla sat down, pumped the lever on her computer chair, and adjusted her knit skirt. "But you enjoy being miserable."

"Not anymore."

"Whatever."

The phone rang and Andy answered. After a few minutes, he said, "I'll let her know. Call us back before they leave."

"Was that Nelson? What did he say?" Marla sounded upbeat, but to Andy she looked tired and worried. She had waited all morning for Darryl and Aunjanue to find the boys and arrest Markiza. And then she did her best not to scream and shout when she found out that the Russians had set up another rendezvous for the detectives later on in the evening. But Andy new the stress had drilled a hole in her defenses. Not only was she jumpy, but Marla had also lost her ability to concentrate.

Andy said. "It's going to be fine. Aunjanue and Darryl were told to go to a motel and wait to be picked up. Nelson promised to keep us in the loop."

"You must be on something, because how else can you believe it's going to be fine? You know that wire in Aunjanue's hair probably won't transmit from never-never land. I hate this. I want Sans."

"Me, too. But they'll have some serious eyes. The feds even have a helicopter ready if necessary." Andy watched Marla slump in her chair, readjust its height, and then get up to pace.

"I've got an idea," Andy said, pointing to a tall stack of files and envelopes. "Why don't we get cracking on those? I started working backgrounds weeks ago and got through about half. Maybe—"

"Give me a break. Our people are out there twisting in the wind and you want me to look up the histories of street cons?"

"Informers, if you please. Look, even if the dynamic duo breaks this case wide open," Andy, noticing the wide-eyed, arched look on Marla's face, added, "which of course they will, we still have to nab the mole. Two of our people died because of him or her. And Sans is in the hospital. Besides, can you think of anything better to do with your time right now?"

"Okay, but instead of picking the usual informers to research, let's do each other. Sans said to look into anyone at all who had contact with MAGS, and no restrictions on dates. Am I right?"

"But doing each other just sounds dirty, Marla."

Marla refused to bite, "I'll investigate you, and you can go through my profile with a fine-toothed comb if you want. Humor me a little today."

Andy shook his head, "Go ahead and do me. But I've already started looking into something else. No offense, I'll get to you later."

Andy fired up his computer and opened a folder of saved searches. When he reached Senator Lex Kastle's name, he clicked on it. There had been almost too much information on the senator's golden days in high school and college. But when he tried to find anything at all about Kastle's childhood, he ran into a wall. And another, and another. All he wanted was date of birth, parents' and friends' names, and schools attended. On many levels, it didn't seem prudent looking up the senator's early years, but the fact that they weren't readily available drove the urgency on.

Andy had a choice. He could waste more time probing a guy who had a one- percent probability of being the mole, or he could move onto others far more likely to present traces of suspicious behavior. Maybe Marla was right. The histories of street-cons-turned-informers would dislodge all kinds of inculpatory Intel, but to be the actual mole in Markiza's world, you would have to be someone with real-time access to MAGS. *Like the senator.*

Andy could not let go. Some kind of cop-trained, second-sight kept him from closing the file. Andy justified his actions by mouthing silently that no one, no matter how high up, was allowed a pass, not even a state senator. No sooner had Andy resolved to push for the full disclosure of Lex Kastle's background, than he remembered the price he would have to pay to be able to dig deeper. The last thing MAGS needed was to owe the feds one more favor, but what choice did he have? He called Nelson and twenty minutes later Andy was logged onto an encrypted website. Tapping in several sets of numbers and letters, Andy found himself so far behind the security wall that, initially, all he could do was stare cross-eyed and groan.

Marla startled him. "You are one boring cop," she yawned. "I'm getting more coffee. You want some?" Getting no response from him, she added, "I started with your early years and now I'm into summer, I mean last summer. Why are you making noises?"

"Be careful what you wish for. I've never seen such a clusterfuck," Andy sighed.

Marla shrugged and walked towards the kitchenette.

By keying in the senator's name, Andy was rewarded with links to hundreds of folders. When he opened one at random, he found dozens of files. All of them were labeled with gobbledygook names, varying only slightly from one to the next. Did every politician merit a dossier of this magnitude? He clicked on the search box and typed covert operation. Ninety minutes later Andy realized that no, most politicians weren't worth the bother. Most.

He highlighted the salient points and reread the text.

. . . Before running for senate, Alexander Kastle worked as an FBI adjunct-agent in covert operations. From 1992 - 2000, Kastle profiled Russian gangsters working the docks in Miami harbor. His keen interpretations of movement and action, along with precise profiling, helped identify seven major players in international human smuggling operations. Subsequently, the United States Department of Justice sought and received an order from the Foreign Intelligence Surveillance Court (FISA Court) permitting electronic monitoring of such suspects.

All seven traffickers were arrested and tried in federal court. Only six were found guilty and sentenced to life in prison without parole. They are currently incarcerated in federal penitentiaries across the US.

On one hand, this all made sense. Senator Kastle's passion and fury to end human trafficking on US soil must have began when he saw up close the true legacy of modern-day slavery in the US: people mired down in misery, frequently beaten and starved, and as often, forced to work as drug mules or sex slaves, or indentured servants in factories and fields. For these reasons, the senator fought to persuade the rest of Congress to create and fund operations like MAGS.

What did not make sense to Andy was how in the world, back in 1992, Kastle, a recent law school graduate, acquired the skills or experience to profile Russian gangsters. Had he been recruited years earlier by the FBI and only went through the motions of being a law student?

Andy read on. Kastle had graduated in the top ten percent from University of Chicago Law School. Classes and grades could have been falsified, but not the improbable and very competitive position of president of the *University of Chicago Law Review,* which he served on for two years.

Next, Andy clicked "childhood" in the search window and hit the mother lode.

Alexander (Lex) Kastle, formerly Alexei Kasati, was born in St. Petersburg, Russia. When he was eight years old, he and his mother, with the aid of a Russian Ministry of Culture attaché, escaped to the United States where they sought sanctuary from the terrible abuse inflicted upon them by their husband and father, Mikael Kasati. The older Kasati spent his adult life in and out of prison. A tyrannical gang leader, he was suspected of eight contract killings. Shortly after his wife and son disappeared, Kasati booby-trapped the Kremlin, hoping to get away with millions of rubles. The bombs never went off, but his four lieutenants were shot dead by government officials. Kasati escaped by means of an underground tunnel. He was spotted in Moldavia in 2002 and, again, in 2006. Again, in Mexico and Texas in 2009. No further information is available on Kasati.

"Marla, you are not going to believe this," Andy said.

"I'm having a hard time believing something else," Marla quipped.

"What?' Andy asked.

Marla tapped her computer screen with a pencil and without looking at Andy said, "Where did you go on the day Lydia died?"

"What are you talking about?"

"It says here you took one of the decoy vehicles, specifically the one you usually drove to go back and forth to the Russian warehouse."

"Why are you asking me this?" Andy said.

"Because I want an answer. Tell me, where."

"I can't. Not right now. But after tonight—"

"Why is there no paperwork for the time you returned the car?"

"Because...because I didn't file anything." Andy shook his head. "It was a bad day. Okay. The worst one of my life. I guess I was really upset. Later—that day—the next, are all fuzzy to me. I really don't remember much until I woke up on Monday morning with the worst hangover of my life."

"But you remember what you did before you got drunk."

"That doesn't sound like a question."

"For the last time, where did you take the car that morning, and what time did you return it?"

Andy looked at Marla. He had to make her stop talking; he was on to something big—not quite sure what—but something with which to nail the son-of-a-bitch. Whatever Marla wanted from him, he couldn't give it up. Not just yet.

"I'm waiting," Marla finally turned and looked him.

"Lydia wanted a favor. I was worried about her," Andy said.

"You, worried about Lydia? I recall that back then, you wouldn't even give her the time of day. Come on, Andy."

Andy had to say something. "Lydia wanted to meet with Sasha and asked me to set it up. Technically, I was still the Russians' techie monkey. I pretended that a part that could convert analog audiotapes was missing. With the manager's permission, I ordered the cable. Lydia drove over with it a short while later in a courier car. But right before she got there, the Russians took me outside . . . to a van and made me watch. It happened so fast. One minute she's gabbing with

Sasha, then he's down and she takes off like a bat out of hell. We went after her. She was so fucking far ahead of us, and then for some unexplainable reason, she must have lost control—"

"Happy now, Marla?" For once, Andy did not seem chipper.

"You saw Lydia die? And you didn't say anything? To anyone?" Marla's voice was low and even. She eased her chair back slightly and put her hands on top of the desk.

"I know it looks bad, but that's all I can tell you right now. I…she…oh, crap," Andy said.

"Stop moving," Marla said straightening, one hand on her drawer pull.

"Why?"

"Because my desk drawer is an arsenal. It's well stocked and fully loaded."

Andy got up and started towards her.

"I mean it, I don't want to shoot you."

"Marla, seriously, what are you doing? It's me, Andy."

"Right now, I am not sure who you are or what you've done. You've been acting strange, and you didn't tell anyone that you were there, that you saw what happened to Lyida. So here's what you're going to do. Pick up the phone, Andy. Real slow."

"I quit drinking for this? Who do you want me to call, Marla, Ghost Busters?"

"Call Nelson. If I can't have Sans, then it's the FBI."

After the FBI agents took Andy away, Marla put her head down on top of her desk and began to sob.

TWENTY EIGHT

What surprised Tadzio most about running away and hiding in a fast moving truck was the thrill of watching another person's every move, when the guy didn't even know you were in the vehicle. Tadzio was so completely conditioned to being the one under the microscope, that he didn't dream he could ever be a voyeur himself. The young boy wasn't sure if he liked the new role or not, or if it was right or wrong; he didn't really care because he could not tear himself away from listening to and examining anything and everything the UPS driver did. And that turned out to be quite a lot of things, even as they raced down the interstate, weaving in and out of lanes.

Tadzio wished he could take out his sketchbook and draw him. The man was quite old, probably forty, maybe fifty. He was a little on the heavy side but moved like he wasn't. His head was covered in thick brown and gray hair, and his handlebar mustache matched. Tadzio studied the face in the rear view mirror. Thick eyebrows hung over hazel-colored eyes that looked everywhere but at the road ahead.

Almost as soon the driver had hopped in the truck, a cell phone chirped. After answering it, the driver let out a low whistle. Then with the phone propped between his ear and neck—the latter was very red and lined—he reached down and pulled up a tablet that turned out to be a flat computer. Using both hands he searched the small device as someone barked orders from the phone's tiny speaker. The UPS driver had pushed his knee up onto the steering wheel and was driving with it.

When he finished talking, the driver threw down the cell phone in disgust, repositioned the computer on the floor, lowered his knee, and began driving with one hand. With the other, he fiddled around looking for a radio station. When he landed on one he liked, he turned the volume up high and began singing along with the music. The sound of loud drums swelled the speakers. While he drove, the wooly-head bobbed up and down and sideways, fingers rat-a-tatted the steering wheel. From time to time, Tadzio could see arms swinging in and out rhythmically. Once, the man's torso jerked up from the seat and his head nearly collided with the ceiling. If the driver didn't have to drive, Tadzio knew, he'd surely be dancing.

Sometimes the driver scratched his arm and then his armpit; twice he reached back and tried pulling up on his belt. Between the pulse-pounding music and the full blast of the air conditioner fan, Tadzio was able to start eating his sandwich again. He was sure he wouldn't be heard chewing over the noise. But he hadn't counted on not smelling.

Tadzio had taken his last bite and was about to swallow it, when he heard deep inhaling. Oh, oh. The driver sniffled loudly and looked down at his feet. Tadzio heard him say, "Shit. Smells like dirty socks. Or dead fish." With that, he opened his window wide open. "That's better." Tadzio nearly choked as a blast of warm air and the wail of persistent sirens displaced the rock and roll atmosphere of the truck.

The boy wanted very much to stretch. His right pant leg had been cutting into the underside of his knee, but he was afraid to move. Every time the truck sped up or slowed down, the fabric scorched his skin. Tadzio had given up on the idea of the driver ever stopping to make another delivery. With one hand, he pressed on the floor and pushed his hip up slightly to release the fabric. But the floor was moist with humidity so that when the truck suddenly braked because traffic had slowed to a crawl, he felt himself lose purchase and fell back down. That would have been okay because it sounded just like a package shifting. Unfortunately, one did shift—so much so that it fell off the shelf and slammed his hand. The sudden pain brought with it a shriek so piercing, that it surprised even Tadzio.

"What in the world?" The driver squinted into the rearview mirror and shouted, "Who's . . . What, what...are you doing back there?"

Tadzio felt the truck begin to weave back and forth followed by a stream of relentless honking. After a few minutes, with Tadzio still crying, the driver pulled to the shoulder and stopped the vehicle. They stared at each other for a full minute in the rear view mirror. Finally, the man shook his head, unbuckled his seat belt, and grabbed a packet out of the glove compartment.

The back doors opened and the driver jumped into the truck. He squatted down next to Tadzio and talked in soothing tones. He examined the boy's hand with his eyes. He asked him to move it. When Tadzio answered back in Russian, the man frowned and then laughed. He squeezed and opened his own hand several times, pointing to Tadzio to do the same. It appeared that the small hand was not broken even though a

toddlers played nearby with a teenaged girl. Their mom sat in a corner crying softly.

"Why don't you rest and wait on this sofa for awhile," the woman said to Tadzio. We've called for a translator. She'll be here in about an hour. I have more paperwork to fill out. Somebody will come by soon with games and books for you. Oh, and you'll eat soon too." She mimed spooning soup from a bowl. "It'll be fine, you'll see." Tadzio shrugged his shoulders and watched the children fight over a toy. This place was for babies. Why was here? How long until Lydia got here? He lay down and cried softly, just like the woman in the corner. Then he was asleep again.

Tadzio woke up when two men dressed in dark suits, wearing dark sunglasses, strode though the front doors. The man that accompanied them was making so much noise that even with his eyes shut, Tadzio knew that it belonged to his old friend, the UPS driver. Pretending to be asleep, Tadzio slit his eyes open and followed the movements of the well-dressed men. One of them said something to the woman who had talked nicely to him, and he saw she was upset. Soon they were showing her badges, but that just made her more mad. She used her cell to call someone and when she was done talking, they showed their IDs, once more time. After a while, she pointed at Tadzio on the sofa. They just stood there. But the UPS driver started towards him. When he was close, he knelt down and began talking softly.

"Boy, it looks like you bought yourself a heap of trouble. See those guys back there? Yep, they're FBI agents. But you know what? I'm in trouble too. So, why don't we put our heads together and see what we can make out of this mess." Then he ruffled his hair again like he had at the restaurant. Tadzio should have known the man would be back. He was getting closer and closer to Lydia. He sat up and smiled. Finally, they would take him to her now. Maybe he should find a mirror and comb his hair. Tadzio looked back over to the FBI agents. Something one of them said caught his attention.

"We need his sketchbook, ma'am."

TWENTY NINE

Deputy-director Stacy Nelson said hello to Andy and frowned at Marla.

"Naah. I will not be treated like I did something wrong. Andy has an awful lot to explain," she said, pointing at her teammate, who was staring at the floor and shuffling his feet. "It's true, I love the man, worked with him for years. *But they're out there,* and I am making sure nothing goes wrong tonight. Please get him out of here, now."

Without a word, Nelson escorted Andy out the door and returned fifteen minutes later. He found Marla crying.

"He's not the mole, Marla," Nelson said.

"What if he is?"

"He's not."

"Then why did you take him away?" Marla asked.

"You made it impossible for me not to. I'm following protocol. Besides, he's still here."

"Where?" Marla tried to push against Nelson, but he blocked her way.

"In the hall with one of my agents. Leave him alone for now."

Marla opened her mouth, shook her head, and then started crying again. "You know why I did this. Oh, what the fuck." Marla turned her back on Nelson.

"Did you really expect me to throw him the hoosegow? Maybe cuff him to a chair? Hand him some dried bread and a spoonful of water?"

"You two in this together? Is that how it's going down?" Marla stomped over to her desk and grabbed her satchel.

"Look, I'm really sorry. I can't tell you about it. Not until this is over. Just take a deep breath and remember who you are. Who Andy is. What MAGS stands for. Please."

"Whatever this thing is, does Andy know about it?"

Nelson nodded gravely.

Marla asked, "Does everyone but me know about *it*?"

Nelson's jaw dropped and he rubbed his face. His look was sorrowful and his answer muffled. "No, not everyone."

"Why him and not me?" Marla asked, clutching her satchel close.

"Would you believe me if I told you that he stumbled on it? Now please put your things down and walk with me. We have some work to do," Nelson said.

Nelson strode to Andy's computer and motioned for Marla to follow him. "Andy said he found something and wants us to read everything he highlighted in a document." Nelson clicked on a file called *LextheSlick*.

"Oh, great. I finger Andy, and he thinks it's Kastle. No . . . wait. What am I saying? I've been suspicious of that man for ages." Nelson stuck his tongue in his cheek and looked up at the ceiling in mock disgust. "No, really, ask anyone. He's always bugged me," she said.

"Why, Marla?"

"Well," Marla set down her satchel and pulled a chair next to Nelson's. "First off, for being in his condition, he's insouciant." Nelson frowned. "It means nonchalant. I just think that a man of his position, and having endured that terrible accident, might be a little more earnest."

"Maybe it's the face he shows to the world to hide the pain underneath," Nelson said.

"I get that, but I think it goes even deeper. If you were really humbled or changed by your new circumstances, wouldn't you be slightly afraid, or even moderately paranoid? For example, a rape victim sees fiends around every corner. Well, even after he lost the use of his entire lower half, the senator doesn't see anything untoward anywhere. It's as if he's a got an insurance policy against future catastrophes. Now, you tell me. How does one get a policy like that?" Marla kicked off her pumps and clicked open Andy's folder.

Thirty minutes later, Nelson got up to stretch. "You and Andy may have good instincts, but all I see here is a very committed human-trafficking hunter," he said as he walked over to the vending machine.

A moment later, handing Marla a cup of frothy latte, Nelson added, "We have a senator who once worked for the FBI, tracked slave dealers, helped put them in jail, then got himself elected to congress by promising to diminish human trafficking into the US. He lost his legs but not one shred of confidence. The man is still a star. Huge, even by super hero standards."

"I think you're wrong, and I'm going to prove it. If Andy is innocent, I owe him that much."

Nelson read a few more documents before getting up to leave. As he was shrugging into his coat Marla pinned him with an incredulous stare. "Get your butt back here and tell me what the hell is wrong with your department."

Nelson had the decency to look worried. "What did you find?"

"Don't you people talk to each other? Cross-reference key words? Take notes? Pay attention?" Marla's breaths came in cyclical gasps.

"Look at these, there must be 2500 documents. Many people worked on this, you can't expect—"

"Read this," she pointed at the screen. "Saint Petersburg is considered federal land consisting of Saint Petersburg proper and nine municipal towns: Kolpino, Krasnoye Selo, Kronstadt, Lomonosov, Pavlovsk, Petergof, Pushkin, Sestroretsk, Zelenogorsk. Alexei Kasati and his mother were from Pushkin," Marla said.

"So?"

Marla opened and closed several documents. "Remember, it said that Kastle's work put six traffickers in jail? Where do you suppose the seventh one, the one that got away, was from?"

Nelson read and shook his head. "Pushkin. All right, but how does that—"

"And what was his name?" Marla said.

"Mikael Kasati. Shit. Kastle fingered his own father in a slavery scheme. But then he beat the rap. Hmmm, so you think—"

"Here, go back to 1976 when Kasati tried to blow up the Kremlin. All Russian police records refer to the escaped mastermind as Mikael Kasati. Except for one, where they call him by his gang moniker."

Markiza.

Marla preened while Nelson slapped a fist into his hand.

She said, "Sometimes, deputy-director, the rank and file has to take a leadership role. In less than five hours, Aunjanue and Darryl are going to the showdown. I say, find Kastle and make him spill everything he knows."

Under her breath, Marla whispered, "I'm so sorry, sorry, sorry, Andy."

THIRTY

Darryl sat quietly in the corner of the motel suite and watched his partner's personality whipsaw between Felicia and Aunjanue. As Felicia, the beleaguered moll of famous drug lord Roman Delgado, the actress demeaned the furniture, sniped at lamps, glared at the entertainment center, and corrected the restaurant menu lying on the dresser. Felicia strode back and forth, and her voice rose and fell according to how blasphemous she felt. Intermittently, she slammed the phone against the desk or kicked the trashcan over. She also stomped her lovely feet and threw notebooks, but when Felicia slapped at a row of metal hangars in the closet, Darryl had to plug his ears. It seemed like forever before the ear splitting, high-pitched echoes totally left the air space.

It was easy to tell when Aunjanue was back because that persona would stand very still at the mirrored closet door examining something deep inside her eyes. Perhaps the detective was searching for a soul inside Felicia's character. Apparently never finding one, Aunjanue always smoothed down her hair, felt for the chip, and took a deep breath before proceeding to kick something else over.

Waiting for the Russians was exhausting. Once an hour for the last seven hours, someone claiming to be *Dimitri* rang to say it would be just a short while before a car came for them. They wiled away the time mostly by role-playing. Sometimes together, and sometimes separately. When they tired of the routine, the detectives took breaks to read magazines and surf the Internet. Darryl played Friends with Words on his phone; Aunjanue preferred the *London Times* crossword puzzle, which she had a habit of always carrying in her purse. Marla called a couple of times on Aunjanue's cell to cheer them up, and Andy showed up on Skype reciting stupid bathroom jokes. They didn't ask why Marla hadn't joined him. The detectives were bored and edgy. The Felicia character came and went.

Darryl looked up from his game and sneaked a peak at Aunjanue. Throughout the day she had given nothing away. Always cool as a cucumber, reserving all of her energy for the kill zone. Aunjanue was so much like Lydia. He'd seen her in action. One minute she was haughty and obnoxious Felicia, the next, sleek and silent like a panther, and just as deadly. Just like Lydia. Yes, they were so much alike.

But were they one and the same person?

Damn, Andy had planted the termite in Darryl's head. Never resting, it ate away at his brain, frazzling his confidence and focus. But Andy hadn't actually said that Aunjanue was Lydia. No, he wouldn't have done that. What he had said was what if Aunjanue wasn't who she said she was. Then who could she be? Maybe there was a way to find out.

Darryl thought back to the days when he and Lydia worked stakeout detail near the homeless compound on South Beach. To make the time go by, they devised juicy topics to chew over. Anything and everything but what they were actually doing. Usually, they took turns picking a subject.

Lydia's choices ran the full gamut of socio/political affairs. Darryl narrowed his spectrum to sports, sports celebrities, and dating customs. They hardly ever philosophized outside of work, nor did they ever manage to solve any of the world's major problems when they did. But the discussions became a type of cleansing ritual that helped prepare them for the eventual challenges that lay ahead. Lydia said it was like sniffing coffee beans after sampling various perfumes at the department store counter. The coffee beans reset the olfactory palate. Random, inane chatter cleared the cobwebs from the brain, sharpening the senses and heightening awareness.

Darryl hit on the idea to rekindle their old tradition while they were waiting to be picked up. It might help to relieve the tedium, he thought, and if he played his cards right, maybe it would do something else.

"Hey. Let's talk," Darryl said.

Aunjanue looked up quizzically. "About what?"

"When Lydia and I had to hole up somewhere for long periods of time, we came up with these life subjects, things we could hash out to freshen up the atmosphere, so to speak. You know, bring some light into the darkness, entertainment into the flatness, stimulation—"

"I know what you two did. I read it in your file," Aunjanue said.

"Isn't anything sacred? I had no idea our debriefings would get so much scrutiny. Anyway, since you know so much about it, let's give it a try."

"Fine by me," Aunjanue sounded skeptical.

"I'll pick the first topic. How about . . . yeah, let's discuss the differences between men and women. That should keep us busy for awhile."

"You're kidding? Right?"

"Just want to hear your take on it. You tell me what you think, and I'll tell you how it really is." He liked her laugh.

"You're on. To begin with, women have bigger brains and are not afraid to show their emotions."

"Whoa. Bigger brains? It's a medical fact that men's brains are much larger," Darryl said.

"I should have said that women are smarter than men because their brains work more efficiently. Scientific discoveries have shown that women have a higher ratio of output to input. Men might have bigger brains overall, but the space devoted to important stuff like emotion and memory formation, language and communication, is actually larger in a woman's brain. Truth is, brains are hardwired for Stone Age needs. That's why men are always getting boners—"

Lydia would have said that. A lot of women would have said that.

"Poor choice of topic. Let's see…do you have kids?" Darryl said.

"Chicken. What? *No.* Do you?" Aunjanue was shaking her head.

"Me, neither."

"Did you go off your ADHD meds today? Because the directions you're taking—I can't keep up with them." Aunjanue said.

"But I thought your communication brain was *so much bigger* than mine." Darryl chuckled. "Seriously, I figured if I knew a few more things about you, I could find better things to discuss."

"Fire away. What do you want to know?"

"Coming here, did you have to break some poor guy's heart back in Chicago? Or is the miserable fool still waiting for you?"

Aunjanue said, "Is this your way of asking me if I'm married or serious about someone?"

"I guess."

"No. There's no one like that in my life. There used to be, but that was a long time ago."

"I bet you're one of these types that's married to the job. Is that what happened with your last beau? Couldn't compete with all of the intrigue and danger?"

"Beau? One minute you're like the Robin Williams character on Mork and Mindy, the next, you turn into a Jane Austen character, full of manners and courtesies."

"I'd say all that fancy talk is just a whole lot of avoidance on your part."

"Yeah, well, a newbie has to keep some secrets, or where's the fun in getting to know her."

This wasn't getting him any closer to the truth. Time to change tactics.

"Okay. Then tell me, why do you do this kind of work? Why the FBI?"

"I scored high on the tests and in the beginning, at least, I wanted to save the world. That, and craving something exciting and important to do in my life. Your turn."

The matter-of-factness, spare details—all Lydia.

"I'm a cop because I'm good at it. I like the people I work with, generally. I've had some close calls, but nothing that would call for hanging up my boots."

"But why did you choose law enforcement in the first place?" Aunjanue asked.

"Same as you, I think. For the good it would do. And for the adrenaline rush. I stayed because, well, I fell for someone in my department." Darryl folded his hands into a steeple and brought it to his lips. He smiled with his eyes and said, "Thought I would be able to see more of her, if I stuck around. Soon after, I made detective. That's when things got really got interesting."

"You stayed because of a woman? I don't believe it."

"There's more happening in heaven and earth when a man's heart is set a-fire, than women could ever dream of."

Now, wait. Where the hell was he going with this? Aunjanue was right. He needed to focus.

"So why are you in Miami? What persuaded you to leave your home turf to come all the way down here to track down Markiza?" he asked.

"Why Darryl, haven't you guessed by now?" Aunjanue flashed him a sly come-hither smile. "You did, of course. After briefing me for four hours—my boss and yours—they left me with two boxes of files, including bios on everyone in MAGS. When I saw your face, I was sold. I had to take the job just to find out if you were really as good looking as your photo."

Darryl knew she was yanking his chain. And if she weren't, it would have made no difference. He was used to women flattering him, but unfortunately, the praise never had the desired effect. When he was kid, he was considered homely and too dark, even by members of his own family — although they never came out and said it to his face. His ears stuck out, his nose stuck out, and he was short until he turned eighteen; that's when he grew six and half inches to 6'1. By then his head had grown and his face had also filled out, and nothing stuck out anymore. Instead he was left with broad shoulders and some fine looking bones, covered by exotic dark skin. Now when women that he had known as girls — girls that would not give him the time of day in high school— came around to Anita's to quietly ask about her handsome detective son, it was simply too late. The only woman who did not flatter him openly and brazenly was Lydia. Somehow she knew better.

Except that one time.

Again, it was during the homeless serial-killer investigation when Darryl had asked Lydia what in the world had possessed her to take on that dirty, smelly detail. She said that once she was shown a photo of her handsome future partner, she would have signed up for life, if that were what it took for him to notice her.

This was all too familiar.

And that sealed it for him. Lydia and Aunjanue had both used almost the exact same words. They were the same person. Lydia was alive, living and working under an assumed name and a fabricated, new face.

Darryl let the knowledge slowly course through his bloodstream, but when it began flooding the regions of his brain, he felt panic rising. Luckily, his thought processes were cut short by an insistent banging on the door.

A Russian man stood scowling in the hall, muttering orders in guttural English for them to leave their electronic devices and to follow him into the parking lot. Shortly afterwards, Darryl and Aunjanue clambered into the back seat of a late model Volvo, where their escort drove them to a deserted warehouse parking lot. There, the new transportation turned out to be a beat-up, white-paneled van with what looked like the first Russian's twin behind the wheel. While Darryl and Aunjanue stared uncomprehendingly through the back doors of the vehicle at two green plastic lawn chairs, they were each handed a pair of dark sunglasses. Until then, Aunjanue had been uncharacteristically quiet and cooperative.

"You expect me to sit on that? No pillow or nothing?" Aunjanue swung at one of the lawn chairs with her purse. "Alan, are these people from Mars? Do they not see what I am wearing? I didn't come all this way just to be treated—"

"It's okay, Felicia," Darryl said in a soothing voice. "It's what we get in the end that counts. And right now, just like us, they can't be too careful." Darryl waved his arms in the air. "This whole cloak and dagger show is to protect both sides."

Felicia remained unconvinced. "Mr. Treadwell, I don't mind wearing unattractive eyewear that you might find at an ophthalmologist's office, but plastic chairs?" Darryl offered his arm and Felicia climbed up into van into the van and sat down, but not before first making a lot of noise scraping her chair back and forth across the bare metal floor.

When the doors shut behind them, the first driver hopped in the passenger seat, and the van rolled out of the parking lot. They made a slow, exasperating trek around Miami. At least Darryl thought they were still within the city limits. But who knew? The new driver took his sweet time driving them around in circles. He slowed down, accelerated, and backtracked. Darryl was sure they had never gotten onto the interstate because the van never picked up speed. And they had driven over busy streets for a long time. In the beginning, the lack of soundproofing brought with it an almost constant whir of car engine noise, the honking of cabs and city buses, slamming brakes, and the wailing sounds of sirens. For the last thirty minutes, there had been fewer and fewer passing cars.

They'd been trapped in the van for more than an hour and a half. They might not have their cell phones, but Darryl wore a watch. A real Rolex, borrowed from the property room at the police station. And he knew they had left the motel a little before nine; it had just turned ten-thirty. Trapped and hot and miserable. Partially his fault. Each time he had asked the Russians how much longer they were going to be playing at this game, the air in the van got a little warmer and stickier. Once, that had really lit up Felicia.

"Are you all crazy in the head, or what?" She screeched. "We know what you're doing. But why are you doing it? You think turning the AC off, going back to dinosaur Soviet tactics is supposed to wear us down? Really? Why would you be stupid enough to think that? Can't you understand that we are the customers here? You are supposed to keep us happy. And cool. Tell me, you morons, just when did being able to dish out oodles of cash for domestic slaves lose its appeal?"

The Russian barked out something gruff and unintelligible; Darryl whispered in Felicia's ear, and she whispered back, "Shiiiit."

Darryl had found the slimmest source of illumination slipping through the crack between the back doors whenever they drove under streetlights. He was using the light to study Aunjanue's face and thought of Lydia. He was relieved to no longer view his old friend in the way he had imagined back at the motel. Because back there, just before they left, Darryl had decided that if Lydia could go under the knife to change her race and completely disown who she was at the core, she'd have to be mad. And then, if she went back to the job, to work side by side with her old team—as if nothing had ever happened —then she couldn't rightly have a conscience. Aunjanue might have some secrets, but he could never believe the worst of Lydia. Sure, there were a few times when her unorthodox methods for solving pesky problems raised eyebrows from superiors, but that did not mean she was a deranged megalomaniac. Not something scraped off the under-bellied, barnacle side of lunacy. Not the Lydia he knew and loved. No, that woman died in a fiery crash, and he would have to let her rest in peace.

THIRTY ONE

They fell into a stillness that crackled with despair and told them that shiny little bits of pretty truth were not enough to live free because the night would take its share and destroy any ghosts they hid behind so he would never know the acreage of her vengeance and she would bury all of that terror and it would never grow into love or worthy passion but would wilt and decay and get eaten by worms as she had not existed when he did not see her.

When you sit on a plastic chair across from a man for an hour and a half without talking, you learn many things about him.

If you know what to listen for, then every single movement: a head turn, one nearly imperceptible body shift, and multiple sighs in a row of which the man is not even aware, will tell more true tales than if he were speaking out loud. But Darryl had been giving up bits and pieces even before they climbed inside the rattletrap, when they were still back at the motel. And yet, it was afterwards, during the long and winding, out-of-the-way road trip, where she finally got what she desperately needed.

With each pause and start, Darryl's involuntary movements told Aunjanue all she needed to know. That even after she volunteered the damning piece of information, when she told him she took the job just so she could see his adorable mug in person, Darryl's heart had eventually struck a bargain with his brain, and he no longer believed she was Lydia. It had been a necessary and expedient concession for both of them given the enormity of their mission. Aunjanue knew Darryl's resolve was only temporary, and like an angry storm slowed down by a landmass, once it moved over warmer air, its rage would widen and swallow up the night. But for now, they would be okay.

Ever since Andy told her about the yearbook discovery in Minneapolis, Aunjanue knew Darryl would be obsessing about her identity. He was a good detective and he'd want to know facts, but this time his heart would lead the search. If he could, Darryl would will her back into existence, so that his one true love, Lydia, could have another chance at life. In his imagination she'd be able to fulfill her dreams, and this time he would not let her go. For seconds, even minutes, he could withstand the betrayal. Then he'd snap like an angry live wire because she had not trusted him enough to tell him what she'd done. Or why. No, it was more that she didn't involve him in the decision to become someone else in the first place, that Darryl wouldn't be able to forgive. Afterwards, the pain would escalate, forcing him to go back to the drawing board. *Who was the real Aunjanue? What was hidden in her past? Why had she come to Florida?* His mind would whiplash like this until she put an end to the misery.

She'd had to. It was essential for Darryl to operate on all cylinders. He needed his confidence back, free from the shackles of doubt. Because if there were even a scintilla of a chance that her partner would go into the sting battling a psychic war of mutually exclusive desires and impulses, he would endanger the mission. They would never find the boys, never arrest Markiza, and would probably get killed in the process. In the short term, she had to convince him that she was Lydia. It was the only way. But what if she was wrong? What if she didn't know him as well as she thought, and her little mind-game backfired — ah hell! Anything was better than this.

Aunjanue had anticipated Darryl's gambit at the motel room. She let things unfold naturally. He had been clever and coy, gently prying out of her the strings he thought would tie her to her old self. He was smart but hadn't she warned him? That women were smarter. But it wasn't that at all, was it? She always had the advantage. She had always known who she was and what she was doing, and Darryl — only guessed. Over and over again.

When Darryl asked her why she agreed to go after Markiza, she had a dozen answers ready. But she whipped out the one that would temporarily stun him and then ultimately catapult her partner back to sanity. If she handed him the same reason for being in Miami that Lydia had when he asked why she took the homeless serial-killer detail, Darryl would finally determine that Aunjanue and Lydia were one and the same person. And in the very next instance, he would recoil from the notion. It was the human psychological defense system doing what it does best. Burying the impossible on the altar of ridiculous beliefs.

He would see that thinking Aunjanue and Lydia were identical was on par with accepting that your mother, your sister, your best friend, or child was a serial killer. The heart would not recognize the worst-case scenario; otherwise it would explode and die. At all cost, it would protect itself, first and foremost.

For Darryl, for now, Lydia was dead. She had died when her car rolled into the ravine and burst into flames. She was gone.

Aunjanue had also taken advantage of the strip of light penetrating the crack between the doors. Occasionally it fell on Darryl. She watched him and listened. He had equivocated. She saw that in the way Darryl folded and unfolded his limbs. Finally, his breathing transformed from shallow and rapid to full and slow. And now that Darryl had received his come-to-Jesus moment, he would hang onto it. For a while, and maybe even long enough.

Miraculously, the vehicle began slowing down. She heard Darryl exhale. Time to meet your maker, Markiza.

"Alan, I know we don't always see eye to eye. Heck, I don't understand why Roman doesn't let me fire you. But you're okay most of the time. Listen, remember when we talked to Roman at the motel? He said loud and clear that I should get the six boys I want. It was my house and my domestics. So don't argue with me when we go inside. Understand?"

"I was there too, Felicia, when Roman called. I also heard him say, 'be reasonable, darling. Be very reasonable.'" Darryl said.

"I am reasonable." Aunjanue's voice rose and she spoke rapidly. "I'm very reasonable. All I want is six boys, three young ones and three teenagers. And they better have teeth. All of them. I've seen pictures of the Ruskies on the

Internet with their snaggle-toothed smiles. Nah-ah! Dentistry is expensive. I'm not buying some used goods from a Salvation Army discount center. All I want —"

"Quiet. You talk too much." The Russian pulled his keys out of the ignition and slid out of the driver's seat.

"Alan, I'm going to see that he gets fired."

THIRTY TWO

Tadzio was beginning to think he had made a huge mistake by running away from Markiza. All he wanted to do now was go back, and wondered if he still could.

In the morning when the UPS truck pulled up, Tadzio thought he had been looking at freedom. Now he wasn't so sure. Maybe Sasha had been wrong and Markiza right. That there wasn't any such thing as freedom, and that the Russian's protection was all he would ever need in this world. *Because nothing else existed or mattered.* Hadn't Markiza always drilled that into the boys? And judging by this complete failure of a day, that certainly seemed to be the case.

Ever since he hopped into the UPS truck, all he did was ride around in different vehicles, going from building to building getting handed over to somebody new, always getting asked the same stupid questions that he did not understand and could never answer. Now it was past his bedtime and they were still talking to him. After all this, he wasn't any closer to finding Lydia or a good home, or even a guarantee that he could go to school one day. He needed so much help, but he wasn't getting it. So what was he doing here?

There were four of them now in the new room at a place called La Quinta. Before they had taken off their sunglasses, the two tall men in suits could have been brothers. Afterwards, Tadzio found some definite differences in their faces. The one who was leaning over, pouring himself another cup of coffee, had round, clear brown eyes set very wide apart, and a long pointy nose that flared from the nostrils. His face was oval and he slurped loudly because the coffee was hot. He didn't stare as much at Tadzio as did his friend. That man had a square face with brown eyes too, but they were sleek and wide like a varmint's, and his nose was snubbed and he didn't drink coffee. His old pal, the UPS driver was there, too. Under the bright light of the desk lamp, Tadzio noticed he had eyebrows like a beetle's, and in sharp contrast to his big grey mustache and wooly head of hair, they were almost black. Whenever he frowned, the brows became one and, if he weren't so weary, Tadzio might have laughed. The man reminded him of grizzly bear with eyebrows.

Now and again, the driver would wink at him and smile conspiratorially. Like they were in this together. But Tadzio knew they were as unlike as could be. Once, the man took out his wallet and pulled out a plastic pack of photos. They were of his wife and two sons. He had looked away quickly because he was afraid he would burst into tears. He used to be part of a family, but now Tadzio was all alone in the world, and more than anything, he wanted to stop thinking and go to sleep. But he couldn't and would have to stay alert because now he had a new mission. He had to figure out how to get back to the warehouse.

The fourth person in the room was a small young woman who rubbed her hands constantly, like she was about to discover something important, and spoke a language he understood. Russian. Her face was bland because she never smiled, but she had nice blonde, shoulder-length hair that curled at the ends. She wore a tan blouse and brown slacks, and always looked a little off to the side whenever she asked Tadzio a question. Mr. Pointy-Nose asked the question first in English. Each time she nodded and repeated it in Russian.

In the beginning, Mr. Pointy-Nose wanted to know everything about the sketchbook, like how long had Tadzio been drawing, what the sketches meant to him, and when and where had he seen the license plate that he drew in precise symbols on one of the pages.

Tadzio had repeated several times that the license plate belonged to a truck driven by a woman named Lydia. She always arrived with packages at the building where he lived, and usually she talked to his friend Sasha first. They always spoke in hushed tones, but once he heard her telling Sasha that he could come live with her. Tadzio said that Sasha had been killed, and Lydia had gotten away in a blue car. Until then, she had always driven a UPS truck, disguised as a man. This last part always had Mr. Snub-Nose clamping his teeth.

After a few failed attempts to hear what they wanted, whatever that was, Mr. Pointy-Nose wrote for a long time in his notebook. When he looked up he had pulled on a thin smile and spoke. Blondie interpreted.

"These men want you to know that they are very sorry for bothering you with all of these questions. Before they can know where to bring you next, they have to be sure they've understood everything. They want to take you home, eventually. Wouldn't you like that?"

Only if that meant living with Lydia, Tadzio thought, but would they ever understand that?

The interpreter listened to the next question and said, "They know the numbers of the license plate you drew are important, their computer explained that to them. They don't know why, though. So you have to go over everything that you told us one more time, just to make sure there wasn't one little teeny, small thing that you might have noticed but forgot to tell us about."

Tadzio looked from person to person in the room, hung his head, and began to wail. Blondie jumped and the UPS man rushed to his side. He held Tadzio tight until the sobs turned into sniffles. Then he turned to the men who stood like robots, and said, "You've been asking all the wrong questions. He's a scared little boy, for Pete's sake. Find out why he ran away in the first place."

Mr. Pointy-Nose arched his brows and nodded to Blondie.

Something snapped in her. Blondie knelt down and took Tadzio's hands gently into hers and looked into his eyes. "You must have been terribly unhappy. Is that why you ran away?"

Tadzio dropped the interpreter's hands and crawled onto the bed next to where the UPS man had sat down. He leaned into him and in a voice that sounded like it was already asleep and dreaming said, "Because Markiza sells boys. Markiza killed my best friend Sasha after he found out he was friends with Lydia. He found out she was trying to help us because he saw my drawings. It's my fault Sasha died. If I hadn't made so many sketches, maybe—"

Tadzio was suddenly alert because it had felt like the room had started to vibrate. He looked at the men. Something in them shifted because their faces twitched and their eye became unfocused. It was because of something he had said, but which part?

The tall men were on phones now, talking sharply, taking notes. After a few minutes, Mr. Pointy Nose came over and sat next to him; he was holding his sketchbook open and Tadzio felt a pen being pushed between his fingers.

The man spoke softly now, the interpreter followed in Russian. "These men want to help you. They have promised to look for Lydia, but to do that, they need for you to draw one more thing." And then he stood up and his smile was broad. "Please."

Seeing two-dimensionally was second nature to Tadzio, and right now he was really grateful for that special talent because it meant he didn't have to talk any more. He just had to draw a picture of the special place where they kept the rest of the boys. It dawned on him that the men in suits must have already gone to the warehouse in his sketchbook. But no one was there any more. They wanted to know about another place that Markiza might use, and how to get there. He was shown photos of street signs and he saw what he had to do.

In careful strokes, he drew the letters that made the names of the intersecting streets in Hialeah.

Afterwards, the tall men rustled around the room, talked on phones, and pulled on their suit coats, and left. Blondie tucked Tadzio into one of the beds and said the social worker would be back soon to get him.

Social worker? Liars!

When the interpreter left for a moment to go to the bathroom, Tadzio plumped up his pillow, tucked the comforter into a body shape, and sneaked out of the motel. He learned to do that when he used to leave his bed and crawl in next to Sasha. So he didn't have to feel so lonely.

Outside, the moon was waning under a cloudy sky. He stood under the motel awning watching the parking lot. He saw the tall men next to big black vehicle. SUV, he had heard the Russians call them. He was small and stealthy and knew something about sneaking into trucks. Tadzio was completely wide-awake now.

THIRTY THREE

Marla turned in her office chair and stiffened as soon as she heard Nelson stride through MAGS' pneumatic door. He was spitting orders into the tiny microphone of his cell phone but the device was not cooperating. Nelson's clenched jaw and repeated hand gesture to brush invisible hair from his forehead told the administrator that the FBI agent was on the losing end of a battle. When he hung up, he looked around the room like he might be searching for an ally. Since they were the only people on the entire second floor of the Miami Police Headquarters, she figured Nelson was also scoping out a place he could hide after he delivered whatever it was he didn't want to say to her.

Finally, Nelson scratched his earlobe and affected the well-rehearsed stance of an innocent bystander who just happened to be in the wrong place at the wrong time. "I don't want you to panic but—"

"What, what happened?" Marla walked backwards, letting the space between them widen and hugged herself against an approaching blitzkrieg.

"We lost the signal. My men were getting a strong read from the GPS wire in Aunjanue's hair, and they tracked it for sixty-five minutes. It was challenging because the Russian driver zigzagged all over Miami. The misdirection might have been to throw the scent off in case he thought he was being followed, or simply to confuse Darryl and Aunjanue. Then about five minutes ago, the signal failed." He shook his head, his eyes buried in Marla's arm. And it hasn't come back."

"How could that happen? It's two blocks, they only had to keep two blocks between them, and didn't you tell me there was another scout car somewhere in front? How—?"

Marla sank into her desk chair and tried not to scream. Instantly, she was on her feet and pacing, fingertips smacking together. "Tell me every single thing," Marla said.

Nelson assumed a placid expression and pulled out a small spiral notebook. "As I was saying, the Russian used delaying tactics by driving around in circles, backtracking, cruising down busy streets, speeding in and out of alleys. After a half hour of that, the van did a slow loop through the northwestern quadrant of Miami. First actual stop was at an all-night food joint in Allapattah—by the sound of it, the goons actually pulled up to the drive-thru window and ordered Cuban sandwiches. Didn't offer Darryl and Aunjanue anything, and they didn't ask.

"Next, the van headed downtown, drove around the Civic Center a few times, turned up Biscayne, and swerved onto Sunny Isles Blvd. At that point we stopped and waited for them to come back. Sunny Isles Beach is Russian territory but all up-market; only way in an out is down this unobstructed mile-long strip. The Russian would have noticed two unmarked cars in an instant. When he was back on Biscayne—"

"Where did they lose contact?" Marla asked.

"I thought you wanted all of the details."

"You take too long. You must be a Pisces. So where was it?"

Nelson said, "No. Aires with Pisces rising. Marla stopped pacing and sucked in her breath loudly, tapping her foot. "El Portal, right between Liberty City and Little Haiti."

"Which way were they headed?" Marla stopped pacing long enough to hear the answer.

"East."

"What's east?"

Nelson looked relieved, like he was coming to the end of his interrogation. "West Little River, Brownsville and Hialeah. Look Marla, I got both cars searching, we haven't given up."

"But you only sent out one receiver. So unless your scout can see through walls after they hide that van, we're left with one car with a tracker that's not tracking."

Marla stretched her teeth over her lower lip and bit hard; afterwards she had to rub away the impression they made with her finger. "We need some righteous help here, and now."

Nelson was talking again into his cell. Marla swallowed several times and said softly, "Andy."

The mobile device crooked between his shoulder and ear, Nelson opened the door and Andy walked in. "Way ahead of you, Marla. Sometimes it's not just the rank-and-file that knows how to get a jump on things."

When Marla screwed up the courage to look at her friend's face, she saw a wide grin that reminded her of the freshness of youth. A time that was completely innocent, expectant, and generously sheathed in mischief. It was a look that said Andy understood her, he had also forgiven her.

"Andy, I'm sorry."

"We'll have a sword dual in the parking lot, later. Just like Errol Flynn and Basil Rathbone in Robinhood."

"Shut up, Andy," Marla hissed. Andy grabbed Marla around the shoulders and drew her into him. When he let go, she was looking at the floor, trying not to empty the wading pools inside her eyelids. "Come on, let's try to find them, just in case the signal doesn't come back," he added.

"I'm glad Nelson didn't believe me and that you're still here. You're the only one who can do this. Figure out what kinds of locations they'd need to house boys and make widgets and all that," Marla said.

Marla, Andy, and Nelson walked over to the LCD Smart Touch Table and pulled up the Miami neighborhood map. With her fingertips, Marla enlarged the old abandoned industrial park where Andy had worked for more than a year. It was in Doral, northwest of the police station and 10 miles from where Aunjanue and Darryl were last spotted, in El Portal. Ten miles in another direction.

"Turn the page, Marla." Andy pointed to a cluster of red markers indicating industrial park locations. "See, most of these are contiguous business districts, stretching nearly a mile; they start in Hialeah and run south to Doral. I don't think Markiza would hold up in a centralized area. He likes stand-alone buildings surrounded by lots of empty land space. And it has to be fairly new to accommodate a facility capable of running a factory, and big enough to house hundreds of boys. Because even if the supply of boys is smaller now due to sales or whatnot, he's got to be ready for the next shipment."

"It also has to be off the beaten track but close to the interstate, in case they need to make a run for it."

Marla slid over to another page that showed recent commercial property sales within a twenty-five-mile square area. "In the last six months, there were eighteen properties sold, eleven were stand-alones; only six were big enough—sixty to one-hundred thousand square feet."

Nelson asked, "How many near the interstate?"

"All of them," replied Marla.

"Can you see which ones took possession within the last month?" Andy asked.

"It's not listed that way. But if you want to know which ones started using utilities like electricity, let me make a call to Florida Power and Light." Marla was already dialing.

Ten minutes later, she had come up with three names. Andy pulled up Google Earth and studied all five locations. Nelson and Marla waited.

Nelson twitched, but Marla put up her hand. Andy was meditating.

"If I had to guess, I'd say give this one in Brownsville a hard look even though on the face of it, it's an unlikely candidate. They'd attract a lot of attention because the Russians arc, well, white, in an all-black neighborhood, but the street is cut off from everything else. I mean you'd really need a good reason to go there. It's hard to get to because of how they cut up the neighborhood years ago to build the interstate. And even harder to get in if you do manage to find it." As Andy enlarged the page they saw a tall cyclone fence. "It could be electric."

"I like this one too." Andy stretched the image of a square concrete slab in the middle of a field in Hialeah.

Again, this one is remote and close to the interstate, but it's also less accessible because of all of the construction on that side of that interstate. It's just that—"

"It's all on one level," Marla quipped.

"That's exactly it. The one in Brownsville used to be a used car lot, with a service station and all. It's two-storied, at one time the showroom was on the first floor with offices upstairs. They'd make good sleeping quarters for a bunch of kids.

"The Hialeah building looks and feels too exposed."

Marla let out the air she had sucked in and held for the last few minutes. "That's it, then. Go call your men, Nelson."

When Nelson had left, Andy smiled conspiratorially at Marla. "You got that man eating out of your hand. How does one manage to intimidate the bejesus out of the FBI?"

"He's not afraid of me, just knows when I'm right."

"Are you kidding me? Intimidating people is part of your charm."

"Not everybody." Marla allowed a quiet rip through her thoughts, momentarily conjuring Lydia's image.

THIRTY FOUR

The warehouse was a cold concrete building with a long, industrial roll-up entrance, a few narrow service doors, and no windows. Aunjanue could make out that it was also an isolated, one-story surrounded by a tall cyclone fence. Behind the building a few straggly trees dotted the landscape. She looked up. The moon was a bright crescent and all the stars had halos around them. The dark glasses were playing tricks on her. She listened. A light wind moved through the darkness carrying with it an orchestra of humming insects and the call of nighthawks. The drone of a distant motorway reminded the detective just how far from home they really were. If something went wrong here, no one would ever know. She fought the urge to touch her hair.

While she and Darryl walked towards a skinny metal door at the far end of the building, the driver and two other men followed closely behind them. Where had they come from? Aunjanue knew better than to think this might be the last surprise of the evening.

Her heels caught several times as they headed down a path of broken concrete. Not cracked or dislodged due to frequent use or exposure to the elements, but deliberately fractured because something that used to be there got bulldozed. She filed away this and other things knowing

Darryl was doing the same. Old habits. But the spotty information would prove stupid and useless once they busted the gangsters. And if it happened she and Darryl were not successful this time around, yet again, it wouldn't matter either, because of course, the Russians would pull up stakes and move elsewhere. But for now it kept her mind occupied and sharp.

More importantly, once they were inside, a tableau with all new details would present itself to be analyzed and catalogued. She would have to do it quickly in case they were forced to go to plan Z. That place of last resort you couldn't readily discuss because you could never actually plan for it. The best training and experience could not imagine every contingency. After you're forced to give up your favorite tools: communication devices and handguns, only life-and-death situations can show you how to compensate.

The door swung open and another Russian appeared taking their glasses, motioning them to pass. They all walked up a short flight of steps and just like a disciplined infantry line, waited patiently in front of a wide metal door. When it clanked all the way open, the line moved in just before the door slid closed again.

The room was a too-long, narrow box whose corners seemed to sag from the forced design. It looked like a double-wide closet. The walls were bare except for a scratched mirror on a wall behind a gunmetal desk. A bare bulb hanging askew from a frayed cord provided the only illumination. Next to the mirror, stood a floor-to-ceiling splintered wooden door that looked like could it could lead to an escape route. Or would have, if one of the two Russians who had moved in to flank the monolith sitting behind the desk, wasn't blocking it now. Two more Russians stood on the monolith's other side.

Under a tightly fitting black turtleneck, a barreled chest protruded and forearms as big as ham bones claimed most of the desktop. Markiza looked like someone carved out of marble by a statue maker partial to planes and angles. He had a comic book face complete with well-defined cheekbones, a lantern jaw, and yes—a deep cleft in his chin. His skin was ghostly white with few lines or creases; instead, two blue veins anchored each side of his wide forehead. Only his hair belied human ancestry. Thick silvery waves as soft and creamy as swirls on a cake, hung down to his shoulders. Aunjanue was certain that when the kingpin got up he would stand at six-three or taller. He was a solid three-hundred pounds. Pretty remarkable since it had been more than a few years that Markiza celebrated his seventieth birthday. His nearly colorless eyes glowed like flashlight beams and, at the moment, they ogled the strange creature that danced from foot to foot like she had ants in her pants.

"Even from jail, Delgado manages to keep the prettiest girl," Markiza said with barely a trace of an accent.

"Hey, no one keeps me. I'm not some concubine," Aunjanue said. "I am Roman Delgado's *girlfriend*. But, of course I know you meant it as a compliment. So let me return the favor."

Aunjanue looked around the room. She held the gaze of each Russian for a moment while her peripheral vision scanned for bulges under their clothing; satisfied, she returned to fix her eyes on Markiza and smiled broadly. "I must say, I'm impressed too. You are a big man," she said while exhaling a remarkable amount of air from her lungs. "Maybe the biggest I have ever seen. I bet you won all the arm wrestling contests back in Russia."

Aunjanue stepped away from Darryl and rounded the table to stand close to the Russians on Markiza's far left. "And I have to say that your assistants here, they are as polite as can be. I used to think that all Russians were such geeky-acting dunderheads. Shows my prejudice, right?" She opened her purse and took out a compact. Before proceeding to check her make up, Aunjanue winked, at no one in particular.

"As you know, Roman's friend Felicia has exceptional hiring standards. For her new line of domestics, she requires six boys, all healthy, and in a range of ages." While Darryl talked, Aunjanue began smiling at the man closest to the door. The young Russian flushed scarlet as she reached over and lightly touched his hand.

Darryl cleared his throat several times. Aunjanue dropped her hand and gave him an innocent stare. "Three under the age of ten and the other three must be in their early teens. And they must have strong teeth. Felicia cannot abide missing enamel. Of course, if they need braces, we'll take care of that."

Darryl threw Aunjanue a look of disapproval when he saw her tap the Russian's upper arm with her fingernail. He was about to say something to her when Markiza's cell phone rang.

Aunjanue heard Markiza whisper in Russian, "He's back? Well, well. I'll be right there. Wait, what about my son?" Markiza listened with eyes closed. He added, "Does he think I have all night?" And he hung up. The kingpin turned to the man on his right and said, "We're leaving for a minute to handle a small, pesky matter." Nodding to the next man, he said, "You grab some chairs from the closet for our guests and tell them to be patient. I'll be back soon."

After Markiza and his lieutenant left, Aunjanue saw the guards shoot each other furtive glances. When he came back with the chairs, the Russian frowned as he placed them against the wall across from the desk. Something unexpected has happened, she thought. They seemed nervous, suddenly. Even the friendly guard would not look glance her way. She heard Darryl whisper, "What are you playing at?"

She sat down next to Darryl and said, "Just measuring the temperature in the air."

"How hot is it?"

"I think most of them carry their pieces in shoulder holsters, except the driver—he keeps it in an ankle holster. And my new young friend, he's clear. What about Markiza, what do you think?" Aunjanue asked.

"It's in the back of his pants," Darryl said.

"Damn, I'm on the wrong side of the room," Aunjanue said.

"Let's hope it doesn't come down to that."

"We'll know when they bring the boys in. After we talk about money, let's give it no more than ten minutes. If the troops aren't here by then, you know what to do."

Aunjanue felt that Darryl was being too complacent. He wasn't emitting an "I can do" vibe. And right now she needed him fearless. Because fearlessness could take you places most people mostly shunned.

Almost fifteen minutes passed before Markiza lumbered back through the door. His expressionless, pale face was even more stone-like than before. His eyes swept over the detectives without really noticing them. He scratched his chin like he was trying to decide something.

"Will they go to school? Maybe it's too late for the older ones, but the younger boys need some education," Markiza said.

"What? Aunjanue was on her feet again. "Are you crazy?" The air stilled and the Russian lieutenants glared at her. Even thought they did not understand her words, they heard the unmistakable disrespect in her tone. "Come on. They're illegals."

Markiza shooed the air between them like it was a swarm of flies. "It's your business what you do with them. But do you really want to be surrounded by idiots? And I didn't say you needed a public school to teach reading and writing."

"My goodness, what a speech." She looked over her shoulder at Darryl who sat impassively, eyes seemingly fixed on the floor, but most likely peering under the table at the driver's ankle. She turned back. "I didn't know the sale came with instructions."

Markiza tried unsuccessfully to stifle a scowl.

"Oh, don't get your knickers in a knot. I've already lined up private tutoring for *all* of the boys, and they'll watch plenty of TV where they can pick up language skills and manners, and all that good stuff. What? Did you think I was born without a heart?" Aunjanue detected something like a sigh of relief expelling from the statue.

Markiza pushed a button on his cell phone. "Bring them."

Aunjanue felt her resolve shift of its own accord when she saw the boys trickle in. They were so skinny and young and tender. Plan Z would not guarantee their safety.

The three older boys stood tall and erect in a line in front of Markiza's desk—he was now up on his feet, towering behind them, his massive arms crossed over his chest, jaw clenched. But his eyes were trained on the door, which opened once more, to let in the younger ones. Two, jaundiced-looking towheads, no more than six years old, waddled to stand next to the others. When the door swung open for the third time, Markiza stepped on the doorsill blocking the boy's entrance. He leaned down and whispered something to him. Aunjanue watched the Russians; they were still tense, one blinked incessantly.

She didn't recognize him at first. The dark hair was cut shorter, and he was taller which made his stocky body look muscular instead of chubby. Aunjanue walked up and down the line. She told Markiza to have the boys open their mouths so she could inspect their teeth. She inquired about the youngest ones, saying she didn't think their skin looked too good. Markiza said that was because they were from the Baltics, of Mongolian descent, thus the darker skin. She was pretty sure they either had hepatitis or their kidneys were failing. But she let it go. When she finally got a chance to examine the last boy they brought in, she did so by bending down and peering into his eyes. She swallowed hard and pointed to his mouth. The boy obediently showed her his teeth. They were perfect.

Aunjanue straightened and walked back over to Darryl. She pretended to shiver, and put her arms across her shoulders. "Gosh, it's so cold in here. I wish I'd brought my jacket." *Code for "what the fuck?*

Aunjanue carefully followed Darryl's eyes as they slipped over Markiza's face. The kingpin was finally displaying an emotion. Anger. "What's wrong, you didn't like this last one? He's my best boy, aren't you Tadzio? Not only does he know the computer, he is also an excellent artist. Let's show the nice lady your sketches, boy."

One of the lieutenants walked over to Aunjanue and pressed a sketchbook into her hands. When she was finished looking at the last drawing she smiled warmly and put her hand on Tadzio's shoulder. With every eye in the room on her, Aunjanue spoke earnestly in English, "I agree, this is a very, very talented young man."

When Tadzio returned to the warehouse, Markiza hadn't yelled at him or hit him; he did none of the things someone who is crazy mad at you does. He only asked where he had been. Tadzio explained that he ran away as far as the interstate and stayed behind the ditch in the bushes. When it got dark and cold and he was out of food, he came back. He told him how sorry he was. Then Markiza wanted to know why he ran away. Tadzio said he went looking for a school. Fine, is all Markiza had said. And then he pushed him into the sale line.

Tadzio knew her the minute he stepped into the room. She had the same clear eyes he had sketched dozens of times. Today they were surrounded by a ton of make up, but he was used to that. Lydia had put on many disguises in the past. Still people can't change their eyes. Not even colored contact lenses could hide what they said when they looked at you. And her look, even for that one small instant said that she had come for him, it was the same look she used to give Sasha. But what was he supposed to do? This was a sale, after all. He needed a sign.

It came when she stopped turning the pages. She was talking now—he knew enough English to understand she was complimenting him. But when he saw her looking at one page and tapping another, the one where he had just finished a new series of drawings about his recent escapades—running away and jumping into a UPS truck, eating lunch with a bushy-faced man at a truck stop, and getting questioned by tall men dressed in suits, wearing sunglasses. Tadzio thought about how lucky he was that Markiza hadn't seen those images.

Yes, she was saying that he had talent. But she wasn't referring to his artistic skills.

THIRTY FIVE

"How long has it been? Andy!"

Not again. Andy looked up from the computer screen at Marla and shook his head. "Three minutes."

"No, really, how long since the last time I asked," Marla said.

"I'm sorry, I was wrong. Make that three minutes and five seconds." She was starting to drive him nuts.

Marla got up and walked over to Andy's desk. "What if they die?"

"Marla—"

"I can't stop the movie in my head. I just see them trapped in this Russian web of gangsters with guns, where they're made somehow . . . maybe Kastle gets there before our guys . . . and then they get their gooses cooked. Andy, what if they die tonight? What if it's their last night on earth?"

"Please don't do this. They are out there because they have the know-how. They're well trained and they've done it before, under similar circumstances. They're the best in the business."

"The best? No. Lydia was the best. And they killed her. And that new agent, Aunjanue? She's so far from home and family, and in the middle of the firing line. She's totally defenseless."

Andy swung round and round in his chair. His whole body ached for a drink. He was afraid that if Marla didn't stop yapping at him, he would eventually be forced to go into Sans' office, open his desk drawer and uncork one of the Cuban bottles of rum. The only thing stopping him now was the niggling thought that Aunjanue and Darryl might be working up a jones for a lot more than a bottle of liquor.

"Aunjanue."

"What," Marla said.

"You said she was so far from home. Defenseless. Neither is true, Marla."

"What are you babbling about?"

"Let's take a little walk, stretch our legs a bit. I'd like to tell you a story."

They walked around MAGS and up and down the corridor outside of the elevators. Andy talked and Marla listened. He told her everything. How Lydia faked her own death and then changed her face, all of it to be able to live and plot to get Markiza. Marla's reaction, similar to a patient who gets shot up with tranquilizer before a procedure, frankly surprised him. Marla had calmed down instantly, her self-destructive spiral vanishing into thin air. But, hadn't this happened to him too. Hadn't he reacted in the exact same manner when Aunjanue told *him*? Whatever she had done, how much she had deceived them, mattered not. Because the upshot was that Lydia, their Lydia, lived. Suddenly Andy felt better. The urge to drink was wearing off.

Andy said, "See, this is why I'm not worried. Our woman is so determined to avenge Sasha's killing and save all of those boys—I just know, even if she's alone, even if something, God forbid, happened to Darryl, there is something in her DNA that will continue to keep her safe until she gets what she's after."

"Well, that just makes so much sense. You know I liked Aunjanue instantly. I even I think that I loved her the minute she walked into MAGS. She told me she was crazy about my hat! Only Lydia would say that. Because she was *Lydia*." Marla was completely still for ten seconds before she lost it. "Oh, no."

"What?"

"Darryl. Oh, my god, does he know?"

Andy shook his head. "Nope."

"Oh, that's bad. It might be worse than bad."

"You got that right. But for the moment, let's not go there. Just swim in the joy for a minute. Then, I have another task for you."

He gave Marla a few minutes. She was making adjustments in her mind, just like he had that morning when Aunjanue made him coffee at his house. The information was welcoming and as good as it gets, but in order to have it completely stick, all kinds of minutia had to be thrown out of the brain files first.

When he thought Marla was ready, Andy said, "You know that stuff you found in my folder on Kastle? You missed something important because I noticed that you didn't open a certain file in a folder called, *What If*. I was just piecing some things together when you decided to call the dog up on me."

"Shut up." Marla looked to where Andy was pointing, read a few sentences, and shook her head. "This is about the accident."

"Remember what you used to say about Kastle when we called him our very own super hero?" Marla looked uncharacteristically blank. "You said, 'even the super heroes of mythology had to fall into the abyss before they could rise up and save the world'."

"I hate to contradict myself, but wasn't that exactly what Lex Kastle's did? By losing the use of his legs, didn't he fall to the bottom only to pull himself out and be the stronger for it?" Marla asked.

"What if he came out a defector?" Andy watched as Marla tried out the concept in her head.

"Think about this: Lex gets run down by an impossible-to-find van driven by an unidentifiable driver. There is little or no follow up, mainly, according to the reports, because Kastle didn't want it. He said he could not move on if he were always thinking about his assailants and what they were up to next. Afterwards, our big sting—a year in the making—goes south. Then Sasha and supposedly, Lydia, are assassinated. Next, MAGS gets de-funded. I've got another theory. What if that accident was no accident? What if it was a warning?" Andy said.

"You mean like, *if you don't stop fucking with us,* we'll paralyze the rest of you?" Marla said.

"Exactly. I heard the senator had an excruciating recovery. According to the nursing staff notes, it was one of the most painful on record. For almost a year, no amount of painkillers did any good, whatsoever. Then, miraculously, his nerves started to heal and the parts that could still feel, stopped throbbing, mostly.

"What if he were so traumatized that just the thought of ever hurting that much ever again, made him do something completely against his nature?" Andy said.

"You mean like aligning himself with the dark side. You think he bought himself protection by selling out MAGS? Or . . . Like Stockholm Syndrome? Shit." Andy bit back a chuckle. Sometimes it seemed that Marla hated being right.

"Kastle did have all the means in the world. Might have had the motive too," he said.

"We have to prove it. Speaking of which, have they found him yet?" Marla asked.

"He's not at his house, and no one's seen him at work since noon. I could get a court order to track his GPS, but I don't think there's enough time. And if he's our mole, I don't think the senator would risk a tracking device that would lead to the Russians. Markiza would have made sure of that."

Andy's cell phone rang. As he listened, he kept his face neutral just in case Marla started in again. The detective mused that after this was all over, she might want to think about working at a library where the only shockwaves she would ever feel would come from falling stacks of books.

"Brownsville was a bust. They're off to Hialeah."

"With our luck, that's wrong too," Marla said.

"I don't think so. That was Nelson. He said an FBI agent from Kidnappings and Missing Persons called a few minutes ago. The agent said he'd gotten a tip about a trafficker. Seems like a young boy speaking very little English stowed away inside a UPS truck. He had lots of drawings with him, and one was of a UPS license plate. After the driver discovered the boy, he reported him to the police but not before showing the license plate drawing to his boss, who called the division manager.

"A couple of hours later, the driver got an unexpected visit from the FBI. Apparently, the numbers tripped a switch for Kidnappings and Missing Persons, but no one could figure out why. The agents picked up the driver and together they collected the boy from child services. After a preliminary interview with the kid, the agent in charge began to think the kid was a run-of-the-mill truant. Then they got an interpreter—"

"The kid was Russian?"

"Actually Polish, but he spoke Russian. Afterwards, the agent and his partner drove to a location that the kid gave them, actually drew for them. They were just following up a lead and were not prepared for this gargantuan warehouse with an electric fence—"

"Don't tell me, in Hialeah." Marla finished.

"Yeah. When they realized they were over their heads, they went into their search engine and plugged in a name the kid gave them. He had told them this incredible story of boys being sold to families to work as slaves. Are you ready? He said the trafficker was called Markiza," Andy said.

"What are these '*kidnapping, missing persons*' agents doing now?" Marla asked.

"Waiting for the artillery to arrive."

Marla grabbed her sweater and headed for the door.

"Where are you going?"

"To Hialeah, of course." Do you want to drive, or should I, Andy?"

THIRTY SIX

Lex Kastle arrived at the far end of the warehouse and let himself in with a passkey. He wasn't ready to call Markiza yet. Mostly because he hadn't decided whose side he wanted to be on today. Standing at the edge of his destiny, Kastle had the power to put an end to MAGS, once and for all. Or he could just as easily swing the pendulum in his father's direction.

Acrimonious voices, one female, grew louder as he wheeled down the hall towards the conference room. Kastle had never felt more tired. He hadn't slept for weeks while he searched for meaning, hoping for some sign of clarity to present itself. Even as he made lists and tried to parse right from wrong, and weighed loyalty versus righteousness, his inability to choose was starting to fray at his sanity. How could he stand by and allow the trafficking to continue? He'd seen the boys and knew from experience that some of them were very sick, and that they would die if they weren't taken to hospital. His rational self always held that Markiza was evil and needed to be stopped. But the counter weight lay in his heart, and it whispered like prayers that without Markiza, all traces of himself would vanish, up and away in a puff of smoke.

Markiza. His father. Flesh and blood. If he were seeing a therapist, he would tell her that despite everything Markiza did to rape the world of its goodness, combined with depriving his son of a safe and secure childhood, in that man's presence, the senator never felt lonely. With Markiza, he shared a domain of history that would always be their inexplicable relationship.

A year and a half ago, the senator was a different man. He was like someone floating through life without an inner core and lacking the essential ingredients to form a solid identity. He had always easily and quickly morphed into whatever anyone wanted him to be. Smart college boy, enthusiastic teacher, and passionate statesman. If someone even suggested he was good at something, he would make that thing his whole life. Like the time he gave a speech at a high school commencement. A colleague and fellow teacher at his high school pointed out that Kastle was not only a dedicated teacher but also a polished speechmaker, thorough and captivating, not unlike Bill Clinton. He told him he'd make a terrific politician. Other teachers and some students chimed in, agreeing. The following semester, Kastle was running for congress. Kastle's real gift was in knowing how to fill the hollow parts of himself with smarts, looks, charm, and a good job.

That all changed the day the kingpin stormed into his office and erased layer after layer of protective veneer. Maybe Kastle had been able to fool others, but Markiza, providing lucid evidence and ruthless persuasion, proved to the senator that he, Alexei, always had and always would belong to his father, to his world. This nearly cost him his life. And he wished it had.

Afterwards, even after loosing all feeling below his waist and the ability to walk or sire children, Kastle chose to cleave to the aggressor. Ever mindful of the bloating sales of boys from abroad to US slave holders, activities that the senator supposedly lead the charge to curtail, whenever Markiza asked for his advice, he had never felt more alive and useful. That their collaboration cost the lives of Lydia and Sasha hadn't hit him as hard as he thought it would. But a month ago, something else began to undercut his loyalty.

Tadzio.

Kastle watched Markiza fawn over the young boy in a way that came neither naturally, or easily for him. Always gruff and cool, the old man began spending more and more time with Tadzio. They shared meals together and the old man bought him books, toys, DVDs. The coup de grace: he taught him how to play chess. Kastle had been a few years younger when Markiza showed him the battlefield of tactics and strategies. The board game that originated in India around the seventh century was really a game all about war and military success. Any kind of success.

Kastle didn't know how Tadzio felt about Markiza, but if he were ever to develop feelings for the old man, that would be the end. Markiza wasn't motivated by sympathy or love, he only related over common traits. If he thought Tadzio loved him, his father would break the kid's heart.

Maybe he already had.

So now, sitting in front of the two-way mirror, Kastle was stunned to see Tadzio in the sale line. An unusually beautiful woman was bending over him, acting concerned. Something about her wasn't right. While she acted interested in her purchases, her body language poured sexual invitation towards a couple of the lieutenants, who, if they weren't careful, would soon be drooling all over themselves. Markiza wasn't on his game and didn't seem to notice. He must already be regretting his choice to give up Tadzio, Kastle thought. What in the world had happened to cause the kingpin to give up his favorite boy?

Back to reality. What to do? Of course he knew Darryl, he'd seen him in casual attire more than once at MAGS. But Kastle still couldn't get over the dame. Where had they found her? Escort service? Game show host? That's whom they got to replace Lydia? Really?

Kastle had enough of watching the charade. Time to call pops.

THIRTY SEVEN

Darryl liked to watch himself from a distance, from a third person point of view.

Before any battle, his routine was to run a self-status check using an old hypnosis technique that he perfected years ago at an elite training camp. Seeing himself standing or sitting next to Aunjanue or mingling around the Russians, gave him a clear sense of his place within the room and, more importantly, enabled him to calculate his future performance based on a series of imagined scenarios. What he saw was a crocodile and it pleased him. Because Darryl King liked playing the crocodile to Aunjanue Desmoné's panther.

It was hard breaking the habit of making comparisons, but just like her predecessor before, Aunjanue was built for strength and speed. Even now, every muscle in Aunjanue's body tensed and stretched, readying to unleash mayhem at anything within striking distance. But he would always remain the ambush hunter, camouflaged and lying in wait.

The Russians watched Aunjanue's every erratic move. They knew she was entertaining and nutty but weren't quite sure if that meant she was also dangerous. They tried to stay alert even as she held them spellbound like lemmings on a Saturday morning cartoon show. While she twirled and vamped, Darryl knew that in his dark charcoal suit, with his slow-talking and slow-walking manner, he was mostly missing from the room. Trickery and deception was a magic act. Darryl was the last person they would have to worry about. He wouldn't be noticed until he was biting and tearing into flesh.

Aunjanue stood up and placed a hand on her hip. "They will do," she said. "Alan, pay up and let's go home already. I am *sooo* tired." With that she looked over at the youngest boys and gave them her prettiest smile.

Darryl got up and walked over to the gunmetal desk and set down his satchel. Markiza opened it and counted the first three stacks of bills. Bored, he signaled to the lieutenant on his right, and the man quickly emptied the contents of the satchel into a nylon gym bag.

Markiza handed the satchel back to Darryl and addressed Aunjanue. "I trust this seals the beginning of a long and fruitful relationship. We need to toast this momentous occasion with the finest Russian liquor."

Aunjanue stopped smiling. "I told you, I'm tired and want to go home. Now. And what did you mean exactly by *long and fruitful?*"

"You can tell Delgado that we are equals now, and he needs to show me respect." Markiza was sitting calmly behind the desk, but Darryl noted his eyes betrayed something else.

"What you guys do together is your business. As far as I'm concerned, this transaction is finished. Time to go." Aunjanue shrugged her shoulders high and stretched her arms all the way back, her fingertips tickling the young Russian's chest behind her. "It's been a long, long day, hasn't it, boys?" she said.

Even though Markiza hadn't moved a muscle, his whole body telegraphed exasperation. "When he wants something, the jailbird comes to me and expects results".

"You see," Markiza pointed to the boys, "I give him results. But when I needed something last year . . . a little help in establishing my business, your boyfriend Roman flicked me off like I was only a speck of dirt on his shoe."

Darryl took a few steps backwards but stopped before the chairs and remained standing. He crossed his arms giving Markiza time to pee over the hyperbole. Sure enough, the old man pushed himself away from the desk and half rose with bear hands clutching the edges. "He thinks he's better than me, doesn't he? Why? Because I sell children. Yet, he sells drugs to children. Do you see a difference? Of course not. Because there isn't one." Markiza sat back down.

Darryl watched the next scene unfold in front of him like jump cuts on a reality show. Aunjanue, as the character Felicia, refused to wipe the look of defiance off her face despite the dressing down. One of the lieutenants led the line of boys past the tall door into a corner and ordered them to sit down on the concrete floor. Still ignoring Markiza, Aunjanue began whispering silky words to the young Russian standing next her. Then Markiza's phone rang, and he sat back down to answer it but turned his chair to face the mirror. The way he absentmindedly fussed with his hair and seemed to look through the mirror instead of at his own reflection, gave Darryl pause. He soon realized that someone could be standing on the other side of the wall—because of course—it was probably a two-way mirror. He hoped Aunjanue would be able to understand what was being said on the mobile.

Aunjanue was only faking fidgety, but she sensed Markiza was actually nervous. When he answered the phone, he didn't say hello, instead, he listened intently and then asked, "What took you so long?"

She couldn't hear what the caller was saying, but Markiza's comebacks sprayed like spit. "You're positive? Roman's lawyer checks out?"

Aunjanue crept closer to the young Russian who stood halfway between the door and the desk. He grinned broadly, and took a step towards Aunjanue.

It was easier to hear the caller now. "I've seen him at the cop shop. But I don't think he's police. I sort of remember him with another man, a well-dressed client brought in for questioning. I recognize that lawyer suit."

Someone, possibly in the building, had a chance to give up Darryl but didn't. Did he really not know him, or was he stalling?

"What about the girlfriend?" Markiza asked.

"Can't be . . . not sure . . . more checking."

Markiza turned back from the mirror and stared straight at Aunjanue. He began in a low voice, "Is she who she says she is, or not? That's all I need to know."

Aunjanue giggled and turned away from Markiza towards the young Russian. But in reality she had scooted farther back towards Markiza and now could make out most of the words the caller said.

"Remember . . . followed Sans? That . . . apartment in Biscayne? My men managed to get video feed . . . after Sans' departure. She was . . . dressed in a . . . might be . . . or . . . not . . ."

"If she's a player then she's got Delgado and Treadwell fooled. Could be . . . a long-time sting. Or coincidence."

"I don't believe in coincidences," Markiza said.

"If . . . a fed . . . speaks Russian . . . careful . . . I'll get back to you." the caller said.

Markiza clicked off and turned around. Aunjanue shifted again, this time her eyes boring into Markiza's. "Okay, fine. How about that drink."

Darryl hoped Aunjanue learned something useful but her actress face didn't give up anything. He looked at his watch. Ten minutes had come and gone since the transfer of money. It didn't appear the cavalry was coming for them.

Markiza's chair scraped back from the desk. He opened a lower drawer and pulled out a bottle without a label filled with clear liquid. Next, he produced three shot glasses and lined them up. Then they all watched as Aunjanue fell to her knees and keened.

"Oh, crap. Where is it? It had better not be busted. Never know with all of these people milling around —"

"Get up Felicia. What do you think you're doing?" Darryl hissed.

"Not until I find my genuine Swaroski crystal earring. It was a present that Roman had shipped all the way from the Czech republic. I know it's not diamonds, but it still means a lot to me."

Aunjanue got on her hands and knees and crawled between Darryl's legs. She whispered, "I think they made me, but you're golden. Time for Plan Z."

Markiza stood and, as one, the guards took a step forward but stopped when Aunjanue shrieked.

"Thank god. Here it is." She got to her feet and put a large, beaded crystal hoop back in her earlobe. "Okay, men, get these youngins' out of here and let's start drinking." She looked over at Darryl who did not appear happy.

Aunjanue shrugged. "Come on, Alan. We don't want to hurt anyone's feelings. And besides, what's wrong with being a little sociable? I've got to smooth things over for Roman. He'd expect that, right?" She cast a knowing look at the young Russian she had been flirting with.

Darryl shrugged and let Aunjanue pull him back over to the desk where a drink sat waiting. As he raised the shot glass, vapors from the grain alcohol burned his nose and clouded his eyes. Markiza raised his glass and toasted. "To America, the land of the brave. The home of opportunity."

"To America." Darryl and Aunjanue spoke in unison and sipped their drinks.

"Do you ever wonder why someone like me can do business in this supposed bastion of democracy?"

"Are you going to tell us?" After carefully sipping more grain alcohol, Aunjanue used her hands to jump on top of the desk. She scooted on her knees, and swiveled around to face poker-faced Darryl, Markiza, and the mirror behind her.

Markiza looked straight at Darryl. "Because America is the new hunting ground, where a person can once more take hold of the brass ring and do something right out of proportion. And what do you suppose changed everything?" Getting only a quizzical look in response, Markiza drank his shot in one gulp. "I'll tell you. Now, and increasingly, your republic is no more." He poured another drink for himself and eyed the detectives' nearly full shot glasses with something like disappointment in his eyes.

Darryl said, "Where are you going with this?"

"Look around you. Your civil rights erode everyday. Someone is always watching you or listening to what you're saying. When you're on your smartphone or computer, another electronic device is noting what brand of toothpaste you use and what's in your bank account."

Darryl thought either the kingpin was starved for an audience with whom he could share his glorified ideas, or this was a tactical maneuver designed to trip them up.

"Are you kidding? Since when is that news? Besides it's a two-way street. When companies spy on you they find out what people actually want and need. From there, you get an immediate spike in production of better styled, easier-to-use products and services. Everyone wins," Darryl said.

"Not *two-way* street but a *two-tiered* system. You know what I'm talking about. It starts with proprietary lanes at the airport. Preference given to alumni's kids at top schools. And we all know that when it comes time to helping out natural disaster victims, that there will always be a slight tilt to the rich and the established. Oh yes, I know something about societal bias. I am a Russian."

The driver came back and nodded to Markiza. The big man snapped his fingers and the boys got up to attention and began following the driver out the door.

"The boys will get in the van and stay there until we are finished drinking." He looked at the driver. Levko will keep them company."

Something was up. Why separate them from the kids now? Unless . . . and then Darryl saw the crocodile's head bob to the surface. With the driver gone, four-to-two was a slight improvement over five-to-two.

Markiza swallowed his drink and slammed his fist into the table. Aunjanue jumped and spilled most of the contents of the shot glass on her dress.

"Where was I?" Markiza waited a beat. "Watch and see. Within ten years my business will be normal, because people at the top, people in authority with money, will demand its legitimacy."

Darryl swallowed half of his drank and said, "This isn't like the controversy surrounding the legalization of pot. Where possession of small amounts in some states has been decriminalized. We're talking about human trafficking. Buying and selling humans will always be illegal," Darryl said.

Markiza smiled at his hands and then rubbed them together. "Slavery is a lot like the flu. You can use fancy drugs to try to kill it, and you might keep it at bay for a while. But don't you know that the flu virus never dies? It fools you because it only crouches and hides; in walls, inside dresser drawers and cabinets, behind clothing and blankets. One day, when the conditions are just right, the flu returns in epidemic proportions, and everyone thinks it's some new-fangled disease. A brand new plague visited upon mankind.

"It's the same with slavery. In one century, the trade flourishes; in another it's outlawed under the guise of social injustice. Still, there are those who were never convinced that its eradication was justified and have passed on these beliefs to their heirs. And it's those future generations, reeking of family money and influence, that will revive slavery, or indenture, or whatever you want to call it, because of one thing: untold profitability."

"I mean no disrespect, but do you know how crazy that sounds?" Darryl said.

"Ah." Markiza sighed like he was really enjoying himself—hard to know if it was the subject matter or the moonshine. "Haven't you ever fantasized of owning a passel of hapless white slaves to do with anything your little heart desired? Come on, Mr. Treadwell, just picture the sweet revenge, not to mention so much mind-numbing savings in labor costs."

Darryl tried to ignore the rush of alcohol spreading across his neck and shoulders and focused on Markiza's insinuations. The kingpin's words—race baiting—were meant to inflame, that much was clear. But to what purpose? It had to be a stalling ploy to get him, the *black lawyer*, to engage and argue until whoever was behind the mirror gave Markiza a signal. Darryl had his own signal. He opened and closed the satchel several times. The case was made of the finest full grain leather on earth, and the hinges snapped and sprang like the doors of his beloved Audi.

———————————

Aunjanue talked non-stop nonsense to her young admirer and found out his name was Petyr. When she finished sipping the last drops from her nearly empty shot glass— most of which she spilled on purpose earlier—she licked the rim of the shot glass like it was an ice cream cone. Petyr never took his eyes off her. When she heard the satchel open and close several times, she turned forty-five degrees so she was facing Petyr straight on when she said, "I'm going to miss all of you young men. Too cute to believe."

Darryl downed his drink and leaned into Markiza's face. "Frankly, I'm glad this is finally over," he whispered conspiratorially.

"Explain why." Markiza poured Darryl another shot. "190 proof. You don't want to waste it."

"Oh, you can probably guess. Delgado and Felicia. I get so tired of all the drama. He can be such a miserable son of a bitch, unless, of course, he's spoiling her. And then you see what happens." Surreptitiously, Darryl slid his eyes over to Aunjanue. Markiza shook his head slightly. "But I actually think this went pretty well. Felicia's usually a lot fussier."

Aunjanue inched across the desk until she was close enough to poke Petyr's thigh with the heel of her shoe. Then she kicked it off and the two of them chuckled as it thudded to the floor. She kept wiggling her way across the desk and let her other shoe fall. Even though she wasn't facing the kingpin, only vapors separated her seat from Markiza's hand, and her shoulder—if she leaned in a bit—was close enough to brush his cheek. Never taking her eyes off the young Russian, Aunjanue swung her left arm and the empty shot glass back towards Markiza. He poured and she waited until she heard him set the bottle down. She giggled as she raised her hand up shakily; if she wasn't careful the entire drink might land in the kingpin's face. Which is what happened when she hurled the shot glass directly into Markiza's eyes.

An iron-fisted grip grabbed Aunjanue's hand and smashed her fingers into the desk. And, again. Finally, the iron fist lifted high and plunged down into her bruised fingers like a dislocated scaffold hurling its way down to earth. But the fist made contact with the shot glass instead. Because Aunjanue snatched her hand away just in time, ignoring the searing pain radiating up her arm all the way into her neck.

Before anyone else could react, before Markiza could swear or put his hands to his face, or cover his bleeding hand, before any lieutenant could move to help him and stop her, Aunjanue was off the desk. She twisted around so fast that when her good hand reached inside the desk drawer and pulled out a slim Walther PPS, Markiza's hands were already up over his head.

Aunjanue felt rather than saw Darryl drop the satchel and slip the last of its contents into his pants pocket. He punched their erstwhile driver and only remaining guard on Markiza's right side hard in the solar plexus. The man moaned as he crumpled to floor and, then, as if for good measure, he hit his head on the metal caster of Markiza's chair. Behind the desk now and crouched on the floor, Darryl lifted a semi-automatic .45 out of the ankle strap and unsnapped a second one from the Russian's shoulder holster. He slipped that gun inside his suit pocket. Out of the other suit pocket, he pulled out a long plastic restraint and using his free hand and the help of his knee, manacled the Russian's hands in front of him quickly. He threw down several more sets of plastic restraints on the desk and grabbed Markiza's cell.

Aunjanue's voice, once syrupy and flirtatious, changed into intimidating Russian as she ordered the former apple of her attention—a now terrified Petyr—to remove his friend's gun and place it on the table. She reached for it, another Walther, but this one was ancient, from another century.

Something was off. Petyr sat on the floor staring at his feet. His face seesawed wildly between tortured disbelief and fierce anger. And something else. Aunjanue suspected he felt shame and fear. She hoped he would not break down and do the unthinkable. Start crying in front of the other Russians. She'd have to give him something to do.

Aunjanue tossed him three long plastic ties and said to cinch the other man's hands and feet. She added that when he was done tying up his friend to sit down and bind his own feet. Petyr did everything he was told. His eyes flickering to his feet every few seconds.

Aunjanue had a gun to Markiza's head and another one trained on the young goons, but her body was sandwiched between the desk and the kingpin's marble shoulders. If he wanted to she knew, he could buck, grab her around the waist, and break her spine. She might or might not get a shot off.

Aunjanue sneaked a look over at Darryl and felt relief. He also had a gun bored into Markiza's head. Slowly she moved away from the desk. While apologizing profusely, the guard on the floor was using his manacled hands to cinch Markiza's ankle to a desk leg. Darryl indicated two ties. Though Darryl didn't speak a word of Russian, what he could do with hand signals rivaled the efforts of an award-winning animal trainer. She only had time for one reverie, and in it she beamed gratitude and admiration towards Darryl. If Markiza were going to chase them, he would have to do it pulling a metal desk behind him.

In one deft move, Aunjanue used the last restraint to handcuff Petyr's hands. Even as her left hand grew in size from swelling, the pain was subsiding and the fingers felt almost numb.

Darryl slipped behind Aunjanue, gun out and cocked. He opened the door slowly and looked both ways. "I thought I heard something earlier, but the corridor's empty now."

Markiza scraped his chair and made to get up. So far the plastic handcuffs held, but he was starting to struggle against them. The desk jumped and Aunjanue shot him a look.

"You fucking cursed swine whore. Think you're smart, that you'll get away? Stupid bitch."

Darryl grabbed Aunjanue's arm, but she held fast, her gun trained on Markiza's face.

"You want it so bad, don't you? You want to shoot me between the eyes—here in front of my men. Oooh – you can almost feel the blood in your mouth. Tastes fantastic, doesn't it, bitch? But your kind never has the guts to go all the way, do you? Prove me wrong. Come on." The leer on Markiza's face hypnotized Aunjanue. It would feel so sweet, a killshot between the eyes. Hot damn.

"Aunj, I know what you're thinking. No, let's go." Darryl snarled.

Markiza sniggered. "So, you think you can get out of here, stupid cows. There is no way out. Want to know why?"

The rapture subsiding, Aunjanue lowered her gun slightly and nodded briskly.

"First, just like when you came in, every entrance is reinforced with a second, metal door. My men have the codes and you'll need two of them to open any door."

Aunjanue's eyes scanned the room.

"No, not them. I wouldn't trust these simpletons with a key to the lavatory. Second, out there, where you are imagining freedom, you will meet my men. My army. They're already coming for you. And when they find you, they will obliterate your bodies into tiny little shards. Picture yourself in a thousand pieces spread across some slab at the morgue for your loved ones to identify."

"Listen pig, we have our own army," Aunjanue said weakly, as she backed out.

For the first time that night, Markiza laughed out loud and the desk jumped again.

Aunjanue took another step backwards towards the door; she only had a few feet before she would clear it. She kept one gun trained at the Russians on the floor in front of her and the other on Markiza. Right behind her Darryl had opened the door wide open and waited for her to pass. When she was all the way through, instead of turning to follow, Darryl slammed into the door and fell. The shot had been ear splitting.

Petyr, still sitting on the floor, with both feet and hands manacled in front of him, had leaned over and pulled his gun out of an ankle holster. The bullet hit Darryl in the thigh, and his .45 clattered to the floor. Aunjanue had been wrong. Wrong twice. Petyr had been armed, and it wasn't fear or shame on the young guard's face but solid gold determination.

Right before the bullet hit its target, as soon as she heard the hammer pull back, Aunjanue fell to her knees and emptied three rounds into the shooter. She sprang up, picked up the fallen gun, and pushed Darryl into the hall. Quickly she shut and bolted the door. The walls began to shake as Markiza started a volley of hoisting the desk up and letting it crash down onto the concrete floor. Up and down.

In the hall, Darryl seemed to recover slightly and then stumbled against the wall. Blood was a geyser spurting from a hole in the dress pants. The bullet had hit an artery and unless she did something to stop the hemorrhaging, Darryl would bleed out in minutes. Sadly, all Aunjanue remembered about tourniquets was that if you tied them too tight, the limb would become starved of blood and oxygen, and that would result in gangrene and amputation.

She examined her handy-work. In less than a minute, Aunjanue had removed Darryl's jacket and shirt, the latter she had torn into long strings and tied two of them below the bullet wound. The leg had mostly stopped bleeding but Darryl looked bad. She thought for a minute she saw his eyes roll into back of his head. Either it was the pain or shock was setting in. They had to get moving; his leg and their survival depended on it. It was clear no one was coming for them.

Aunjanue tried the phone, but it was locked and useless.

Aunjanue tried to help Darryl walk by putting her arm around his shoulder and waist. She began propelling him forwards, but soon Darryl stopped. She thought he was tired but he started pushing her away.

From inside the suit jacket and without saying a word, Darryl pulled a .45. He held it awkwardly in his right hand and his breath was ragged and uneven, but again he tried to push her off with his elbow.

Aunjanue pushed back. "Give me your gun, you're going to drop it."

Darryl didn't move and didn't release the gun. "No."

"This is no time for heroics. You're useless right now, and you know I'm a better shot."

Maybe it was because Markiza had already unnerved her, but when Darryl finally spoke, the words sucker-punched her brain and made her hurt all over.

"It's you, isn't it?" The .45 semi-automatic was pointed at her chest.

THIRTY EIGHT

"Are you nuts? Get that out of my face," Aunjanue said.

"You know I'm a better shot?" Darryl didn't move. "How would I know that? Huh?"

Aunjanue glared at him. "It's an expression, all right? Look at you. At this moment, I am a better shot," she said.

"I figure one way or the other, it's you. You're either Lydia, or you're the mole. If you're Lydia, I'm only royally pissed. If you're the mole, I'm not giving you anything."

"Listen to me, crazy man. How long do you figure before Markiza, who's built like the Titanic, picks up the desk and hurls it into the mirror, breaks through the wall and comes after us? We never bothered to check the room; there could be an arsenal in there. Or more phones. Right now we have to get to the van and make the only phone we have, work."

She took a couple steps back, rolled her eyes, and studied her shoes. "But I promise you, super sleuth, we'll continue this little chit-chat later." All traces of the Minnesota accent, gone.

"No, that doesn't take you off the hook. I saw you flirt and tease that man, only a boy, really. Petyr. Not much older than some of the captives you say you want to save. And then a few minutes later, you wipe him out like he's nothing."

"Oh, no you didn't. Are you seriously questioning what I did back there? That boy shot my partner, my best friend. So I killed his ass.

"Don't stand there and act like you wouldn't have done the same for me. If I'm wrong about you, then maybe I should shoot you in the other leg." And then she raised her gun to his gun.

Aunjanue was no longer Aunjanue. She was Lydia again and the cat was out of the bag, but the detective had wanted an apology and would have settled for anything, even a shrug. Instead, Darryl handed over his gun and started walking using the wall as a brace. A couple of times he had looked at her with boiling anger in his eyes. Tough, she thought, as she not so gently nudged him forward. But she slipped the .45 back into his suit coat and cleared her throat.

"You're not mad because I shot that kid. I'm warning you, whatever you think you know, or are feeling, save it, because our lives depend on it."

They separated and walked sideways on either side of a narrow hall lit by overhead fluorescent lights that buzzed like insects. It was an eerie echo chamber that made their light footsteps clip clop like horse's hooves. They made their way quickly down the hall until they ran into a T. Before either of them could decide which way to turn, they heard it. Not clip clops, but the unmistakable stampede of Markiza's army.

Aunjanue strode back, pulling Darryl to her side. She tried doors, but they were all either locked or painted shut. Finally they found a shallow recess in the wall and stepped into it. Fifteen seconds later and just before the Russians could turn the corner, Aunjanue fired two shots into the concrete floor. All movement stopped and the only remaining sounds were the ringing and rattling inside everyone's brains.

A voice, affected like a cartoon villain's—except for the broken English—sounded an ultimatum. "You are surrounded. Drop your weapons, put your hands up over your heads, and step out. Now."

"Why don't you step out, you slimy cockroach," Aunjanue barked back in quick and precise Russian.

Another voice, older, sounding concerned and replying in Russian, said, "No one has to get hurt; show your hands and we will take you safely back to Markiza."

As if hearing his name being taken in vain, a full 500 yards away, the screaming began anew, this time accompanied by glass shattering. Aunjanue imagined Markiza getting enough purchase to take out the two-way mirror with his head. She hoped Markiza would pass out and have a stroke at the same time. But he never stopped screaming and the walls continued to shake with the bashing of the desk. Oh my fucking word, he's coming after us with a desk tied to him, she realized.

The Russian voice continued, "You're trapped. We have a regiment coming in from the other direction. In moments, you will literally be surrounded on all sides."

"Before you take us out, many of you will die first because we have two shooters and four guns."

The older man, sounding less concerned now, said, "One shooter, so I hope you're ambidextrous. Oh, wait, one of your hands is hurt and bleeding."

Aunjanue looked down at her hand, puffing up like purple marshmallow and it was bleeding. She hadn't felt a thing. She could still shoot with that hand. Sort of. Two guns against an army. And a very upset Markiza.

"How could you know that? There was no camera in the room."

"No. But if you look carefully, you will find them in the halls. It seems your friend needs medical attention. Come on out, throw down your guns, and we'll get him to a doctor."

Lydia shot four rounds into the walls. She lowered her gun and watched Darryl pull out the .45. His hand was shaking, so was his whole body. *Please don't die on me.*

"I'm sorry. I was wrong. You were right. I'm an idiot," Darryl said.

"Shh. Save your strength. We need a diversion strategy. Why don't I—"

"I've always loved you. It hurt so much, killed me sometimes. You know I was never a better person than when your face was the last thing I saw at night and the first thing I saw smiling in the morning. You were always the one, baby."

"Look, I think I can stall them a bit, and you know our guys have to get here sooner or later. So when I—"

"Always the optimist. Okay, I'll play, but just in case I don't make it and our guys are late, I need to tell you that my best days were with you. I was crazy to let you go." He grabbed her shoulder and sank his head into her neck. "Let's just hope they do what Markzia said. Shoot us up like dogs. Otherwise, the alternative—"

"Jesus, Darryl."

The voice around the corner sounded angry now. "You've had enough time, you give us no choice."

Lydia picked off the first two lieutenants, and the next two barely dodged getting hit before retreating around the corner. She calculated they had less than a minute before she and Darryl would be fired upon from both directions. She was more worried about the new threat coming from Markiza's direction. Now that he was on the move, the cacophony was multiplying. First a scream, then the sounds of scraping and dragging. The relentless noise behind them unnerved her. Darryl didn't seem to notice and he could no longer hold himself upright; his feet and legs were slipping out of the recess. Before that could happen, he shot a few rounds in the direction of Markiza's shrill advance. *We are going to die here.*

Two more Russians rushed the corridor and Lydia fired, but her bullets did not reach them because at that moment Darryl slumped heavily into her and the shots went wild. Even though she missed her targets, the Russians fell flat to the ground.

She retreated pulling Darryl back into the wall recess. Aunjanue sneaked a look at the space separating the hallways. The sound and the muzzle flash were dead giveaways. Someone was firing a sub-machine gun at the Russians. After what seemed like minutes but could only have been seconds, silence fell over the corridors.

Even Markiza fell silent.

"What the fresh hell? Don't tell me that was your diversion?" Darryl gave up and sank to the ground where he sat staring at the open corridor.

"Not my diversion," Aunjanue mouthed.

Coughing and sputtering replaced the silence. The air throbbed with pain. It seemed that the shooter meant more to intimidate than to kill outright. And then a brand new vibration began to echo in the distance. The closer it got, the more it sounded to Lydia like leather peeling away from a slick floor. Rolling. Something was rolling towards them.

Darryl heard it, too. "What is that?" he asked.

Lydia smiled. "It's my dream." She looked at him with longing. "Call me crazy, but I've been having this recurring dream where Sasha and I wander in and out of halls just like these, trying to find something or someone. And a way out. We hear creaking and rolling noises but for some reason, we always to choose to go in the opposite direction. Of course, when I wake up, I look back and we're still in that hall. This hall. I think the dream finally caught up with me."

"You might be dreaming and I might be hallucinating, but isn't that Senator Kastle coming towards us?"

THIRTY NINE

Lydia reloaded one .45 and for good measure dug out the ancient Walther PP from Darryl's jacket pocket. It was lighter and easier to hold and aim with her bad hand. When Kastle turned the corner, she stepped out into the hall with both guns aimed at him. The Uzi lay on his lap; the senator's hands were clasped around a cell phone.

"Friend or foe?" She asked.

"Beats me, I've never really known. But be assured that at this moment, I want to help you get out of here in one piece."

Darryl pulled himself up. "Christ on a cracker! First you, Lydia. Now, the senator. What is this? Dr. Jekyll, Mr. Hyde day? No one could make this shit up."

Kastle looked pained. "Lydia?" He scanned every feature on her face. "Really? Fantastic. Darryl's right. You and I are definitely in a dead heat for top honors in deception."

Lydia heard Markiza say something, it sounded like son, or, my only son. The voice was coming from a cell phone next to the Uzi. Of course, they had been in communication the whole time. Lydia looked at the cell they took from the room. Still inoperable, Markiza must have disabled it from another device. She sniffed and looked around. Something was different, no more scraping. Oh, no. The Russian must have lost the desk. *Where was he?*

Kastle's head snapped up, his eyes glowed with anticipation, and like a burned out light, closed and lost their sparkle. The cell phone clattered to the concrete floor.

"So that's why you shot up the hallway? You're here to deliver us to Markiza personally?" Lydia knew they were done for and the game was almost over. So what. She still had guns and bullets and would shoot until they were gone.

"By the way, there was never a contest, Lex Kastle. Just a bunch of scared little boys who didn't know they were being shipped to America to work as slaves. I thought we were supposed to be on the same side. What happened to you, *Senator*?" Lydia said.

Darryl grabbed her leg. "Hey, I think Kastle's the mole."

"Shut up, Darryl. Just lapse into a coma or something," Lydia hissed.

"See how she gets, when you get her mad," Darryl said.

"Spill, Kastle, or I'm going to blow you away, right here. Sasha died because of you. Tell me, were you dirty right from the start? Even back when you taught high school? All those young kids, is that where you got the idea?"

"Be careful, detective. You aren't equipped to judge. Only someone who grew up like me, or my father, can do that."

Darryl stopped muttering and for an instant Lydia had turned into stone. She was aware of a steady slogging across the concrete floor. But she had to know this first.

"*Your father?*" Lydia pulled the hammer back.

Kastle snorted, "If you couldn't shoot Markiza, you won't shoot me."

"It was him, Lyd. He was behind the mirror in the hall." Darryl said. Lydia lowered the gun.

Kastle looked down and began fingering the Uzi. "Ours is a long and grotesque history. I can't expect you to understand all that inherited blood and family. There was a time when I mistakenly thought I had a choice. It was just an illusion though, along with so many hopes and ideals. When your complete survival depends on identity, what you will do in life becomes predetermined.

"I never had a choice because I was never anyone else but who I am. Who I always will be. The one and only son of Markiza."

"Everyone has a choice. Even craven pieces of dog-meat like you. Markiza is a clinical psychopath, but you . . . you didn't inherit anything; you chose this lifestyle free and clear. Your father might be evil, but you're a cesspool-grade, putrid varmint."

"I'm not going to waste time arguing with you. Your mind is made up, and you'll never be able to see that I might have valid reasons for the things I've done. So, how about we get going."

The senator leaned over and picked up his cell phone and then moved his wheel chair ahead of Lydia and Darryl. He stopped suddenly. With his back to them, he said, "For what it's worth, Lydia, I'm glad you made it out of the canyon. And I swear, no one meant for Sasha to die. Markiza has always regretted that. I think something went out of him afterwards because he stopped paying attention. He's losing it, you know. I thought he was just old. But now I suspect it's because he's tired."

"Not even an iota interested in your family problems, comprende? But I would like to know why you're supposedly helping us now, and how can we be sure you won't change your mind again?"

Kastle turned his wheelchair slightly and craned his head towards Lydia. "I'll show you."

Lydia helped Darryl to his feet and followed Kastle to one of the locked doors she had encountered earlier. Again, she wondered where Markiza was, and why he wasn't yelling or at least talking into the cell phone. But then, he would be listening.

Kastle used a passkey, punched in a few numbers, and slid the metal panel to the side. Aunjanue decided that being the son of the kingpin afforded you the use of one code instead of two. Inside, lay a short, dark, narrow corridor. At the end of the corridor stood a red door. When the senator opened it, the stench was unmistakable. Lydia breathed in sweet, sticky sweat—the fear of the young.

Kastle rolled back and gave Lydia room. She braced for what she would find and stepped into the room.

The boys sat on the floor in ten perfect lines; she counted seventy in total. The boys would have been perfect, too, had it not been for their tear-stained dirty faces and swollen bellies. Lydia took another step. More smells. More than one boy had peed on himself, and now the urine was wicking up their clothing. At the sight of Lydia, their expressions changed slowly from unaffected to only slightly puzzled. They were nearly catatonic with hunger and illness. Pictures of prison-torture victims crossed her eyes and she felt woozy. She walked back down the corridor and stopped at Kastle's wheelchair.

"While I was trying figure out what to do, whether to give you up to Markiza or fight for you, I bided my time by looking inside these locked rooms. I just found them," Kastle said.

"We used to rationalize that we were giving starving Russian orphans another chance at a life. And perhaps we were. You know, a warm comfortable bed to sleep in at night, three squares, education, and regular baths. Eventually, these boys would make it out of servitude, well . . . most would anyway, and begin to lead normal, productive lives. But . . ." Kastle drew a circle with his finger, "Markiza doesn't even know this room exits, or that half the boys in here have fever. My father used to pride himself in serving up perfect, healthy merchandize. Recently, though, he's left the day-to-day operations to idiots because he no longer gives a shit."

"Kastle, Markiza's close. Aren't you worried that he'll come down here and kill you for helping us?" Darryl asked.

Kastle bristled. "You know nothing about us. That man wouldn't harm one hair on my head. Believe me."

"What about us? What's he going to do to us?" Lydia asked.

"Ah, that. Probably just rough you up a little. He has to save face, understand. But, nothing I won't be able to control."

Lydia was left with no choice but to suspend doubt and trust in Kastle's words, because in the next instant she felt rather than heard, the steps behind her. When the kingpin was close enough so that his soured breath radiated heat on her neck, Lydia held her own breath and the guns tight.

How in the world does a 300-pound man, as hard as steel, walk soundlessly through an echo chamber? But that's exactly what Markiza had done. She supposed it helped that he'd first unshackled himself from the desk. Markiza had floated above them like an angel, skipping from pillowy cloud to pillowy cloud. Maybe it was what Kastle said about his father being inattentive and tired. Perhaps the old man was already a goner—his persona—a ghostly doppelganger. She imagined a decrepit villain slogging through a fugue state, searching but never finding his true lost home. Hell.

Very slowly she turned around and stared at the giant. Markiza appeared to be in an altered state. His eyes were glazed over and the hand that gripped yet another Uzi, shook. For a second, Lydia thought about complementing Markiza's stealthiness when she caught site of his bleeding ankle. Instead, she quipped, "Let me guess, the desk looks a lot worse than you do."

"You." Markiza abruptly came to and clamped a hand over Lydia's throat. He began lifting her up by the neck. She knew she could pass out any second and jammed the .45 into Markiza's groin and cocked the hammer.

"That's not the deal. Put it down right now, or I'll kill you, Lydia," Kastle barked.

"Okay."

"Papa, let her go or I'll shoot you in the balls myself."

Markiza wasn't interested in Lydia; she didn't exist. When he released Lydia, she fell to her knees. While Lydia coughed and rubbed her neck, the kingpin set down his submachine gun on top of Kastle's, and sniffed the air as he walked into the room full of boys. He told them to stand up. They obeyed, and Markiza began examining their faces and arms. Then he asked them to take off their shirts and turn all the way around.

When he walked out, Markiza's eyes pleaded with the man in the wheel chair.

"What's wrong with them? Who did this to these boys?" The Russian's words were at once guttural and unsure. "I always took pride in my investments, all healthy, all strong children. This isn't right, Alexei."

"It's over, papa. There's nothing left for us here. You see that, don't you?" Kastle implored.

"We'll go to prison. We'll die in prison," Markiza said.

"Prison's been our home since I can remember, so it's fitting that we die there too."

"Why, Alexei? Why now?"

"You know. You don't want to do this any more. You've lost your purpose. There's no one left to wreak vengeance on because the enemies, all of your old ghosts, they're gone. I've accepted it, you will have to also."

Markiza rallied. "I have an idea. We'll let these good people go." He turned back to look at Lydia and Darryl scowling slightly. "We won't hurt anyone else, and we'll leave the boys. I have money stashed away. We can go now and start fresh somewhere else. I can't bear to lose you again."

"I wish we could. I really do. But it's too late. Who knows, maybe with good behavior—one day—we can be bunkmates."

"No, I think—"

"Listen to your son, it's over. Don't you hear it?" Darryl was coherent and smiling.

Aunjanue's head snapped to her partner. "What?"

"You were right, Lyd. Better late than never," Darryl said.

Lydia strained to hear inchoate shouting and pounding spilling in through the concrete from the outside. Someone spoke, but the words were garbled. A metal ram began breaching the exterior. The building shook. Shock waves pulsated from under the floor. But training and too many disappointments made Lydia doubtful. "Darryl, what if they're not ours?"

Darryl started to speak but could only choke back laughter. The last thing he did was to put up his hands over his head before he slumped back down to the floor for the last time. "If that were true, it would mean Andy went AWOL. Because I'd recognize that obnoxious, high-pitched squawk anywhere."

Oh, no. This can't be happening, she thought.

One by one, orbiting images settled on the front steps of her thought processes, and, suddenly, Lydia became gripped with terror for the first time that night. When men dressed in riot gear, all looking like Darth Vaders came for them, she knew those poor boys would die of fright.

Lydia closed her eyes and watched the night scene outdoors. She'd been through it before. First, she saw a 900-watt Telescopic Tower turning the bleak, dark parking lot into testosteroned-blazing daylight. Next, a picture of a half dozen heavily armored SWAT vehicles lined up across her field of vision. From inside those vehicles, dozens of police equipped with assault rifles, breaching shotguns and handguns, scrambled out and advanced on the warehouse. But when she saw an image of a single soldier outfitted with body armor, ballistic shield, military helmet, and black facemask, moving towards a lone van sitting on the far side of the building, her stomach clenched because she also saw also saw Tadzio's innocent face staring back.

Lydia started down the hall but a strong hand seized her around the waist. She turned around and slapped Markiza across the face. As she took off down the hall, she yelled, "Take care of Darryl, Kastle."

Lydia ran towards the T in the hallway, swept past injured and dying Russian lieutenants, and scrambled out a shattered concrete opening with her hands up, yelling, FBI! When she was sure no one was going to shoot her, she ran to the side of the parking lot and stopped. A SWAT team member was already there, pulling the last of the boys out of the van. He had taken his face shield off and was smiling at them. But Lydia was crying so hard, she almost couldn't make out Tadzio. She swiped at her eyes until she focused on a short, dark-haired boy corralling and patting the others. When he saw Lydia, Tadzio broke away and ran to meet her outstretched arms. Then he motioned for the others to follow. Lydia cried and hiccupped and patted and kissed each bewildered boy. To Tadzio, she whispered, *"Пойдем домой."*

"Let's go home."

FORTY

Liset was standing next to the nurse's station looking down at her smartphone when Darryl spotted her. This time she was dressed in a Prada suit and wore her signature pearls, looking like the vision she truly was. Darryl figured it was easier to look classy once you knew for certain that your husband, the love of your life, was actually going to live. Liset barely had time to look up when Darryl dropped his cane and grabbed her around the shoulders. He limped and stumbled and finally let go when Liset screeched and begged, "Let go, I'm an old woman with bad joints."

Darryl laughed and kissed both of Liset's hands and then her cheeks. He stepped back and picked up the cane.

"Damn, I just heard Carlos is going to be as good as new. Nothing could be better."

"Darryl, sweetheart, he's been waiting for you. Every few minutes he cries to me: 'Darryl here yet? Go see if Darryl came. Did Darryl call?' Sometimes I think he loves you more than me."

"Oh man, I didn't bring anything. Just drove as fast as I could when Marla called and said he was awake and seeing people."

"You're the gift, *loco*. And you are lucky to be alive as well. I heard if it weren't for Lydia, you might not have made it." Darryl took a deep breath and looked away. "Go down the hall, last door on the right. I know it's going to be a love fest for the two of you but please, don't stay too long. Remember he's only been conscious for a few hours."

The rent-a-cop barricading the door to the room was young and beefy. After scrutinizing Darryl's ID and looking at his own list of acceptable guests, he nodded and got out of Darryl's way, barely.

A television set with Rachael Ray demonstrating a black bean salsa recipe was turned up high. Several chairs draped with books, boxes, and pillows angled helter-skelter made for a second barricade. Vases of assorted sizes and shapes filled with very tall tropical flowers sat on the windowsill and blocked out most of the light. Darryl walked gingerly across a floor littered with balloons, stuffed animals, and potted plants. He wondered why Sans wasn't fussing about the mess given how meticulous his home and office usually were.

Sans' head was swathed in a white, gauzy bandage, IV tubes hung like long, skinny straws from both arms releasing saline, nutrients, and morphine. Machines ticked and clicked while stalking every vital movement of the captain's bodily functions. The place sounded and smelled like an overworked medical factory. Another thing that in another lifetime, his boss would have had little tolerance for. But Sans' smiling face explained everything. He'd made it after all and, from now, life would brim on a grand scale.

The man in the hospital bed actually looked quite dapper sitting up and sucking on a lemon stick. Instead of the usual hospital gown, the captain wore a red-flannel, two-piece pajama set. Liset's handiwork no doubt. When she could finally dress up again, so would her husband of forty years. Darryl could just barely make out little black and white umbrellas and Tropicana dancers sewn across his chest.

"You ever see *Abbot and Costello Meet the Mummy*, 1955? Cuz . . ." Darryl swept his arm around the room, "we could do a remake right here. Maybe get for-real salsa dancers from Little Havana to spice it up."

"Come over here and give us a kiss."

Darryl set down his cane and dragged the only uncluttered chair, placing it close to Sans' bed.

"You know, if they do decide to make a movie about your near death-experience, I want Lenny Kravitz to play me because he's almost as good-looking."

"What are you talking about?" Sans asked.

"You can't turn on the radio or TV without your ugly mug popping up, and some hot tamale giving a blow-by-blow of the events of your last five days. Even more coverage now that Markiza's been arrested. I'm pretty sure the analytics will bear me out: right now, you and the unit are more popular than Rihanna and Adele combined."

"Oh, that. Why do you think I'm scoping out the food network? I figure now that I'm famous they will want me to weigh in on the proper ways of making bean salsa. I can help them with that."

Sans turned the volume to mute and looked serious. "Darryl, I can't express how proud I am of you and Lydia and the team. Thanks to all four of you, we just cracked the biggest people-trafficking case in South Florida, the nation, maybe the world. And I just got word that Markiza is spilling over like Niagara Falls. I know he's got an agenda, but that's okay with me. We got leads on trafficking pipelines, offshore accounts, and names of dozens of missing kids and contacts for their families. We're making history, kid."

"Captain, I wish you could have seen Markiza when we shackled him. Actually, it was a little disappointing because he was kind of catatonic-acting after Kastle put the kibosh on everything. Makes you wonder who was really in charge," Darryl said.

"What I can't get over is that little boy. Did you know that in the end he was the one that made sure the kids got dressed and fed? Tadzio watched over them when no one else would or could. And those drawings. Have you seen them—I have them on my phone here." Sans pointed to his cell on a stand next to the bed. "His graphical images of street signs and buildings are what led the feds to the warehouse. But they didn't know what to do until Andy, Marla, and SWAT arrived. All in all, that was a very smart and productive day!"

"For me, the biggest surprise was Kastle. What do you suppose will happen to him now?" Darryl asked.

"He stopped Markiza. That will go a long way at his trial." Sans said.

"It's hard to wrap my head around their family ties. Even after years of separation, Kastle still chose his father and his lifestyle. I just don't get it."

"Don't try to judge them or their situation by anything you were taught at the academy. Markiza and his cohorts endured and survived and eventually became the monsters that raised them. And I don't mean parents but the society itself, which was and in some ways still is an oppressive, demented government."

"But why do you suppose Kastle turned on his father in the end?" Darryl said.

"I could be out in left field here, and don't go posting this on Facebook or Twitter, but I think he did it to save the old man's life."

"Well, I promised the indomitable Liset that I wouldn't stay too long. Guess I'll just head back to the station," Darryl rose from his chair.

"I don't think so."

"Captain?"

"As of now you are on an indefinite leave from police duties. You can go to the station, but I gave strict orders that you will have to turn in your gun and ID when you get there," Sans said without blinking.

"What are you talking about? Sans?"

"I'm citing you with conduct most unbecoming of a police. Until you rectify such matters or make retributions, you will not continue to serve at my pleasure."

"Was it really time for you to come out of the coma? Because at this moment you sound whacked. And for your information, captain, just before I got here, The Citizens for a Free and Democratic Russia called saying I had just received their highest award for bravery, which includes a stipend of ten thousand dollars. All I have to do is go to Russia and speak at some award ceremony. And more commendations are forthcoming, one from the governor and I think the president too."

"Good, go work for them."

Darryl stood and grabbed his cane. He moved unsteadily and asked, "What the hell did I do wrong?"

"You haven't returned any of Lydia's calls."

Darryl absorbed the shock and betrayal in silence.

"Captain, that's not your concern. No one's business but ours."

"Have it your way." Sans reached for the remote and turned up the volume just as Rachael Ray began pouring liquid into a saucepan. The crackling and sizzling drowned out any further conversation between them.

———————

Darryl wanted to punch a hole in the wall or yell at the orderlies, but he settled for going to the lunchroom where he could collect his thoughts in peace. He couldn't eat or drink so he took a seat at an empty table, set down his walking cane, and rested his injured leg on a chair. He closed his eyes and leaned his head back. A few minutes later, he felt a hand on his shoulder.

Andy was grinning that idiot grin he had inherited from sobriety. "So, how's it going bro?"

Darryl sat up, pulled his leg down, and shrugged Andy's hand away. "I would strongly advise against touching me." Darryl thought, please don't do as I ask so I have a reason to punch your lights out, *jerk*. Finally! Here stood an easy outlet for his anger and confusion.

But Andy did withdraw his hand and the easy smile.

"It was always you. Never me or anyone else," Andy said.

"Excuse me?"

"When Lydia first came to the unit we both got crushes on her. But you had it bad. Everyday you brought her a fancy coffee. Each one with more whipped cream and a different flavor than the day before."

"So?"

"When I look back, I think Lydia fell in love the minute she laid eyes on you. But you lost your nerve and dumped her. I guess that was easier to do than trying to work out some daddy issues."

Darryl shot up, fists clenched. "You don't know what you're saying." Bearing weight on his leg was excruciating painful and Darryl slumped back into the chair keeping his head down so Andy would not see his tortured face.

Andy backed up pretending to be intimidated. "That's when she came to me and cried on my shoulder, saying how you didn't believe it would work because she was white and you were black. But we both knew that was only an excuse for your fear of intimacy. Now she's black and you dumped her again."

Darryl unclenched his hands and spread them over the small table. He looked up. "Lydia is not black."

"Black or white, you've been in love with the same woman for years."

FORTY ONE

The room vibrated like someone was running a vacuum cleaner next door. Lydia smiled at the idea of an inmate vacuuming his own concrete floor. Maybe a worker had been jack hammering in the basement earlier, and that activity was still sending micro explosions through the steel framework of the prison. No, Lydia thought. There is no such thing as silence. Every empty room quivers with sound waves, the stuff of life.

Real sounds in the distance. Sharp clicks followed by sucking noises. When he rolled through the doors, Lydia wasn't surprised to see that the senator's hands were cuffed. They all knew what that man could do with an assault rifle.

Kastle's appearance clashed with the room. Painted a warm pink, the walls were meant to calm, to offer a refuge from the usual stirrings of violence and mayhem the psychopathic cons in Dade Correctional Institution were likely to exhibit. Somehow, the orange jumpsuit erased all of the well-intentioned peace, love, and understanding. Instantly, Lydia felt stirrings of misgiving and irritation. Why had she come? And then the senator reminded her.

Kastle's eyes were predatorily narrowed and the corners of his mouth curved down. She had never seen him angry before.

Lydia leaned back in her chair and coolly met his stare. "What? Is it my deodorant?"

"How dare you? Spreading those lies in the media about Markiza. You actually think my father ran over me and then left me to die? That I'm in a wheel chair because of him?"

"Relax, Lex. I want to hear your side. It's important to me."

"Why, so you can tie up some loose ends and finish the paperwork. Or is it to have your curiosity sated? My life is more than a curiosity."

Life around them ceased to even murmur as the room fell completely silent, as if it had died. Lydia made it come back to life. "Give it up, you want to tell me."

Kastle looked everywhere, at the ceiling, the floor, the guard, everywhere but at Lydia, as he began his story.

"A little more than a year ago, Markiza made an appointment to see me. Using a false name, he claimed to be a crew captain with information about smuggled children. I recognized him as soon as he walked through the door. I called him a dirty trafficker and a murderer. I accused him of killing my mother, at least causing her to die prematurely of stress and despondency. She actually died of cancer, but I blamed him."

"He yelled back, told me to shut up. Markiza said he was glad she was dead, but sorry he hadn't tortured her first because of what she had done to him and me."

"Marina?" Lydia prompted.

"I had blocked out the bad things, and I still do sometimes. Marina was after all, my mother, the one who managed to smuggle me out of Russia. In America, I got a fresh start; I could be anything I wanted. I could be safe and happy." Kastle's features softened as he let his eyes meet Lydia's. "You see, you were fooled by me, but I was fooled by the whole world. At least until that moment, when my father reminded me of what really happened when my mother ran off with me. Of whom I was and always would be."

"Tell me about Russia," Lydia said.

"My mother was born into one of the richest families in Russia. Her father not only owned or had ties to major Asian and European oil pipelines, but once, he had also held the post of mayor of St. Petersburg. That man controlled banks, politics, but sadly, not his daughter. Rich wasn't good enough for her. She wanted adventure, danger, and above all, Marina craved power. When she was nineteen, under the pretense of trying to help community, Marina joined a volunteer group that taught literacy in prisons. The minute she met Markiza, she started plotting her new career. Markiza was young, horny, and believed her when she told him that with her connections and his ambitions, they could rule the world. She actually had said that. He actually believed it.

"You have to remember, my father was only a small-time thug back then. A couple of robberies, some opium distribution in the Balkans—small potatoes. It was her idea to bomb the Kremlin, by the way.

"When that literally blew up in his face, Marina suggested they get into trafficking. He thought she meant drugs. But she insisted on selling children. He told me he declined at first because the idea of sex slavery, prostitution of young girls disgusted him. But she wanted to find orphaned boys and sell them into slavery. Supposedly start the lads on a new life. Eventually, Marina persuaded him went along with it. After a few close calls Markiza had to leave the country for a while. After that, my mother took up with a real trafficker— a shithead who was also a meth addict, and who beat her nearly to death. Marina ended up in the hospital, embarrassed; she told everyone that Markiza did it. Later, she got the attention of a sympathetic US Congressman who fudged her visa application, and that's all she wrote. To make it look good, she took me along and we came here."

Again, Kastle focused his sharp grey eyes on Lydia and waited to see if she believed him or not. Not seeing anything in the affirmative, he added, "There are still a few, clean, uncorrupted police in St. Petersburg. If you do some proper digging, you'll learn about the investigations into Marina and her family, the mob connections, the bribes and lies. It's all there."

"What did Markiza do when he found out she took you out of the country?" Lydia asked.

"He set two goals. To steal me back, and to grow into an illustrious criminal, the world's biggest and baddest."

"That day, in your office, what else, did Markiza tell you?"

"Just about every sordid detail of my mother's motivations and actions. How she reminded him daily that she wished she'd had an abortion; once, when I was a toddler, she suggested that they should sell me because I could fetch a million dollars from the right sort. He also reminded me that until the day that she holed up at the US consulate, she never really spent time with her son. I remembered then that we always had nannies, and a private teacher who stayed some nights to prepare dinner and tuck me into bed. When we got to America, Marina put me in boarding schools, and later I was living full time with a paid caregiver. But she made sure to look good by taking me out of school to pose with her for any media events surrounding our 'so-called escape from the evil kingpin'. My mother was good-looking, savvy, and without a trace of heart."

"What did you do afterwards?" Lydia asked.

"I raged and screamed. Once, my aide barged into the office to see if I was all right. Then I pretended to calm down, told Markiza to leave. I said that I would sort things out."

"But I wasn't calm. I churned with the white-heat rage of a lunatic. I felt my skin crawling with poisons. I couldn't breath. An hour later, I walked out into the bright day, into a busy intersection against the light, into speeding cars, until, finally, one could not avoid hitting me. I tried to die that day."

Lydia said, "But there was a witness who said she saw a van double back and run you over again, but for no apparent reason she changed her mind—"

Kastle said, "Yes, and if you read the full report, you will see that she told several versions of the same story. You will also see her boss' sworn affidavit stating that at the time of the accident, he was sitting in his office reprimanding the so-called witness for excessive tardiness and dereliction of duties."

"Lex. None of this explains why you crossed over. After all of your hard work and good intentions, why?"

"It happened slowly. After the surgery and for a solid year, Markiza visited me every day. First, in the hospital, then in the nursing home. After a few weeks in the hospital, when it was certain that I would never walk again, I asked him to kill me. Instead, he gave me reasons to live. Told me the usual crap, that I was bright and ambitious. He said that in time, I would know this too. That even though my legs didn't work, I could still be anything I set my mind to."

"Markiza tried to convince me to study science so I could find a vaccine for incurable diseases. One week it was AIDS, the next, Ebola Virus. He said, 'When you've won the Nobel, nobody notices you're a paraplegic.' He would babble on like this until I told him he had to leave. But he always came back the next day with books, music, and even more ideas. He even talked the doctor into changing my depression meds."

"Wait, how was he even able to see you?"

"He told the hospital staff that he was my uncle from Russia. I never refuted it. Anyway, one thing led to another, and he started talking about his business. He didn't say too much, I suppose he worried that since we were on opposite sides of the law, this might send me over the edge. Eventually, I got inquisitive and asked a few questions. Markiza was delighted and explained what he did and why, told me about the travels, the boys and sales, the cargo ships, the watch list, Interpol, etc. He had some great stories, a funny one about the would-be Kremlin bombing.

"A couple days later, he came in to my room all smiles and said, 'I know what would be really good for you. You and I in business, together, a father-son-venture.' He said that my role would be like that of a double agent, something from the cold war days. He said I would love it. I knew I would be good at it."

"Just like that? You can't be serious?" Lydia shook her head.

"It wasn't *just like that*." Kastle tried unsuccessfully to snap his fingers. "I said that it took a year. You might recall that I was traumatized and vulnerable. I thought I'd lost my father; then when he found me, he managed to annihilate any good memory of my mother. Whatever she had done, Marina was still my mother. What was I left with after that? Sure enough, no legs, no manhood, no family—basically nothing. But on the day he made the proposal, I found a reason to live. I had a goal and I knew for certain that I would never be alone again."

Kastle signaled to the guard that he wanted to leave. Before he was out the door, he leaned back in his chair and said to the ceiling, "Parent and child bonds, when as intertwined and twisted as ours have been, they become completely and utterly impervious to rational thinking and behavior. See, some people are either born with huge deficits in their souls, or become that way because of repeated abuse and abandonment. In my case, the need to fill unexpressed desires outranked everything else."

FORTY TWO

After Kastle left, Lydia stayed in her chair. She had one more inmate to question, but wished she didn't have to wait. The longer she waited, the more likely she was to get up and flee. Protocol dictated that the visiting room be searched before another inmate came through, and Kastle had to be safe inside his own cell before they even started for Markiza. As she sat without moving, the idea of talking to the kingpin began to sicken her. But he had something she wanted to reclaim. Her peace of mind.

He was coming. The sounds were different from when Kastle had been brought in. This time she heard sharp clicking from two separate sets of leather-soled shoes, and a discordant shuffling she guessed came from a third ambulatory man, big with hobbled hands and feet, and what sounded like enough metal and chain to secure a small stable of livestock. As the footsteps neared, she heard him say, "I'm telling you, I am the one who made her famous. If not for my capture, stories about this detective—even though they never show her face—would not be bouncing off every news channel, newspaper, and magazine."

Markiza studied her white, buttoned-down shirt and jeans. "You look terrific," Markiza grinned. "I like you better in casual, unpretentious attire. Not the trashy dress you wore to the warehouse. Although, I must confess, it did suit your character at the time. And I suppose congratulations are in order, after all. You are simply a marvelous piece of work. I could have used someone like you on my team, instead of—"

"Shut up and sit down."

"What's the matter with you? Can't you be polite? It won't kill you."

"Sue me."

"Stop. I need your help. You said you'd listen."

What was she doing here? Why? Why had she agreed to see him? In the email that the warden had forwarded to her, Markiza expressed great concern for his safety. He said he was sure he would be sent back to Russia where he would have to face untold torments. He thought if she wrote a letter on his behalf to the state attorney general and the directors of the FBI and Homeland Security, he would be guaranteed the right to serve out his time in the United States.

She knew better. Markiza had cooperated with the feds and very quickly exposed other Russian criminal activity in Florida; therein laid his insurance against extradition. Lydia knew that being sent back to Russia was paranoia, but she let him feed on it because she enjoyed knowing Markiza was suffering, and because she would use it to get something from him for herself.

But by coming to see Markiza, she wondered, wouldn't it appear that she cared? Lydia couldn't let him think that, even for a moment. He was a murderer. He murdered her son.

Still, she had to keep her eye on the ball. Lydia needed answers and would play along to get them.

"What do you want? Spell it out and be quick. I only have a few minutes," she said.

Markiza relented and sat down, grin erased. Lydia imagined if his hands weren't manacled behind him, he would have spread them out in front of him in mock supplication.

"I have it on good authority that the United States and the Kremlin have been engaged in talks about my immediate release into Russian authorities. That would be disastrous."

"Why, because they would put you to death without a hearing first? Sounds like a very efficient system. No muss, no fuss," Lydia said.

"I wish. That would be merciful indeed, but that's not what's going to happen. The sort of people who want me back will throw my old body into a dungeon and torture me for fun. Then my enemies will put on finery to watch the brutality. But the torture will not be sufficient to let me die quickly. I'll be kept alive for months. You cannot imagine the horror."

She could imagine and hoped her thin smile appeared as cruel as it felt.

"I have another reason to stay. Perhaps I can appeal to you as a parent. You have a son now, Tadzio. I can only guess how much joy that smart, creative boy will bring into your life. So think about how I feel. When I finally found my Alexei, I didn't think I would lose him again so fast. Listen, even if we have to live in separate cells, separate prisons, or different cities, if I'm here in the states, then I'll be able to talk to him, send emails, and make up for some of the lost years. I need you to write me that letter."

The man was a psychopath. She knew it, he knew that she knew. What he did not know was that she had absolutely no power over his sentencing or placement. If she had, he would not have been so eager to talk with her.

Lydia needed the answer to one question. Even though the kingpin had no conscience, at least not the kind most people employ in making daily decisions about work, love, and responsibility, Markiza had personal ethics and a code. Whatever he told her, she would know immediately if it were the truth. Not from micro expressions or subtle body language, but from what would happen afterwards.

Lydia crossed her arms and leaned into him. She whispered. "Why did you murder Sasha? Why did he have to die?"

Markiza leaned in too. And the guards took a step forward. His eyes never leaving her face, Markiza sat back and licked his upper teeth with his tongue. He spoke emphatically, a little too loudly.

"I do not kill children. It's bad for business." As if he was already tired of this line of conversation, he looked away and said in a normal tone, "The plan was for my sniper to wipe you out in front of Sasha, so the boy would finally understand what happens after someone tries to double cross me. Sasha needed to see my strength and power in high definition if I were ever to reel him back into the fold. I gave my man strict orders to shoot you after Sasha was clear. The idiot missed you and killed that beautiful lad. So later, I shot the idiot. Myself. But I would never hurt a child. That's all."

From a secret corner of her mind, Lydia watched Sasha. Tall and skinny with pale, paper-thin skin. He was smoking a cigarette, tipping the ash into her cupped hand, laughing. The image collided with another one of Tadzio. The younger boy with darker hair and skin, and round, clear gemstone eyes, had just run out of a room. Seconds after upending a chessboard and its pieces flying everywhere. "You bad stupid player, not like Markiza or even Sasha," Tadzio had cried out.

It wasn't that Lydia was so terrible at strategy board games; they bored her. She played with Tadzio to have something to do, perhaps bond, but her heart was never in the game and he continued to beat her. She supposed he guessed that she was dallying. And that set him on edge. As did so many things.

What in the world would he be like once he started school? Between the intelligence testing, psychological evaluations, and medical exams, Lydia had not been able to enroll him in school. In the interim, Lydia found some play groups in her neighborhood and insisted he meet children his own age. But those feeble attempts to socialize Tadzio ended up in failure. The first time, Tadzio refused to get out of the car. The next time he ran into the park where he saw other children sitting together to watch a play. But then he refused to leave her side, and before the first act was over, Tadzio was fast asleep on Lydia's lap.

Lydia supposed that she should stop romanticizing the life she could have had with Sasha because it was never going to happen. Most likely, Sasha, a pre-teen, fed on raw street survival and organized crime culture, would've been even harder to control once he discovered girls and drugs. She would never forget her first boy, but Lydia was starting to feel a little better. It was still true that had it not been for her, Sasha would be alive, but the kingpin's assurance that the boy had not been used as an example began to plug up the deep hole of obsession she had dug for herself. Perhaps now, she could move on and become a better mother for the Polish puck. If she harbored any doubt that the kingpin had been less than truthful, it was immediately extinguished once his rant started to overpower her daydreaming.

Markiza's eyes glittered with anger while he yelled and the guards carefully but insistently began ushering the kingpin out of the visiting room. "You tricked me, bitch. You were supposed to help me, but you just used me to fix some mental problems. I'll fix you, that's a promise."

"Yeah, like I'm scared," Lydia got up and placed her hands on her hips.

Lydia strode into the prison parking lot, Markiza's syncopated tirade fading in her ears. There was real joy in being able to best the megalomaniac.

Two down, one to go. Sadly, Lydia thought as she sped down the highway, that in comparison, the first two were easy peasy.

FORTY THREE

After years of emotional wandering, you get a second chance to get in touch with who you really are . . .

You have denied yourself the abundance of nature's offerings . . .

No one's skin is smoother and shinier than after it's been through the fire . . .

Oh, forget it. Darryl would never buy clever maxims that were designed to make the speaker sound precious and the listener stupid. She had to be real with him. She could at least try. But it was going to be super humiliating, especially after finding out that Sans had blackmailed Darryl into meeting with her.

Lydia found a small table at the back of Darryl's favorite coffee shop and immediately began brooding. She knew deep down that Darryl loved her even if he surrounded himself with emotional walls strong enough to withstand the siege of Troy. She also understood that despite the low odds of their romance rekindling, every date, every woman—every time—for Darryl, Lydia would be the mirror, the constant comparison, the test of time. Darryl was in danger of not only not having a relationship with the only woman he really should be with, but at this rate, he'd never have one with anyone else either. Because anyone else would not be her. She rationalized that she needed to save him from himself as much as she needed Darryl to be back in her life.

Lydia drained her cup of tea and watched a shadow fall over her and the table. Darryl stood propped against a chair as he hooked his cane on the back of it. When he folded himself into the seat, she noticed his cup of coffee was only half full. Darryl must have stood or sat somewhere else for a while before deciding to join her. Although he sat squared to face Lydia, his eyes immediately began moving around the cavernous room. They slithered over artwork on the walls, past pastry displays behind acrylic cases, unto the ceiling fans above them. She watched his eyes with renewed interest. Always sleek and bright, today she also noticed that they were webbed, tapered like a cat's at the outer edges. And, not unlike, she mused, the perfect and plastic orbs of the earliest Barbie doll. Except Darryl's eyes could take you places from which you might never come back.

"Before you say anything, it wasn't Sans. I came because I wanted to," Darryl said quickly.

"Really, why?" Lydia was already feeling defensive.

"Why do you think? We have to sort things out. I've been avoiding you and that's wrong. Things need to be said."

"What things?"

Darryl looked away. "I need more coffee."

Darryl came back with his coffee and two pastries. Lydia noticed his limp but didn't say anything.

"Your favorite, French-puffed donut with vanilla icing." He handed her the small plate and said, "I heard you gave notice. Is it because of—"

"You? No. Besides its temporary, Marla and I are going uptown for a while to work with the feds, profiling potential terrorists. You know, Marla assessing threat levels, and me weaving my wizardry to establish modus operandi, location, potential weaponry."

"How long?"

"A year or two, until I can get Tadzio stabilized." She watched his skeptical expression.

"Becoming a parent comes with a long learning curve, especially if you're raising someone as bright and stubborn as Tadzio."

"Tadzio's Polish. He doesn't mind you being black?"

"He doesn't seem to notice. Besides, white families adopt kids of color all the time."

"What happens when he does notice?"

"Who's going to tell him? You? You don't believe I'm black."

"You're not." Darryl swallowed his coffee and grimaced. And not because the coffee was hot or burnt. "Are you going back? I mean to being white?"

Lydia shook her head lightly and narrowed her eyes. "Is that what's worrying you? Why would I go through another invasive surgery?"

"Because you could. You could go back to being what you were before. But that's not true for me. Actually, it would be impossible for me to do what you did. Change races."

"It never was and still isn't a competition, Darryl. I did what I had to do."

"You did what you wanted to do without any regard for black culture or struggle. You never thought about me when you did this, and what it would mean for us."

"You're right about one thing. When I made my decision, I was not thinking about black history and the widespread racism against people of color. I'm sorry about that. And I'm trying to make up for it. I'm doing my best.

"But the other thing: there was no us. We didn't exist. At least not until Aunjanue stepped onto the scene. And then everything changed. You felt something for her, and my feelings resurfaced almost like they had never gone away. That's when I realized I never stopped loving you. And it turns out that you never stopped caring for me either. You wanted me, admit it."

Lydia watched Darryl squirm; he knew she was right, but he wasn't going to admit anything.

"That's before I figured out it was one big con game," he said." Lydia winced.

"You deserved that because you're trying to reduce your epic decision to something simplistic. And do you really expect me to know what I want? One minute, I think, yeah, I can do this. The next, I'm feeling sick. I can't get past certain barriers. I might never."

"This is classic Darryl. Talking in circles, avoiding what's important. Why don't you tell me what's really bothering you." Darryl closed his eyes and became silent. When he opened them again, they were cold.

"Didn't you know that when your face changed, your life would too? That people would see you differently, treat you differently? That your old tried and true responses to negative experiences wouldn't work anymore, because now it was personal?"

"I've already been sucker punched a couple times. I know there's prejudice and I'm riding on a bumpy road, but I'm ready," Lydia said.

Darryl snorted and leaned forward, "I've been black all my life, like four decades. You, you've been an African American for two minutes. You have no clue about what you're saying."

"I suppose you're going to enlighten me," Lydia said.

To her horror, Darryl began crying. He didn't bother wiping his face as big hot teardrops rolled out of his eyes. "It isn't just people who do you wrong, racism is an institution. It's taken up space in all corners of society. To be black is to wake up feeling second-class most days. Take redlining. If you live in a black neighborhood, it means you have no choice but to pay two to three times the average interest rate on your mortgage.

"How about looking for work? Let's say you apply and then you find out that your dream job went to someone else. Later on you'll always wonder, was it because the next guy or woman had better skills, or was it . . . something else?

"Then there's apartment hunting. How many times does it take to get turned down in a nice area, until you move somewhere downscale because that's the only place they'll have you. Or the looks you get when you sit your ass down in a white-suburban restaurant. Don't get me started on trying to get coffee to-go in the boonies."

Physically, it was still the old Darryl she knew sitting across from her, but inexplicably, another being had taken residence inside his brain and was doing all the talking. She'd never heard him open up like this before.

"And look at the crap on television. Black people are either docile or super sassy. To be taken seriously, they have to be musicians or sports celebrities. There's not a damn thing in between. Like people of color don't have normal everyday routines and habits. Like we don't work all day long, go home tired and still have to go shopping for this or that and play with the kids.

"When you experience this day after day, week after week, you start to go crazy. It eats at everything good about yourself. Call it identity PTSD. Lydia, knowing what you did brings it all back in sharp focus."

"Darryl, but when I was white you didn't—"

"Didn't have a problem with that? No. I knew who you were and where we stood. The emotional fault lines were very clearly drawn. Same if you had been black. But this, just . . . looking black, isn't black. Problem is that you're a hot head, and that could get you killed, or me."

"I don't know . . . what to say." Lydia didn't think she had ever felt this exposed. Darryl was right, she hadn't a clue about anything anymore, but what he said next, told her for certain that there were some realities she would never be able to skate around.

"My surroundings are my teacher. I learned long ago that as a black man, I can't do everything white people do. Before I act, I have to think about a million things first. In the past, white Lydia could have gone off half-cocked and people, yeah, law enforcement, all the rest, might've gotten a little shook up. Still, you were never considered a real threat. But now, don't you know that black women are violent? You show your temper and it's going to slow your roll. If you're not careful, badge or no badge, you might find yourself slammed into a cell someday."

Darryl slumped in his chair and knuckled his eyes. When he looked at her again, she saw that he was spent. He could sleep for three years. Didn't matter, Lydia was going to get one more crack at the bat.

"I can't begin to tell you how sorry I am. In the days that follow, I'm sure I'm going to feel even worse. Okay, at first, I thought what I was doing was cute. I admit it. Then I started to take my new face and my place in society seriously. But you're right; I'm way out of my league. It's going to take a village. I'm going to need practice and lots of help.

"There's just one other thing. What we've created here is a Pro and Con sheet. You filled in all the negative slots, and I put my chicken scratch on the positive side. I promise you that I will study the negative consequences of my actions and at the same time, work on being a better person. But I'd like for you to cross over too. It's not all battlefields and landmines. It can't be.

"I love you. I want to build a life with you. Tadzio asks about you all the time. Not sure why, but you made an indelible impression on him during the sting. Darryl, I wish you would get to know him."

"Lyd."

"I'm asking you for a second chance to make us work. But that's it. Don't expect me to prostrate myself. I won't beg."

EPILOGUE

Three weeks later

In Miami it was raining.

Darryl drove to the coffee shop uncertain of his decision. While his mind occasionally raced with exploding thoughts of hurt and anger, the tension and confusion of the past few weeks had finally given way to a dull roar, and something nearing acceptance niggled at his heart. So it didn't bother him that he wasn't completely sure about a resolution, nor was he eager to know exactly what it was he was about to do. It would be what it would be. One thing was certain, life *had* to feel good again.

For weeks, Darryl assiduously threw off veils of secrets and lies, distortions and sabotage from his psyche. He talked at length with his mother, started a daily meditation routine, saw a shrink a couple of times, and each morning added another page to a long and rambling letter that he would never send because he wasn't sure if he should address it to himself, Lydia, Anita, or his father.

As he drove, the wind picked up and rain sluiced his windshield in horizontal swipes. The short-lived ease he felt only minutes earlier disappeared as new worries pelted him like body blows. Because, Darryl realized, the decision his brain and heart had finally melded together would require more sacrifice than even a good Catholic martyr should endure in one lifetime.

Maybe he was only fooling himself. Was he ready for this? And then like clockwork, his mind seesawed in another direction.

How could he live without her, the woman he'd loved for so many years? He forced himself to remember why he had given up Lydia in the first place. Was it because she was the only one who came close to exposing his darkest fears?

Darryl used to think that it would be easier to defecate in public than admit how much he missed his father. Back then, Lydia's genuine love was too hot to handle and it scorched his heart. Her unconditional caring only succeeded shining a bright light on the knowledge that he would never have the all-abiding security and safety of a male parent. He had left her because acknowledging her love was the same as admitting his own loss.

Now she wanted him back.

But she had a new face.

He had damned good reason to mistrust and be angry with her. Lydia not only staged her own car crash, survived it, and then acted without his knowledge or input; she took his race for granted.

She had led him to think she was dead. Gone. Dead. For so long his anger had colored how thankful he was each and every day that she was alive. It made him crazy to recall that he had mourned her death and had missed, yes, truly missed her, and did not feel better until he saw the Aunjanue for the first time.

Darryl squeezed into the last open spot on the street in front of the coffee shop, and sat low in his seat thinking about the day he met Aunjanue.

As soon as she walked into the MAGS, his heart had lightened and his mind relaxed, like he'd taken a tranquilizer. It didn't even occur to him to feel guilty for being smitten with the newbie. In fact, he felt the opposite. Light as feather, free from all worry and doubt.

Because he had known.

Darryl didn't think that at the time he actually believed that Aunjanue was Lydia, her face, nonetheless, had brought him comfort. For all of the surgery she underwent: a new nose and cheeks, and then the darkening of hair and skin, the eyes had not changed at all, and that heart-shaped chin . . . seeing someone who wasn't Lydia but resembled her, even if on a subconscious level, brought him surprising buoyancy. It was wrong to keep that from her. That Aunjanue brought him joy because she was Lydia inherent, just below the surface. Even if he had not completely perceived the notion at the time.

Lydia sucked in her breath, because when the coffee shop lit up with a burst of sunshine turning everything in its wake into sharp angles, Darryl had chosen that moment to walk through the front door. His body was sharply backlit, and he looked like a dark angel with a blazing halo as he approached her. Although he barely limped now, Darryl's stride was slow and deliberate.

"Every time I walked in the door you were here. And then I left because I wasn't ready. On top of that, I was reduced to having to drink coffee at one of the chains," Darryl shook his head.

"Don't worry, I saw you skulking maddeningly past the front windows. Day after day. Three weeks seems like forever to wait for you. I was just about to give up. But you're here, so pull up a chair."

A glint from somebody's jewelry flickered like fireflies between them. They followed the spots of light like cats chasing the red dot from a laser pointer. After a while, Darryl broke the spell.

"Before we start, I have a question. Why Edison?"

"What do you mean?"

"Why did you tell me that you went to high school at Edison, I mean when you were playing Aunjanue? That was some cruel shit."

"Don't I know it. You were supposed to think I was a fed from Chicago, but raised in Minnesota. I memorized the usual stuff: where I went to school, church, names of best friends, hang outs, and so on, but that day I drew a blank. On the way back from Anita's, I think you asked what high school was like, not which one I went to. But I thought I better supply a name, and the answer was knee jerk. Because I did spend one year in Minneapolis when my father took a temporary position there. So, Edison just slipped out.

"Never in my dreams did I imagine that you would find time to go there and check on me. Why did you?"

"It would have never happened if on some plane, all of us, Andy, me, even Marla, didn't suspect you of being Lydia. Well, we didn't know, but the scent was taking us all in different and weird directions. Mine was to stop at your old high school to find your school pic."

"Was it because of Andy?" Lydia asked.

"Partly. He didn't trust you. And then I freaked out when I saw Lydia's pic in the yearbook, and then later, when I went to Andy's and your car was parked out front . . . I didn't know what to think or believe."

"I'm so sorry you had to go through all that. But I don't think that's why you're here today. You've come to a decision, haven't you?"

Darryl looked at Lydia like with a friendliness she hadn't seen in a long time. "I'm not good at saying nice things to people I'm still mad at. But you deserve the truth. When I look at you, I see Lydia more than I see Aunjanue. It didn't happen all at once. But I got some before-and-after photos from Sans. After staring at them for a long time, I finally saw what Michelle did at my mom's party. Remember that insane moment when she mistook Aunjanue for Lydia? It was so bizarre. She saw the truth until we shamed her out of it.

"It didn't happen like that for me, at least consciously, because you were introduced as a co-worker, someone to take my old partner's place. But my sister knew. I think for her, it was an easy and natural editing process. Like the old witch and young woman optical illusion. The brain plays tricks. Michelle was open to seeing you, but I wasn't."

Lydia sat with her brow furrowed and her mouth hanging open. She had not expected this. She stared at Darryl so long without saying anything that he started to look worried. "Did I say something wrong?"

"No, go on."

"I wanted you to know that I see you. You, the real you. The person I've known forever, and loved just as long."

Lydia squeezed her shoulders high and hugged herself. "I feel like . . . I don't know. What you said about seeing me . . . it's the best gift you could give me. Because I thought for a while that I would never be able to explain to another living being what I went through in the beginning. It's an editing process all right. I was so completely terrified of my new face when I saw it for the first time. After all the bandages were off, and the swelling had come down. I thought I was in hell—I didn't know who in the world was staring back at me from the mirror. It was a nightmare, like a bad acid trip.

"So when you ask me if I would go back, the answer is an unequivocal NO. Not unless you chained and drugged me first. Once was enough."

Darryl got up and ordered sandwiches and biscotti. When he came back to the table Aunjanue looked for signs of defection. There were none. Not yet.

"I had a long talk with my mother—"

"Oh, god. Does Anita hate me?" Lydia asked.

"She's on the fence waiting to see what I'll do. I think she got kind of scared after the last time you and I met. She called me that night when I was still pretty raw and intense. Anita was worried that I might hurt myself or someone else. The next day she showed up unexpectedly at my house and told me a story about my father. And that started the change. How I felt about you, myself, and the future."

"Darryl, this story, why didn't she tell you before?"

"She said she had broached the subject with me on two separate occasions, but that I had always cut her off. She might be right, I just don't remember."

Lydia leaned forward and said, "Tell me."

"She started by saying that if she'd had it to do all over again, my mom would not have stayed in Miami."

"What? After your father left? Where did she think she would go?"

"To Jamaica. To go after Cedric."

"Why, after everything he did, why would she pursue him?"

"Because my mom finally admitted that she was the first one to do the abandoning. See, she was always aware of my father's enormous guilt for having so much in America when his friends and family were going without clean water, good schools, medical care, any of the basics in his hometown. He had talked to her for years about them going back together, at least for awhile, and taking the kids."

"So, it wasn't a surprise that he just up and left," Lydia asked.

"He didn't do that. It took a long time for him to finally screw up the courage. Every time he talked to her about it, mom told him the same thing, 'you're selfish, willing to trade your very nice life and family, one that we both worked so hard for, to follow a whim.' She accused him of being irresponsible and not loving his own, immediate family enough.

"What Anita regrets is that she always railed at his words and never listened to his heart. She never put her husband first, but expected him to do that for her."

"Anita isn't someone who would just follow another person blindly," Lydia said.

"No, that's not it. She was talking about give and take. My mom in the end could not risk giving up a solid, stable life in Miami for uncertainty in a third world country, not even for a summer. She refused to try at all. When he realized she would never change her mind, he left."

"How does this make things better? I don't understand," Lydia said.

"Well it does and it doesn't. I still grew up without a Dad, and that loss shaped a big chunk of my personality. For better or worse. But just knowing the context for my father leaving, finally allows me to stop thinking that outside forces are controlling my life. That somehow I'm cursed. I used to carry around this magical-thinking that if my father could disappear without a reason, then so could you. So I left first. My mom's explanation showed me that just like crimes, relationships are built on actions and consequences. Not magic."

"But you stayed married to Karen for twelve years. I'd say you showed extraordinary responsibility and, as I recall, no magic or curse snaked its way into that relationship," Lydia said.

"How could it? Karen never loved me, and I didn't love her either, at least not after the first few years. Ours was not the kind of relationship that could trigger that kind of fear and loathing, because there had never been that kind of intensity. Not like with us."

Lydia was first and foremost a woman of action, not prone to much self-examination. And she wondered if she had inadvertently stoked a hornet's nest. As thankful as she was that Darryl was being forthright and honest with her, she secretly hoped that his sharp self-scrutiny would not go on forever.

"What I did, can you live with that, Darryl?"

"You said you wanted to be a better person." Darryl smiled. "I take that to mean that you are going to work on things like patience. I trust you, I believe you. I have to."

"And what about you, do you want this to work?" Lydia asked.

Darryl got up and slid into the chair next to hers. He put his hand on her arm and squeezed it. Long after, during the drive to pick up her son, she would still be feeling the warmth his touch radiated over her shoulder and neck and face and what that told her.

"I'm willing to fight for us, work on issues. I'm not real good at this stuff, but I promise not to bail the first time I get scared or things don't go my way. So I guess you're going to have to trust me too." When he took his hand away, he asked, "Where's Tadzio?"

Lydia looked outside as a darkening sky filled with saddlebag clouds threatened to unleash another rainstorm on the already drenched city. To her delight she saw another picture: Tadzio running up to Darryl and complaining that Lydia was always late in picking him up. The boy knew just enough English to be able to sandbag her.

"He's at Children's Home Society. It's the final day in a month-long series of evaluations. I get to pick him up and bring him home for good. And I better go, Tadzio hates it if I'm late," Lydia said.

Darryl jiggled his keys. "My car's out front, why don't I drive."

Read an excerpt from **Mickie Turk's**
gripping New Orleans thriller,
The Delilah Case.

PROLOGUE

May 20, 1968

Little Niqui didn't stop to catch her breath or fasten her shoe buckles. She knew the cracks and fissures in the sidewalks by heart, avoided them and ran as fast as she could. Past the quickly disappearing smear of faces. Past the arranged tableau of her childhood. The usual folk estivating like reptiles in the heat. Sipping iced teas on their porches. Endlessly fanning themselves with old newspapers. She never saw them.

But they always noticed her.

Especially today. The seven-year-old bolted up her front stairs and tore open the screen door with so much force that it snapped back against the window shutters like a heavy magnet and stayed there, letting in a spume of dust and all of the buzzing flies. Old men, weary women with small children, pre-teens whose parents didn't own fans, all gaped in astonishment because only once before had the little girl attempted anything so brash and bold.

Where was the fire? And what about Darnell, the block wondered. Why in heaven's name was she keeping him waiting?

Little Niqui flew into the dining room right before dropping to her knees and crawling under the table. When she found what she was looking for, the girl repeated her steps backward and was out in the street before the cone of dust had a chance to settle back to earth. The object of her quest, the new present from Miss Marta, safely swaddled in the crook of her arm.

The six-inch, brand new voodoo doll wore a tuxedo and top hat. Gede's hands were splayed in gleaming white gloves, and dark sunglasses with one lens missing hung rakishly on his head. A short fat stubby cigar poked out of the twisted mouth, and a carved wooden cane dangled from his right forearm. He looked drunk and lascivious, but this deity, the voodoo lwa, was the one you called when there was a serious illness in the family, and he loved the little children whom he defended against the seen and unseen.

Little Niqui was already halfway to Treasure House to play with Darnell when she realized she'd forgotten her protector. She had to run extra hard and extra fast because she knew full well that this mistake would cost her three-and-a-half minutes of play: one-and-a-half minutes back home, a half-minute for the retrieval, and another one-and-a-half minutes back to the place where she first noticed the doll missing.

Little Niqui never wore a watch, never looked at clocks, was terrified of them because everything in her life was scheduled—her mama Nadine, always making sure of that. Instead, she used her internal guides to tell time just the way

Miss Marta taught her. She had taught Little Niqui that once you understood them, the spirits would always be there for her.

Nadine didn't approve of that kind of thinking, but what could she do? Miss Marta was Nadine's voodoo priestess, too.

Once again the skinny girl with legs like a gazelle was running past the neighborhood, a little less frightened now, and a lot more aware of her surroundings. She smiled and waved to the people talking all at once at her.

"You forget something Little Niqui?"

"Gonna catch your death running in the heat."

"Slow down girl, you hear."

"Careful or you'll wear out your shoes."

"Ummmhmm! Brand new patent leather Sunday shoes."

"Don't let your mama catch you."

"I have thirty minutes," Little Niqui said.

"Not no more you don't."

"Show us whatch ya hidin' under that arm."

"Better hurry, Darnell be waiting on you."

Darnell. Her everything. Her one true friend. She was truly sorry to be late. Three-and-a-half-minutes late. Darnell would say hc didn't mind. That was how a true friend acted. Not like that crazy Delilah who would have screamed at her for one silly mistake. You never knew about Delilah, because as much she said she could be counted on, the older girl sometimes wouldn't come around for days, even weeks. And then, you'd have to be afraid of what kind of mood she'd be showing. Once in a great while Delilah could be a peach. That's when she brought them fun games to play and didn't even get too cranky when she lost. That's why she was invited back. But lately Delilah only made Little Niqui feel real bad about herself, even worse than before she showed up.

Her mama never mentioned Delilah, but she made her feelings very clear about Darnell. He wasn't smart enough or good enough. In her estimation, just another neighborhood runt. Still, Nadine believed if left to his own devices, that boy had the power to unravel all the good plans she had carved out for her daughter's future. Hadn't he already discarded her proper title of *Dominique*, for that low class nickname, Little Niqui? As if her perfect angel needed street cred. No, everyone knew that the prodigious child's destiny was to grow up and make a great impact on this 'ole world. Nadine would have to stay cautious. Ummmhmm!

If you had bothered to ask Little Niqui's opinion, she would have told you that her mama was jealous. Maybe Mama knew she loved Darnell as much as her. Maybe Mama knew that Darnell could keep her safe in a way she could not. Maybe Mama knew if she died, Little Niqui would be very sad. But if Darnell died, Little Niqui would die, too.

She might die anyway. More than usual, things were rocketing right out of proportion. Clutching Gede to her chest, the girl tried to squeeze out the memories of the day. It ranked among the worst. And it was happening again. She'd begun detesting every single thing she was forced to do.

That morning she woke up like every day, an hour earlier than the other children on the block, and was chauffeured to a private Jesuit school in the upscale suburb of Metarie. The first half of the day was spent in European-style classes for fourth graders—thanks to her mama's wheedling she had skipped second and third grade altogether. In the morning she studied her primaries: mathematics, English, history, geography, religion. Then after lunch she was passed from nun to nun, for individual tutoring in eclectic areas such as Picasso's Blue Period, or the discoveries of the Italian Renaissance. At three-o'clock she took a French vocabulary test and passed it with flying colors.

Little Niqui had the reading comprehension of a tenth grader, and the I.Q. of the current reigning Mensa champion. She could sing opera, play three instruments, compose music, recite a dozen sonnets, and on occasion, fix her mama's sewing machine and the old electric toaster when they went on the fritz.

When she thought things couldn't get any worse, after her last class, Little Niqui was summoned to the principal's office. He explained that because of her greater than expected academic progress that year, she would be spending the summer taking accelerated classes with a group of equally talented, although slightly older, children on the French Riviera. The principal beamed, saying it would be for the *whole summer*. Astonished to see a look of sheer terror cross those big bright eyes, he quickly added that her mama would be going, too. And that's when she burst into tears and ran into the bathroom to throw up her lunch.

They had a deal!

You didn't break deals, or go back on your word. Even if you were Nadine Doucette. Last winter after they took Darnell away from her, with only Delilah to witness it, Little Niqui jumped off her second-story veranda onto the brick courtyard below. And although she hadn't broken a bone, an examining doctor at Charity Hospital who was no shrink, but could recognize a suicide attempt when he saw one, reported the incident to the resident psychiatrist. A group of specialists was brought in, and, soon after, a conclave convened between the hospital and Dominique's school. And between Nadine and the Black Panthers.

One of the first things the latter group did after they had taken over the neighborhood was become Little Niqui's personal benefactor. Indeed, they supplied the cash for the expensive matriculation, after-school lessons, and of course the car and driver. They bought Little Niqui's mother a new stove and refrigerator, and when she asked for it, paid for the repairs to her porch and steps, and replaced the shutters on the front windows.

The senior members of New Orleans's Black Power movement were also Little Niqui's neighborhood-appointed child advocates. They had a big say in what happened next.

So it was settled that she would continue all of her schoolwork and activities. She would keep curfew and go to church and Bible study on Sundays. The tiny, precocious child also promised no more shenanigans like jumping off porches, or cutting—the ER doctor had also found a half dozen tiny unhealed slits alongside older scars on the back of her neck, mostly covered by her long pony tail.

In return, much to Nadine's chagrin, her daughter would be allowed to play with Darnell for thirty minutes each day after supper. No more, no less, and as much as Little Niqui wanted on weekends, as long as there were no special events planned.

That was the deal.

Until today.

Instinctively, Dominique knew this new life plan was different, that it would do no good to complain to Barry Beales, the leader of the Panthers, because most likely he was financing the trip. She would just have to find a way to bring along her best friend. Otherwise, how would she ever survive the summer?

Darnell sat on the top step carefully unwrapping a piece of chewing gum. Little Niqui watched him for a moment before taking the piece and popping it into her mouth. She never tired of looking at his face, briefly wondering why some of her mama's friends thought Darnell didn't quite "fit in". Almost the darkest kid on the block, nine-year-old Darnell had been born with European features, a short skinny nose, thin lips and steel-blue eyes. His jet-black hair fell in waves slightly over his ears, and, unlike Little Niqui's, it was natural and not processed. To her, he was the cutest creature she'd ever laid eyes on, and she prayed he would always belong to her.

"Come on, let's play." Darnell clambered up the steps and tore into the house. Little Niqui ran after him chortling, trying to catch up. She followed the narrow hallway and ran past three rooms until she found him in the kitchen. Darnell heroically ducked and feinted her grabs by running under the square metal table. When she finally tagged him, he fell into an exaggerated heap on the cracked linoleum floor and pretended to be dead. The girl pulled and tore at his sleeve. She laughed so hard she fell down, too. Then, like a miniature twister, she shot up and screamed, "Catch me if you can!"

The two kids always continued this exchange, in and out of the rooms for fifteen minutes. The house was laid out much like the rest of the shotgun houses on the block: three rooms with an unbroken hallway connecting them. But this one had the camel back edition, where a second bedroom had been built upstairs. It belonged to Davina and Dave Treasure, who a month ago up and left to take care of their ailing daughter near Vicksburg, leaving the keys with their next-door neighbors, the Davis'.

Once, when Larry Davis went to check on the house, he found the back door slightly ajar and that's when he discovered Darnell and Little Niqui jouncing through the front rooms. From that time on, he unlocked the back door at five minutes to seven and came back promptly to lock up at seven-thirty-five. If it so happened that his wife made cherry Kool-Aid that day, he filled two glasses and left them on the kitchen table where the kids would be sure to find them.

Their final ritual, to run up the stairs and jump up and down on the old feather bed, had to be cut short today, but they still managed to get in a game of who-could-jump-farthest-off-the-bed. It was when Little Niqui cleared her friend by almost a foot and rolled to her side, that Gede fell from her pocket and landed on the floor. Darnell swiveled his body and grabbed the doll.

"This new? When did you get it?"

"Yesterday, from Miss Marta."

"But you already got one."

"This one's better." Little Niqui took back the saucy patron of young children, sat up and balanced him on her knees. The children studied the cockeyed face staring at them.

"Why do you need better?"

"You know." Little Niqui twisted her mouth. "I'm getting scared. All the time now."

Darnell turned away to look out the dormer window. The glass was melting. He could feel Delilah's heat all around. "It'll be okay," he said, knowing it wouldn't be. "I'm here. Don't you worry."

"Look at me Darnell." Little Niqui's eyes were wide trying to contain a flood of rushing tears. "Look at me."

"Don't cry. I don't like that crying."

"I'm sorry. Darnell. Darnell."

When he looked back at her his smile was warm. Darnell couldn't bear to see his friend sad. "You have five minutes, then we gotta go." Darnell did own a watch, his own present from Barry Beales.

"You won't ever leave me, will you Darnell?"

"You know I won't." And then looking very serious in the manner of a grown up, he asked, "Have you seen her yet?"

"She'll be by soon."

Their evenings always ended with Darnell patiently reciting every article of whatever Little Niqui made him promise. He put up with it, because it seemed to make her feel better. Secretly he wondered why she bothered at all with the ritual when she already knew the ending to the story.

It most certainly wouldn't be him leaving her.